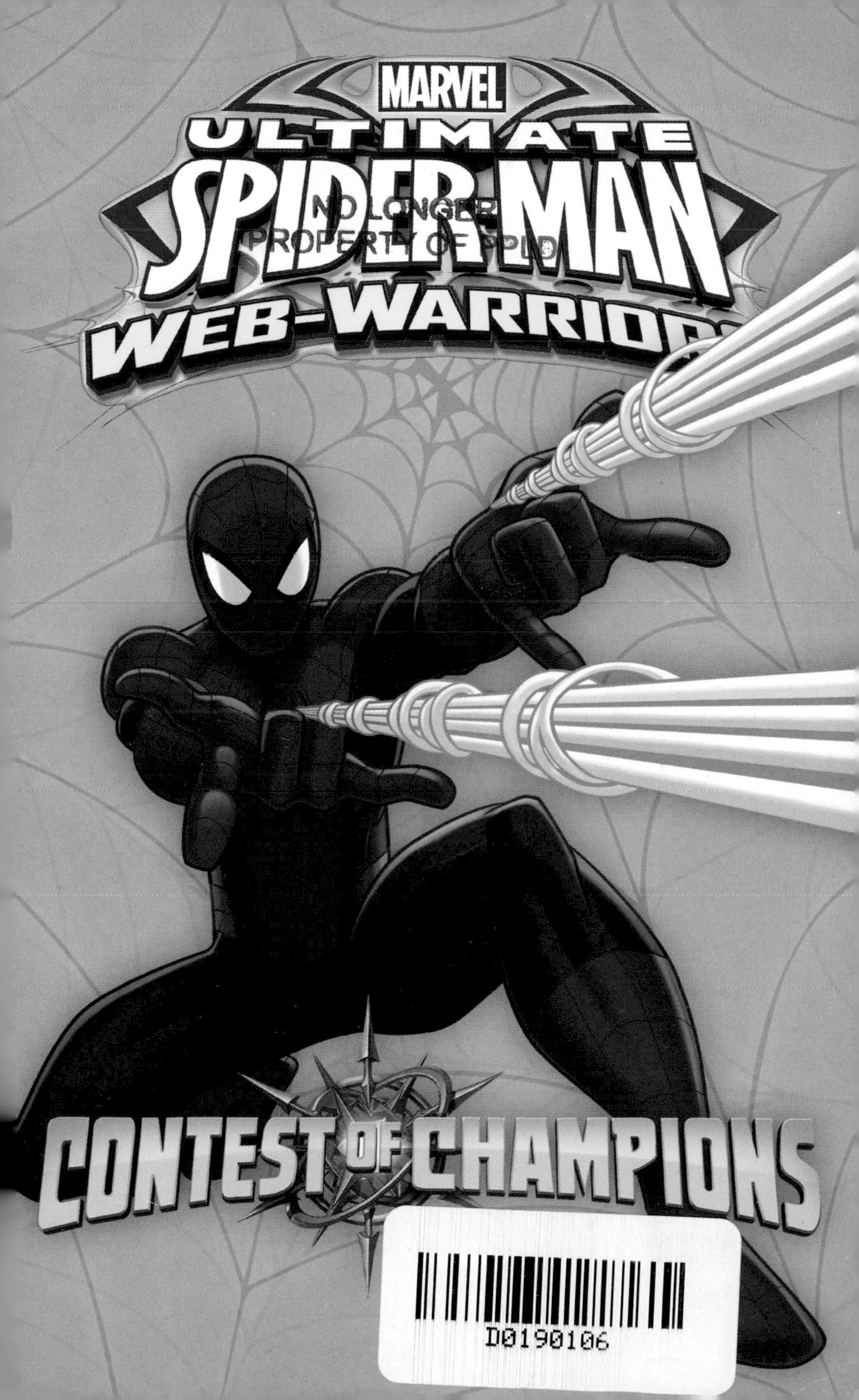
MARVEL
ULTIMATE
SPIDER-MAN
WEB-WARRIORS
CONTEST OF CHAMPIONS

MARVEL UNIVERSE ULTIMATE SPIDER-MAN: CONTEST OF CHAMPIONS. Contains material originally published in magazine form as MARVEL UNIVERSE ULTIMATE SPIDER-MAN: CONTEST OF CHAMPIONS #1-4. First printing 2016. ISBN# 978-1-302-90165-3. Published by MARVEL WORLDWIDE, INC., a subsidiary of MARVEL ENTERTAINMENT, LLC. OFFICE OF PUBLICATION: 135 West 50th Street, New York, NY 10020. Copyright © 2016 MARVEL. No similarity between any of the names, characters, persons, and/or institutions in this magazine with those of any living or dead person or institution is intended, and any such similarity which may exist is purely coincidental. **Printed in the U.S.A.** ALAN FINE, President, Marvel Entertainment; DAN BUCKLEY, President, TV, Publishing & Brand Management; JOE QUESADA, Chief Creative Officer; TOM BREVOORT, SVP of Publishing; DAVID BOGART, SVP of Business Affairs & Operations, Publishing & Partnership; C.B. CEBULSKI, VP of Brand Management & Development, Asia; DAVID GABRIEL, SVP of Sales & Marketing, Publishing; JEFF YOUNGQUIST, VP of Production & Special Projects; DAN CARR, Executive Director of Publishing Technology; ALEX MORALES, Director of Publishing Operations; SUSAN CRESPI, Production Manager; STAN LEE, Chairman Emeritus. For information regarding advertising in Marvel Comics or on Marvel.com, please contact Vit DeBellis, Integrated Sales Manager, at vdebellis@marvel.com. For Marvel subscription inquiries, please call 888-511-5480. **Manufactured between 7/1/2016 and 8/8/2016 by SHERIDAN, CHELSEA, MI, USA.**

10 9 8 7 6 5 4 3 2 1

MARVEL ULTIMATE SPIDER-MAN WEB-WARRIORS

CONTEST OF CHAMPIONS

BASED ON THE TV SERIES WRITTEN BY
THOMAS F. ZAHLER, MATT WAYNE,
MARTY ISENBERG & EUGENE SON

DIRECTED BY
TIM MALTBY, KALVIN LEE & ROY BURDINE

ANIMATION PRODUCED BY
MARVEL ANIMATION STUDIOS WITH FILM ROMAN

ADAPTED BY
JOE CARAMAGNA

SPECIAL THANKS TO
HANNAH MCDONALD & PRODUCT FACTORY

EDITOR
MARK BASSO

SENIOR EDITOR
MARK PANICCIA

SPIDER-MAN CREATED BY **STAN LEE** & **STEVE DITKO**

Collection Editor: **Jennifer Grünwald**
Associate Editor: **Sarah Brunstad**
Editor, Special Projects: **Mark D. Beazley**
VP, Production & Special Projects: **Jeff Youngquist**
SVP Print, Sales & Marketing: **David Gabriel**
Head of Marvel Television: **Jeph Loeb**
Book Designer: **Adam Del Re**

Editor In Chief: **Axel Alonso**
Chief Creative Officer: **Joe Quesada**
Publisher: **Dan Buckley**
Executive Producer: **Alan Fine**

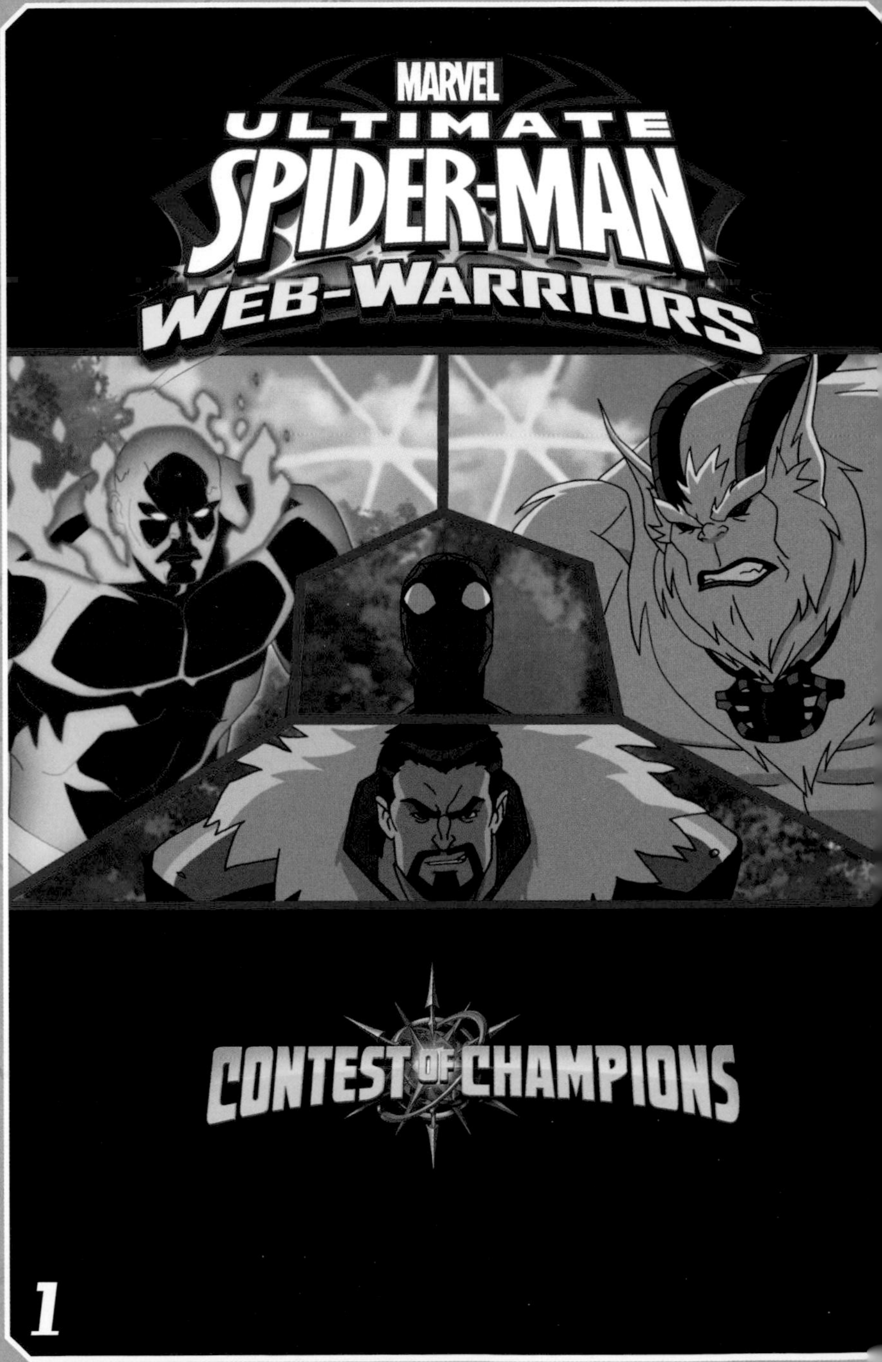
MARVEL
ULTIMATE SPIDER-MAN
WEB-WARRIORS
CONTEST OF CHAMPIONS
1

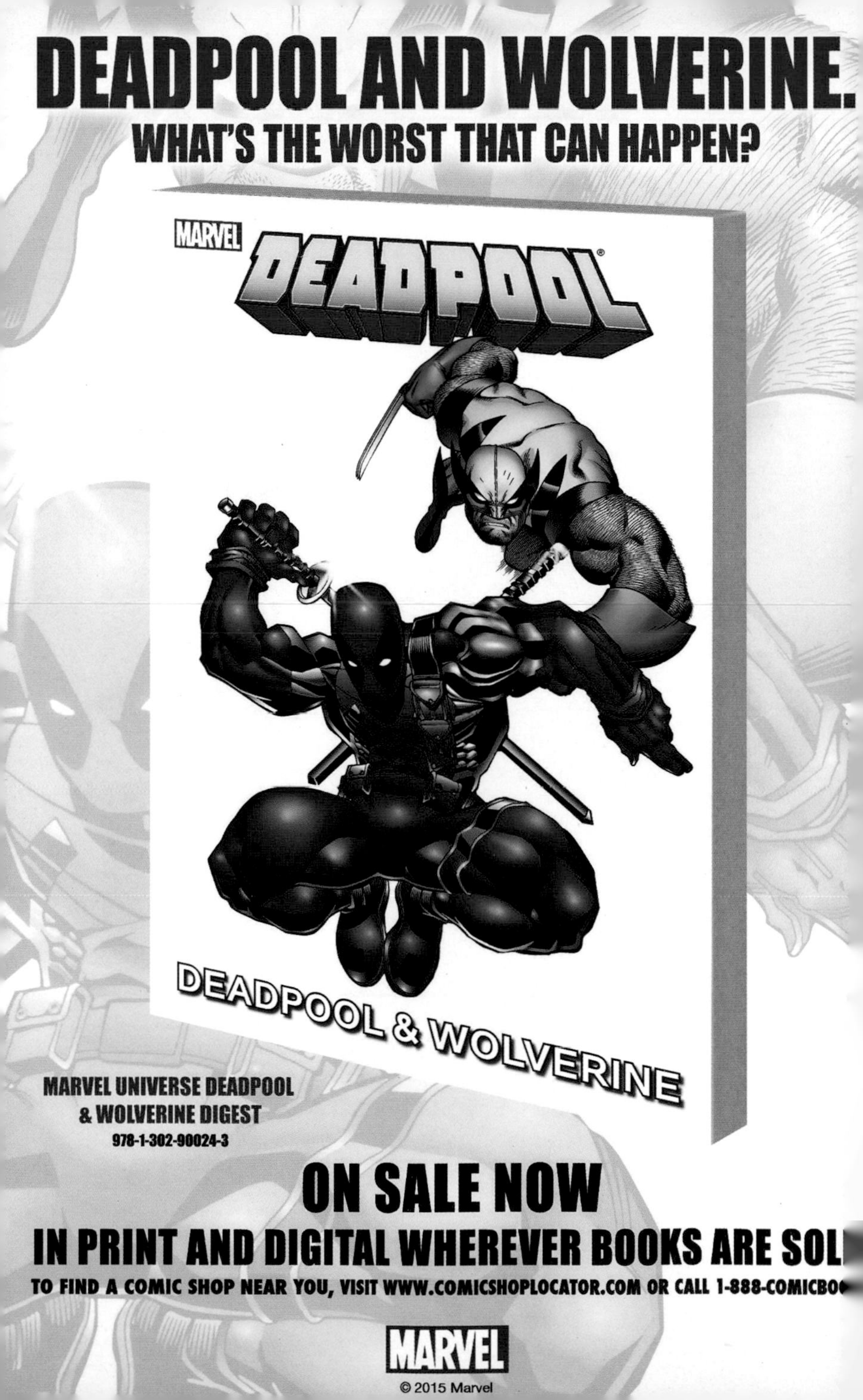
DEADPOOL AND WOLVERINE.
WHAT'S THE WORST THAT CAN HAPPEN?
MARVEL
DEADPOOL
DEADPOOL & WOLVERINE
MARVEL UNIVERSE DEADPOOL & WOLVERINE DIGEST
978-1-302-90024-3
ON SALE NOW
IN PRINT AND DIGITAL WHEREVER BOOKS ARE SOL
TO FIND A COMIC SHOP NEAR YOU, VISIT WWW.COMICSHOPLOCATOR.COM OR CALL 1-888-COMICBO
MARVEL
© 2015 Marvel

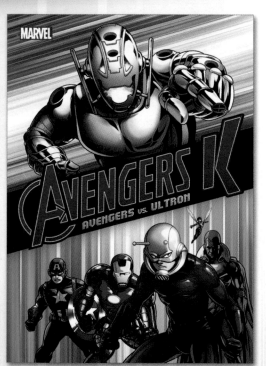

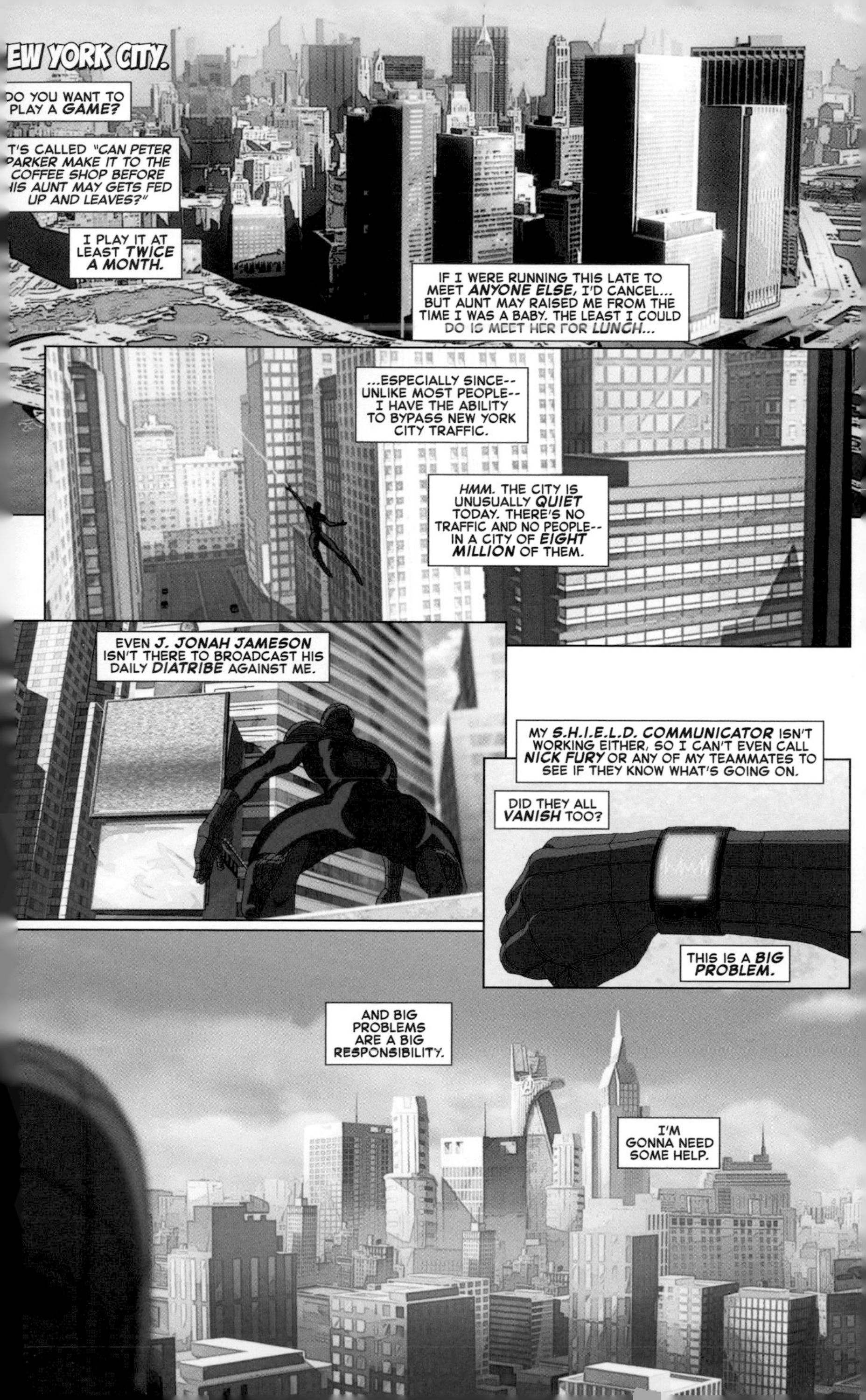
EW YORK CITY.
DO YOU WANT TO PLAY A GAME?
T'S CALLED "CAN PETER PARKER MAKE IT TO THE COFFEE SHOP BEFORE HIS AUNT MAY GETS FED UP AND LEAVES?"
I PLAY IT AT LEAST TWICE A MONTH.
IF I WERE RUNNING THIS LATE TO MEET ANYONE ELSE, I'D CANCEL... BUT AUNT MAY RAISED ME FROM THE TIME I WAS A BABY. THE LEAST I COULD DO IS MEET HER FOR LUNCH...
...ESPECIALLY SINCE-- UNLIKE MOST PEOPLE-- I HAVE THE ABILITY TO BYPASS NEW YORK CITY TRAFFIC.
HMM. THE CITY IS UNUSUALLY QUIET TODAY. THERE'S NO TRAFFIC AND NO PEOPLE-- IN A CITY OF EIGHT MILLION OF THEM.
EVEN J. JONAH JAMESON ISN'T THERE TO BROADCAST HIS DAILY DIATRIBE AGAINST ME.
MY S.H.I.E.L.D. COMMUNICATOR ISN'T WORKING EITHER, SO I CAN'T EVEN CALL NICK FURY OR ANY OF MY TEAMMATES TO SEE IF THEY KNOW WHAT'S GOING ON.
DID THEY ALL VANISH TOO?
THIS IS A BIG PROBLEM.
AND BIG PROBLEMS ARE A BIG RESPONSIBILITY.
I'M GONNA NEED SOME HELP.

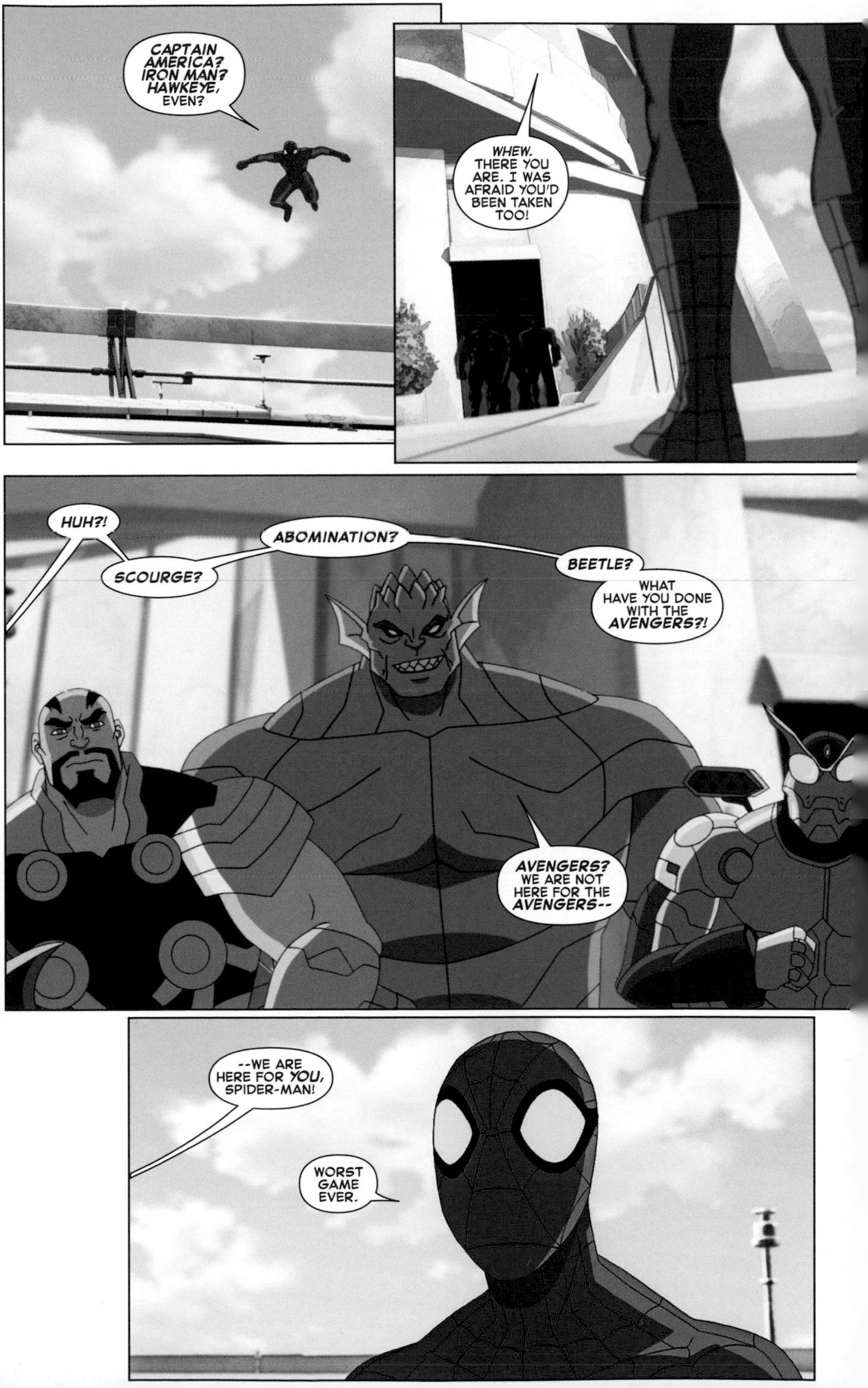
CAPTAIN AMERICA? IRON MAN? HAWKEYE, EVEN?
WHEW. THERE YOU ARE. I WAS AFRAID YOU'D BEEN TAKEN TOO!
HUH?!
SCOURGE?
ABOMINATION?
BEETLE?
WHAT HAVE YOU DONE WITH THE AVENGERS?!
AVENGERS? WE ARE NOT HERE FOR THE AVENGERS--
--WE ARE HERE FOR YOU, SPIDER-MAN!
WORST GAME EVER.

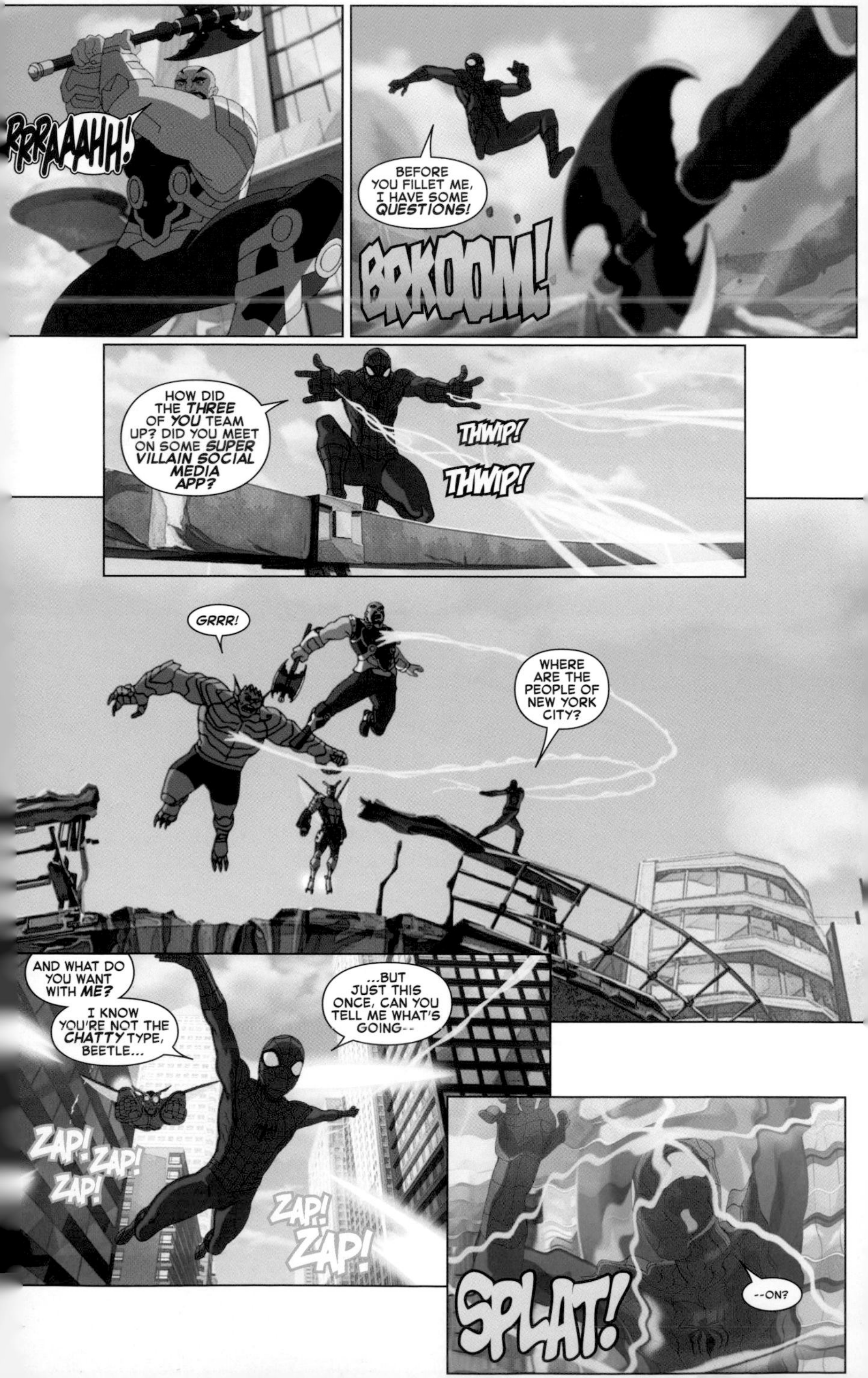
RRRAAAHH!
BEFORE YOU FILLET ME, I HAVE SOME QUESTIONS!
BRKOOM!
HOW DID THE THREE OF YOU TEAM UP? DID YOU MEET ON SOME SUPER VILLAIN SOCIAL MEDIA APP?
THWIP!
THWIP!
GRRR!
WHERE ARE THE PEOPLE OF NEW YORK CITY?
AND WHAT DO YOU WANT WITH ME?
I KNOW YOU'RE NOT THE CHATTY TYPE, BEETLE...
...BUT JUST THIS ONCE, CAN YOU TELL ME WHAT'S GOING--
ZAP! ZAP! ZAP!
ZAP! ZAP!
SPLAT!
--ON?

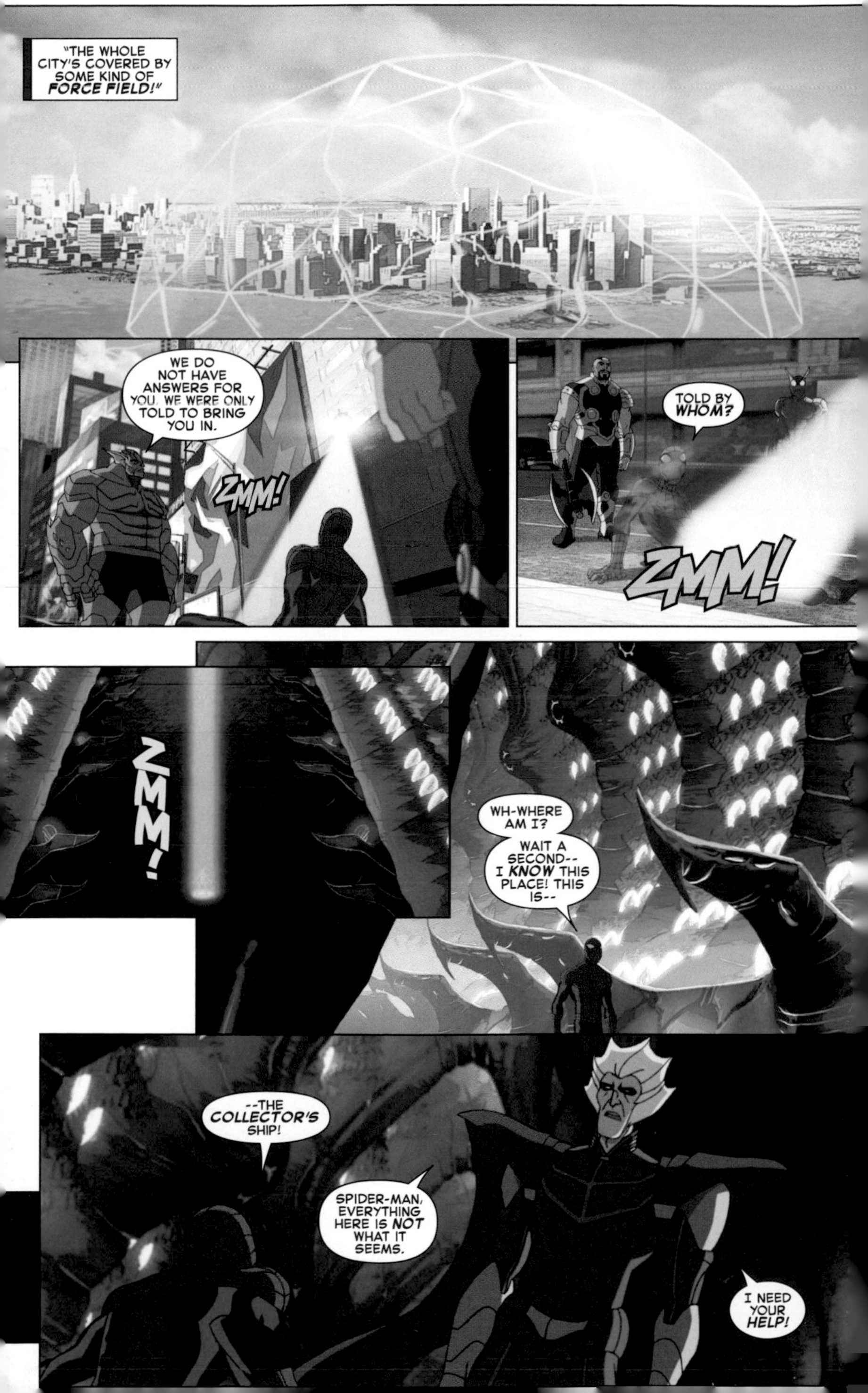
"THE WHOLE CITY'S COVERED BY SOME KIND OF FORCE FIELD!"
WE DO NOT HAVE ANSWERS FOR YOU. WE WERE ONLY TOLD TO BRING YOU IN.
ZMM!
TOLD BY WHOM?
ZMM!
ZMM!
WH-WHERE AM I?
WAIT A SECOND-- I KNOW THIS PLACE! THIS IS--
--THE COLLECTOR'S SHIP!
SPIDER-MAN, EVERYTHING HERE IS NOT WHAT IT SEEMS.
I NEED YOUR HELP!

WHILE ATTENDING A RADIOLOGY DEMONSTRATION, HIGH SCHOOL STUDENT PETER PARKER WAS BITTEN BY A RADIOACTIVE SPIDER AND GAINED THE SPIDER'S POWERS! NOW HE IS TRAINING WITH THE SUPERSPY ORGANIZATION CALLED S.H.I.E.L.D. TO BECOME THE...

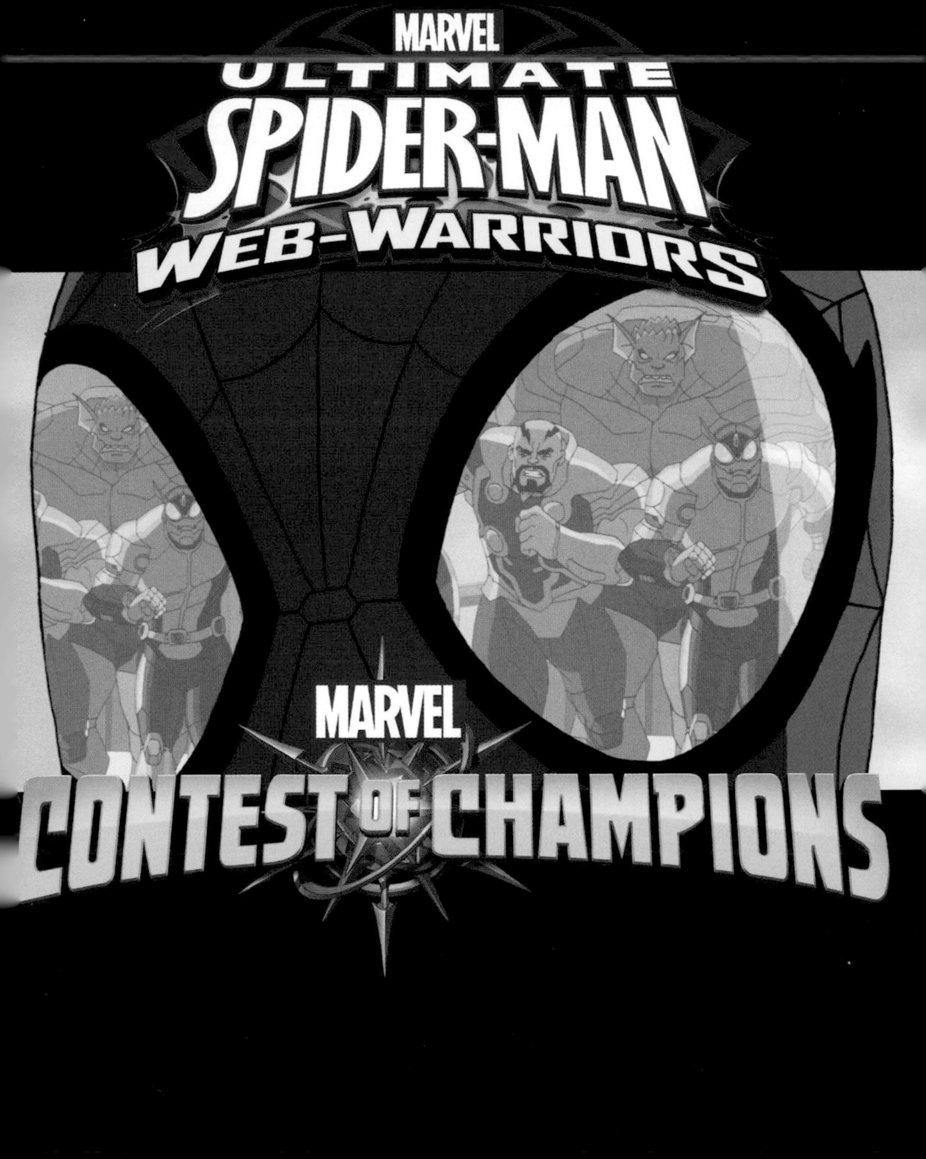
MARVEL
ULTIMATE
SPIDER-MAN
WEB-WARRIORS
MARVEL
CONTEST OF CHAMPIONS

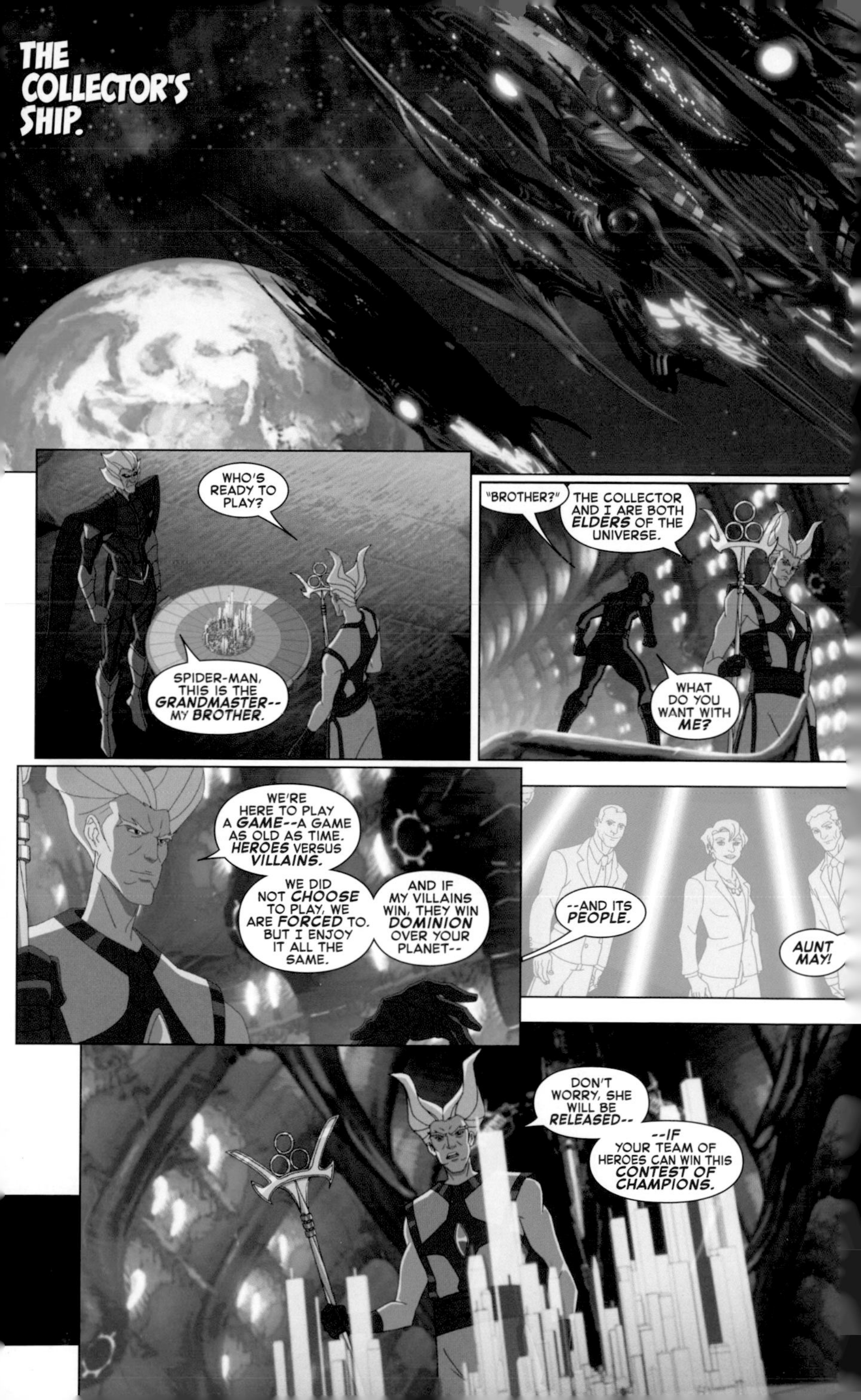
THE COLLECTOR'S SHIP.
WHO'S READY TO PLAY?
SPIDER-MAN, THIS IS THE GRANDMASTER-- MY BROTHER.
"BROTHER?"
THE COLLECTOR AND I ARE BOTH ELDERS OF THE UNIVERSE.
WHAT DO YOU WANT WITH ME?
WE'RE HERE TO PLAY A GAME--A GAME AS OLD AS TIME. HEROES VERSUS VILLAINS.
WE DID NOT CHOOSE TO PLAY, WE ARE FORCED TO. BUT I ENJOY IT ALL THE SAME.
AND IF MY VILLAINS WIN, THEY WIN DOMINION OVER YOUR PLANET--
--AND ITS PEOPLE.
AUNT MAY!
DON'T WORRY, SHE WILL BE RELEASED--
--IF YOUR TEAM OF HEROES CAN WIN THIS CONTEST OF CHAMPIONS.

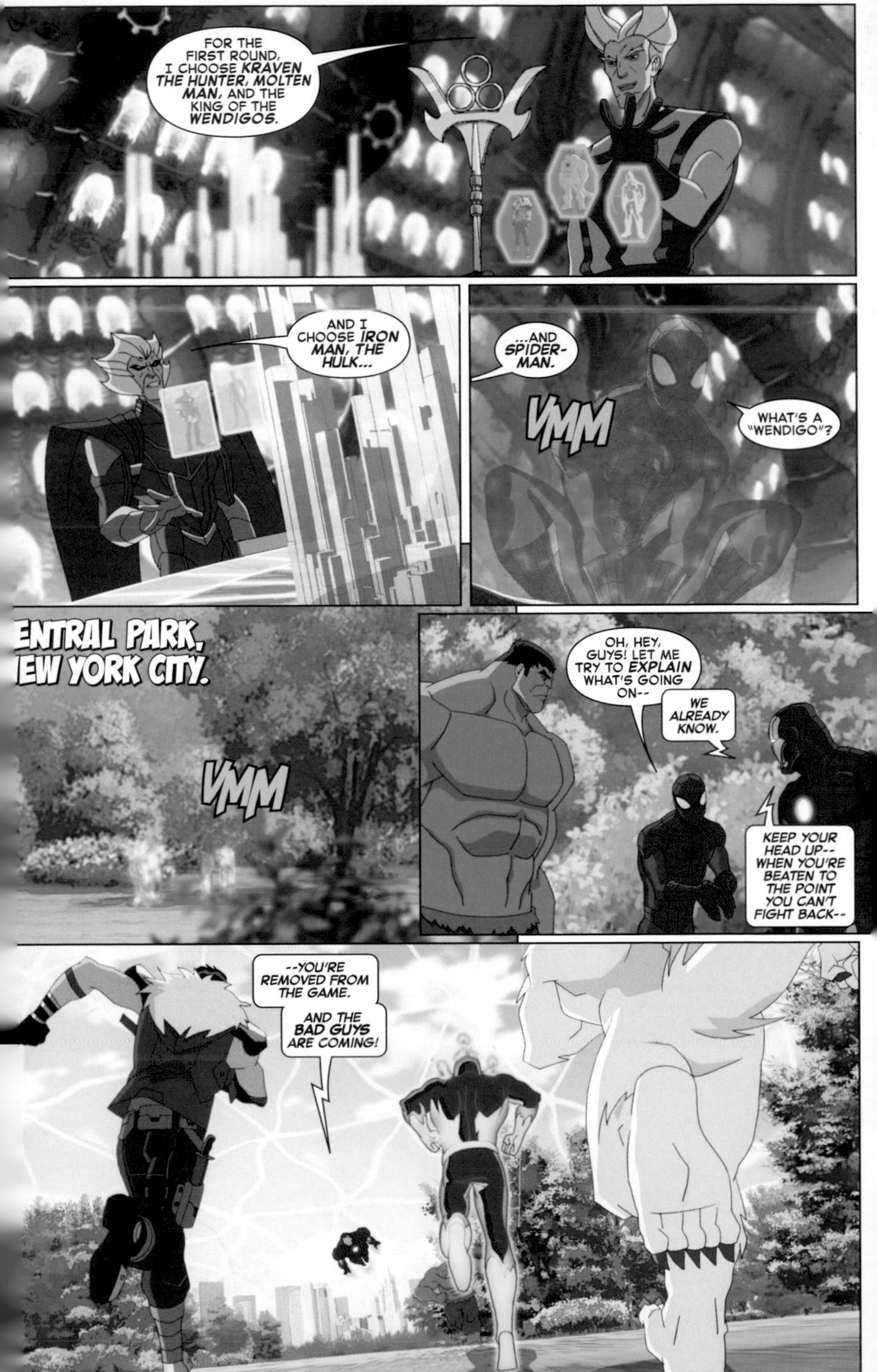
FOR THE FIRST ROUND, I CHOOSE KRAVEN THE HUNTER, MOLTEN MAN, AND THE KING OF THE WENDIGOS.
AND I CHOOSE IRON MAN, THE HULK...
...AND SPIDER-MAN.
VMM
WHAT'S A "WENDIGO"?
ENTRAL PARK, EW YORK CITY.
VMM
OH, HEY, GUYS! LET ME TRY TO EXPLAIN WHAT'S GOING ON--
WE ALREADY KNOW.
KEEP YOUR HEAD UP-- WHEN YOU'RE BEATEN TO THE POINT YOU CAN'T FIGHT BACK--
--YOU'RE REMOVED FROM THE GAME.
AND THE BAD GUYS ARE COMING!

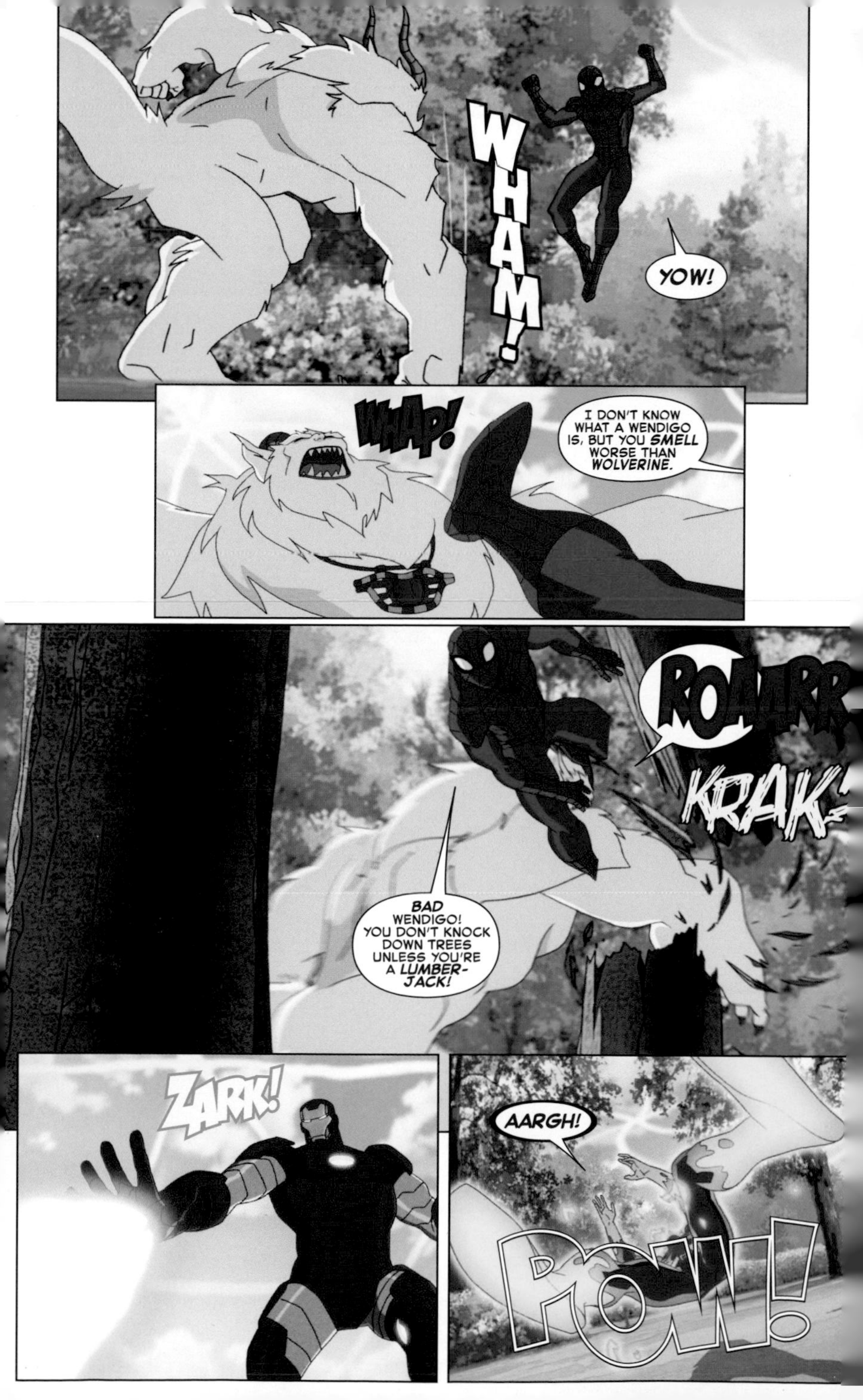
WHAM!
YOW!
WHAP!
I DON'T KNOW WHAT A WENDIGO IS, BUT YOU SMELL WORSE THAN WOLVERINE.
ROARRR
KRAK!
BAD WENDIGO! YOU DON'T KNOCK DOWN TREES UNLESS YOU'RE A LUMBER-JACK!
ZARK!
AARGH!
POW!

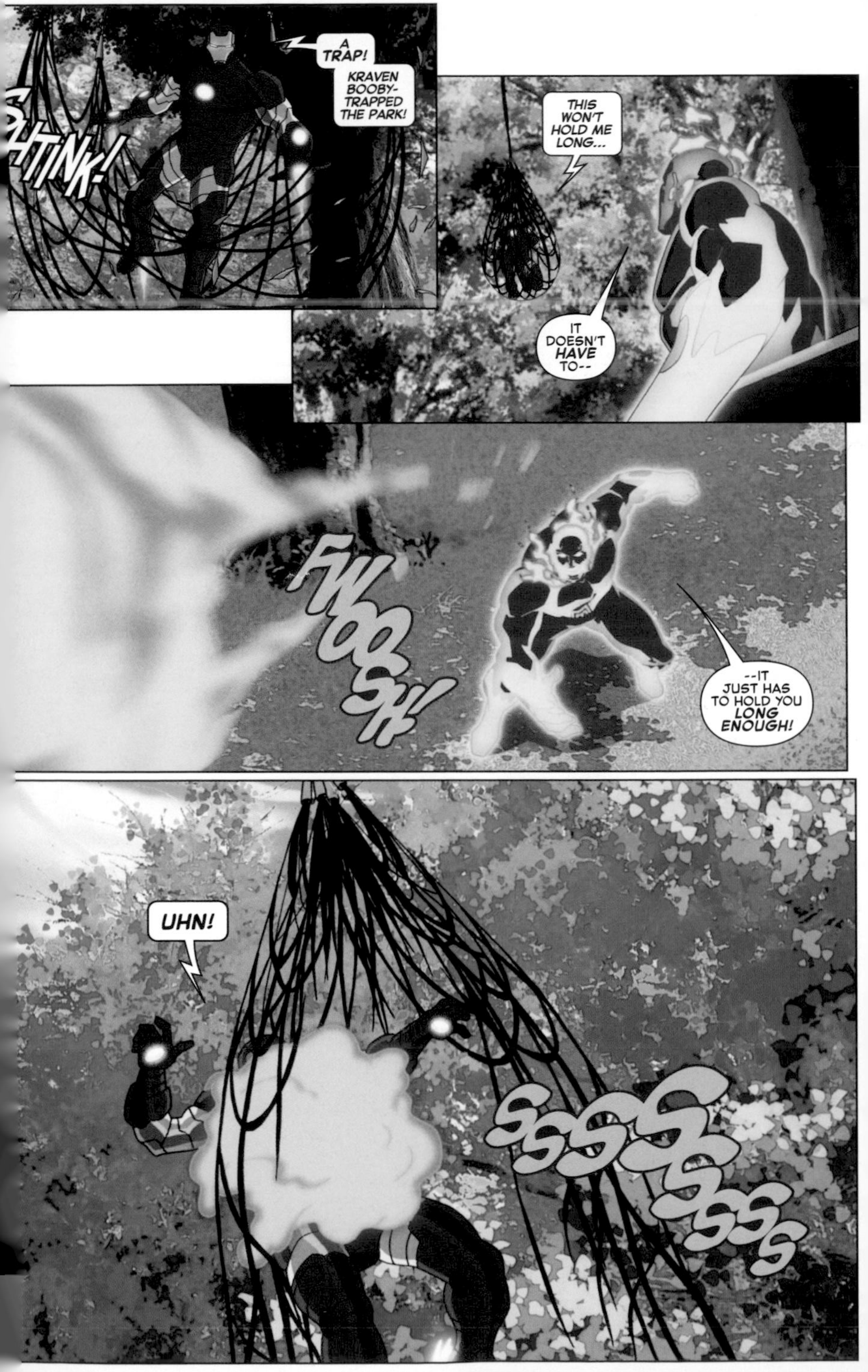

SHTINK!
A TRAP!
KRAVEN BOOBY-TRAPPED THE PARK!
THIS WON'T HOLD ME LONG...
IT DOESN'T HAVE TO--
FWOOSH!
--IT JUST HAS TO HOLD YOU LONG ENOUGH!
UHN!
SSSSSSSSS

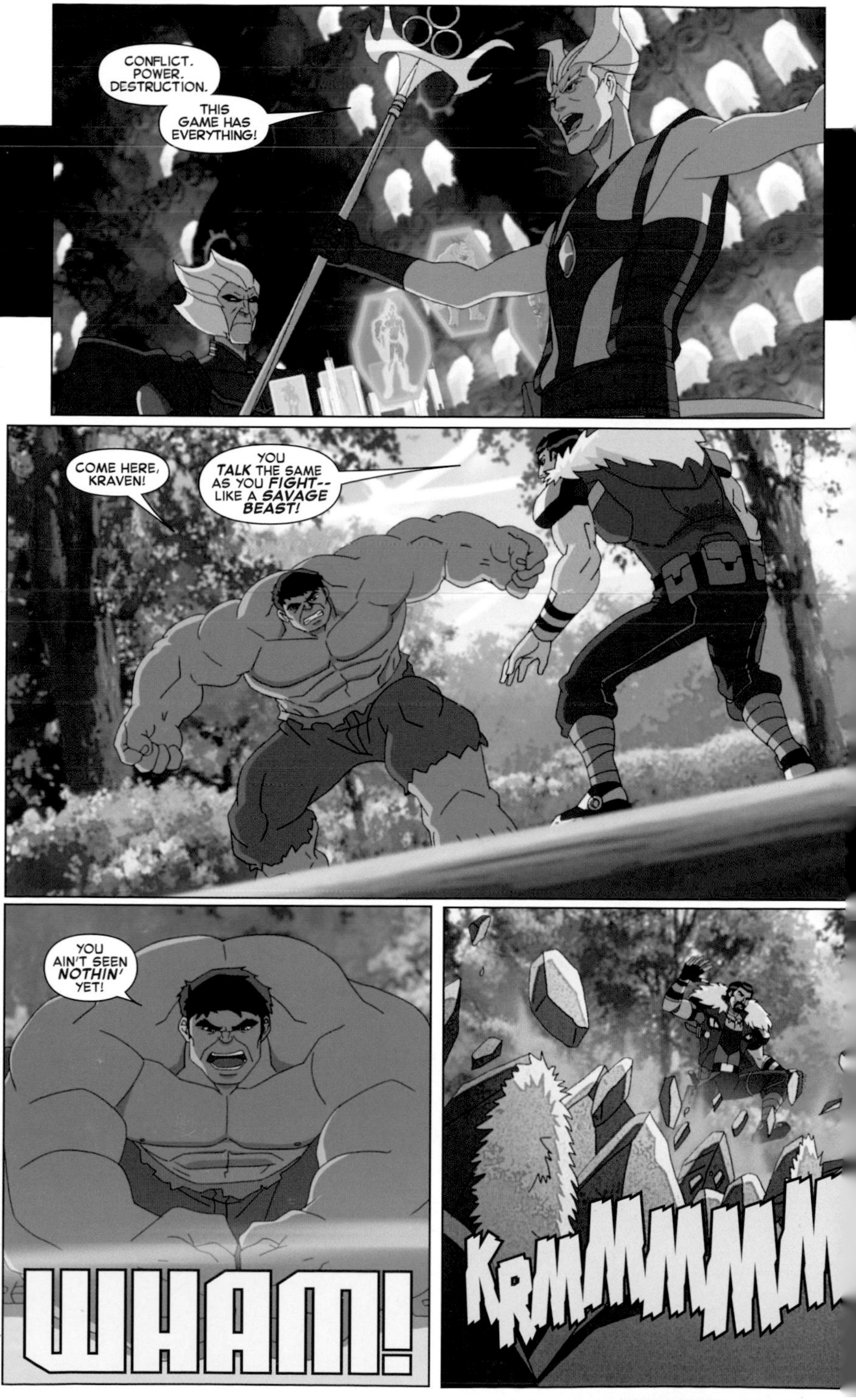

CONFLICT. POWER. DESTRUCTION.
THIS GAME HAS EVERYTHING!
COME HERE, KRAVEN!
YOU TALK THE SAME AS YOU FIGHT-- LIKE A SAVAGE BEAST!
YOU AIN'T SEEN NOTHIN' YET!
WHAM!
KRMMMMMM

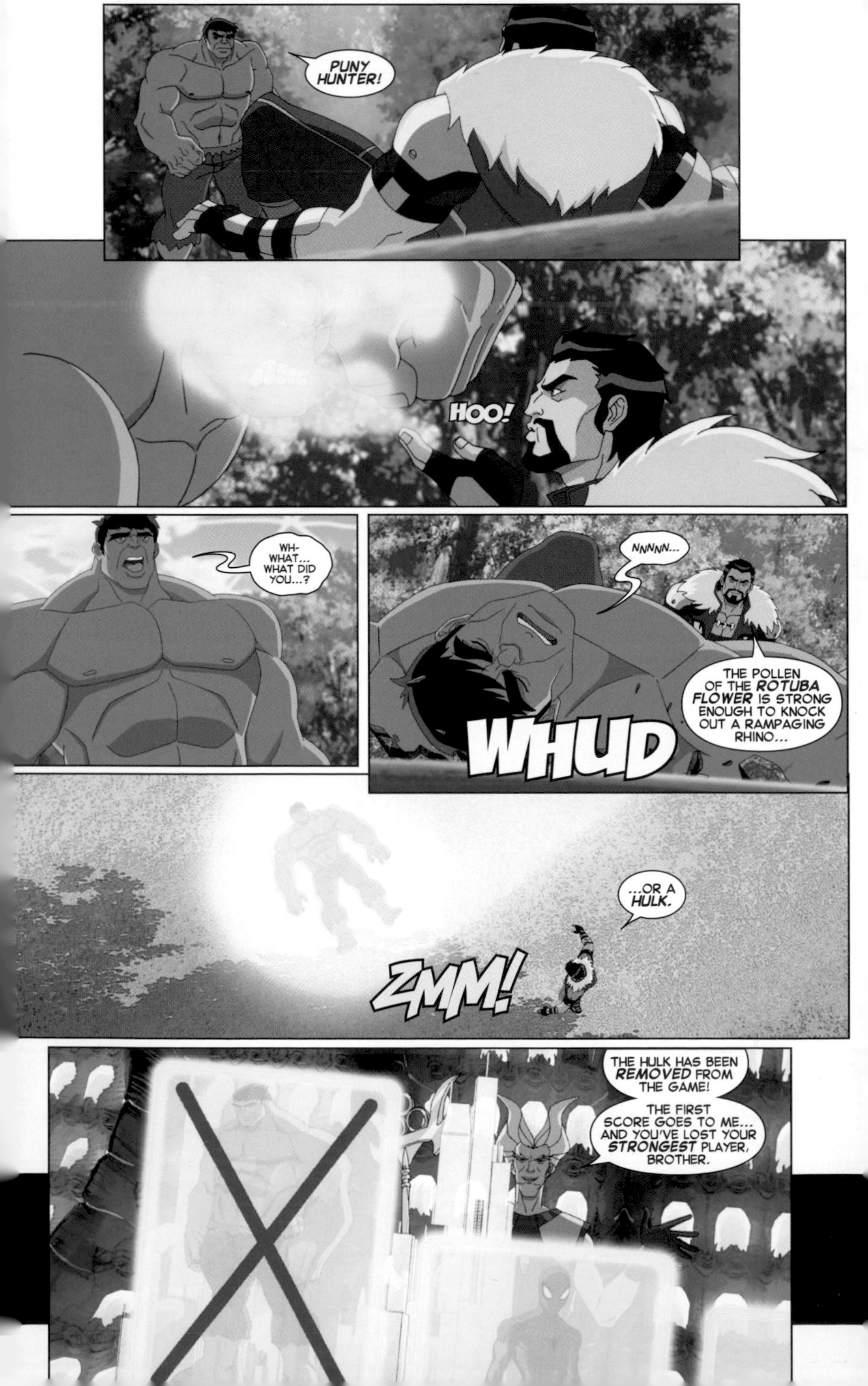
PUNY HUNTER!
HOO!
WH- WHAT... WHAT DID YOU...?
NNNNN...
THE POLLEN OF THE ROTUBA FLOWER IS STRONG ENOUGH TO KNOCK OUT A RAMPAGING RHINO...
WHUD
...OR A HULK.
ZMM!
THE HULK HAS BEEN REMOVED FROM THE GAME!
THE FIRST SCORE GOES TO ME... AND YOU'VE LOST YOUR STRONGEST PLAYER, BROTHER.

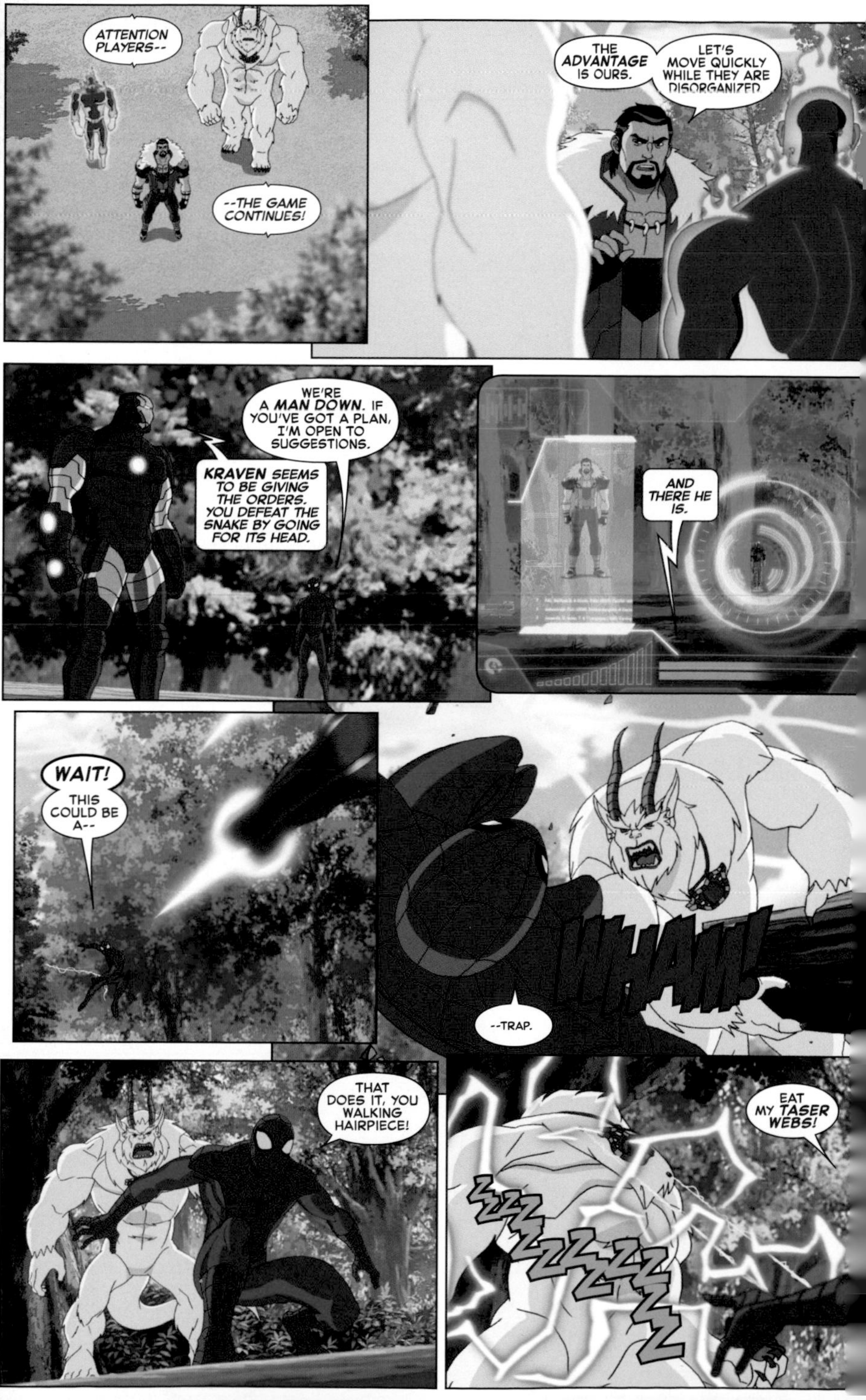
ATTENTION PLAYERS--
--THE GAME CONTINUES!
THE ADVANTAGE IS OURS.
LET'S MOVE QUICKLY WHILE THEY ARE DISORGANIZED
WE'RE A MAN DOWN. IF YOU'VE GOT A PLAN, I'M OPEN TO SUGGESTIONS.
KRAVEN SEEMS TO BE GIVING THE ORDERS. YOU DEFEAT THE SNAKE BY GOING FOR ITS HEAD.
AND THERE HE IS.
WAIT! THIS COULD BE A--
WHAM!
--TRAP.
THAT DOES IT, YOU WALKING HAIRPIECE!
EAT MY TASER WEBS!
ZZZZZZZZZZ

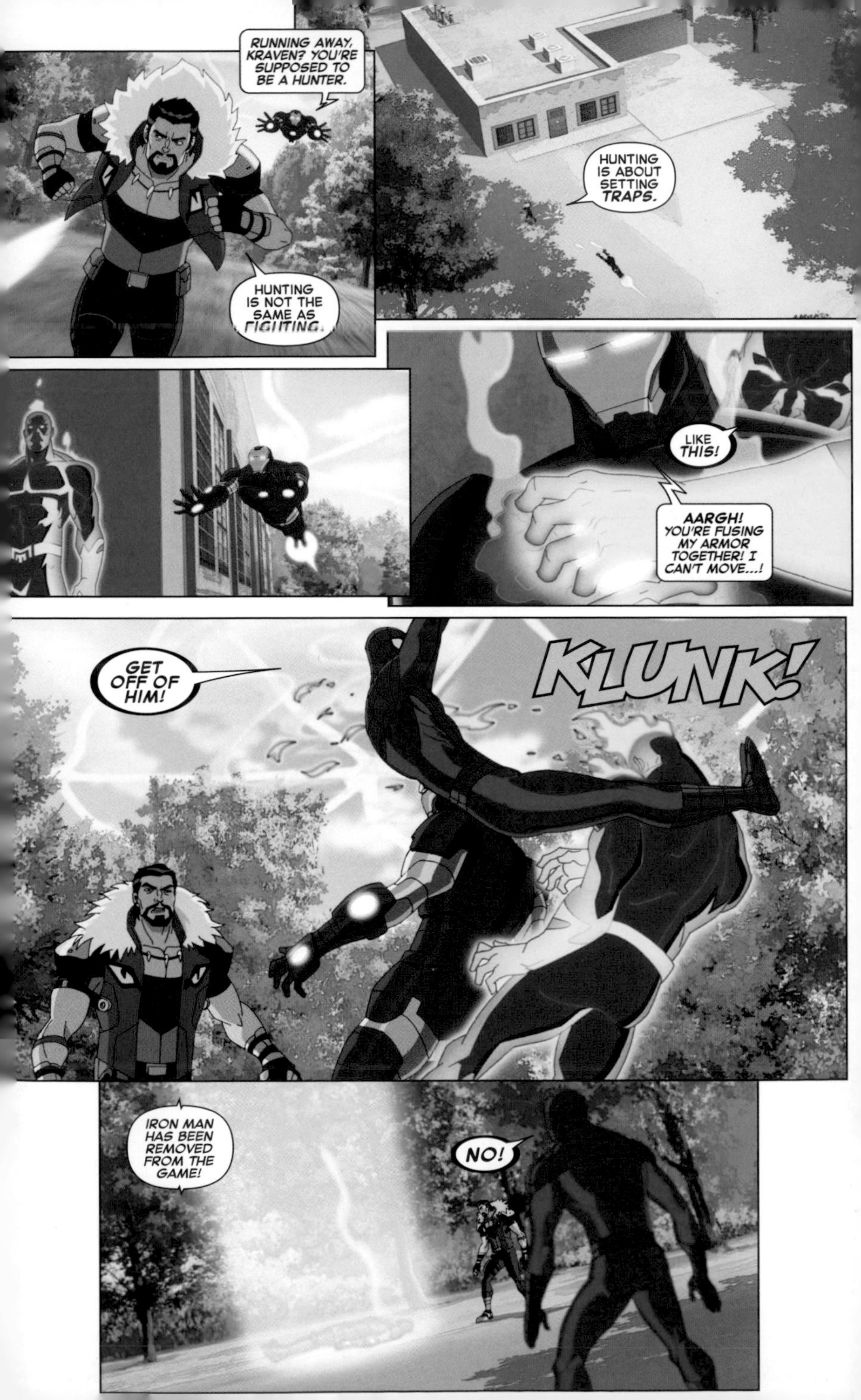
RUNNING AWAY, KRAVEN? YOU'RE SUPPOSED TO BE A HUNTER.
HUNTING IS NOT THE SAME AS FIGHTING.
HUNTING IS ABOUT SETTING TRAPS.
LIKE THIS!
AARGH! YOU'RE FUSING MY ARMOR TOGETHER! I CAN'T MOVE...!
GET OFF OF HIM!
KLUNK!
IRON MAN HAS BEEN REMOVED FROM THE GAME!
NO!

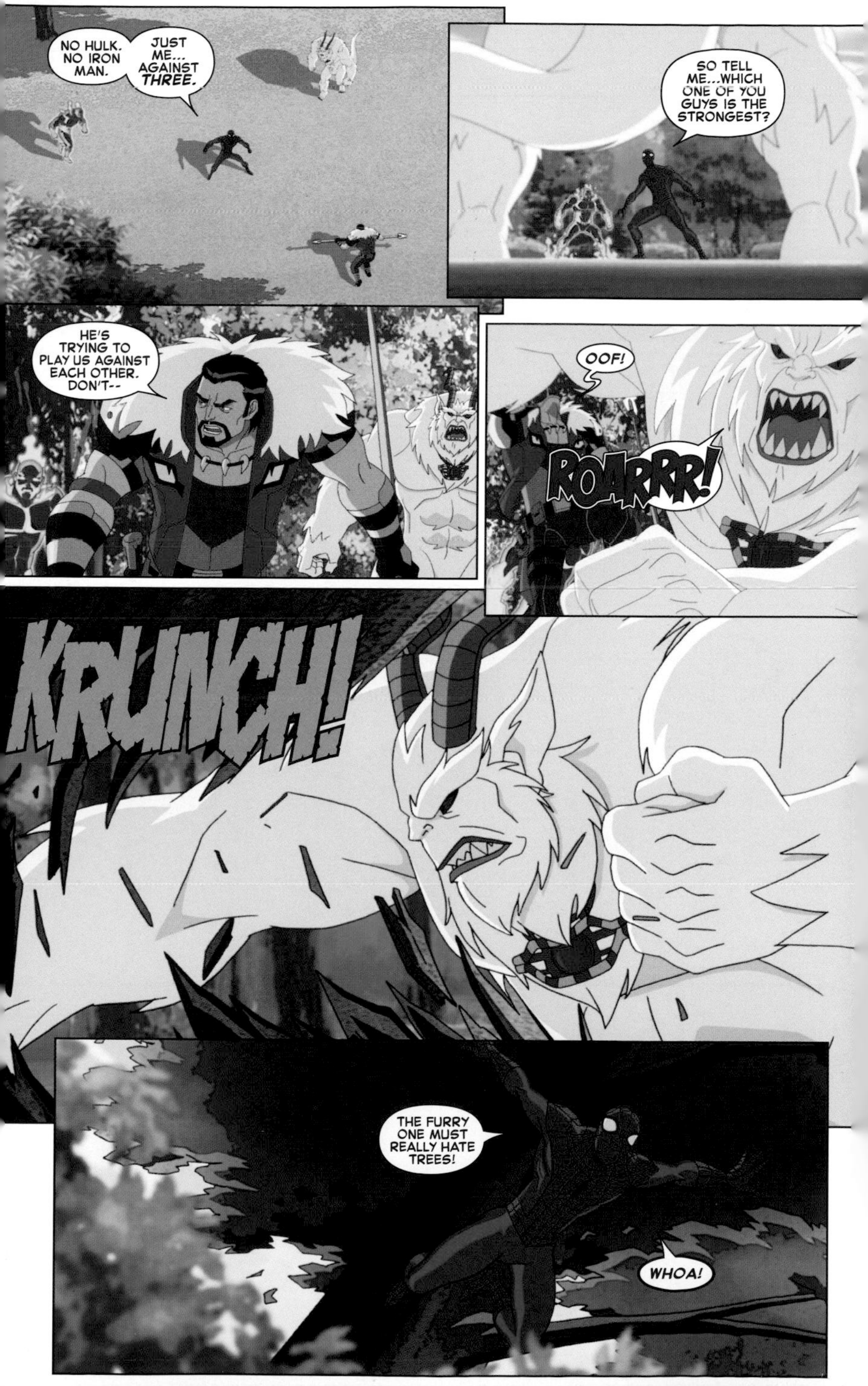
NO HULK. NO IRON MAN.
JUST ME... AGAINST THREE.
SO TELL ME...WHICH ONE OF YOU GUYS IS THE STRONGEST?
HE'S TRYING TO PLAY US AGAINST EACH OTHER. DON'T--
OOF!
ROARRR!
KRUNCH!
THE FURRY ONE MUST REALLY HATE TREES!
WHOA!

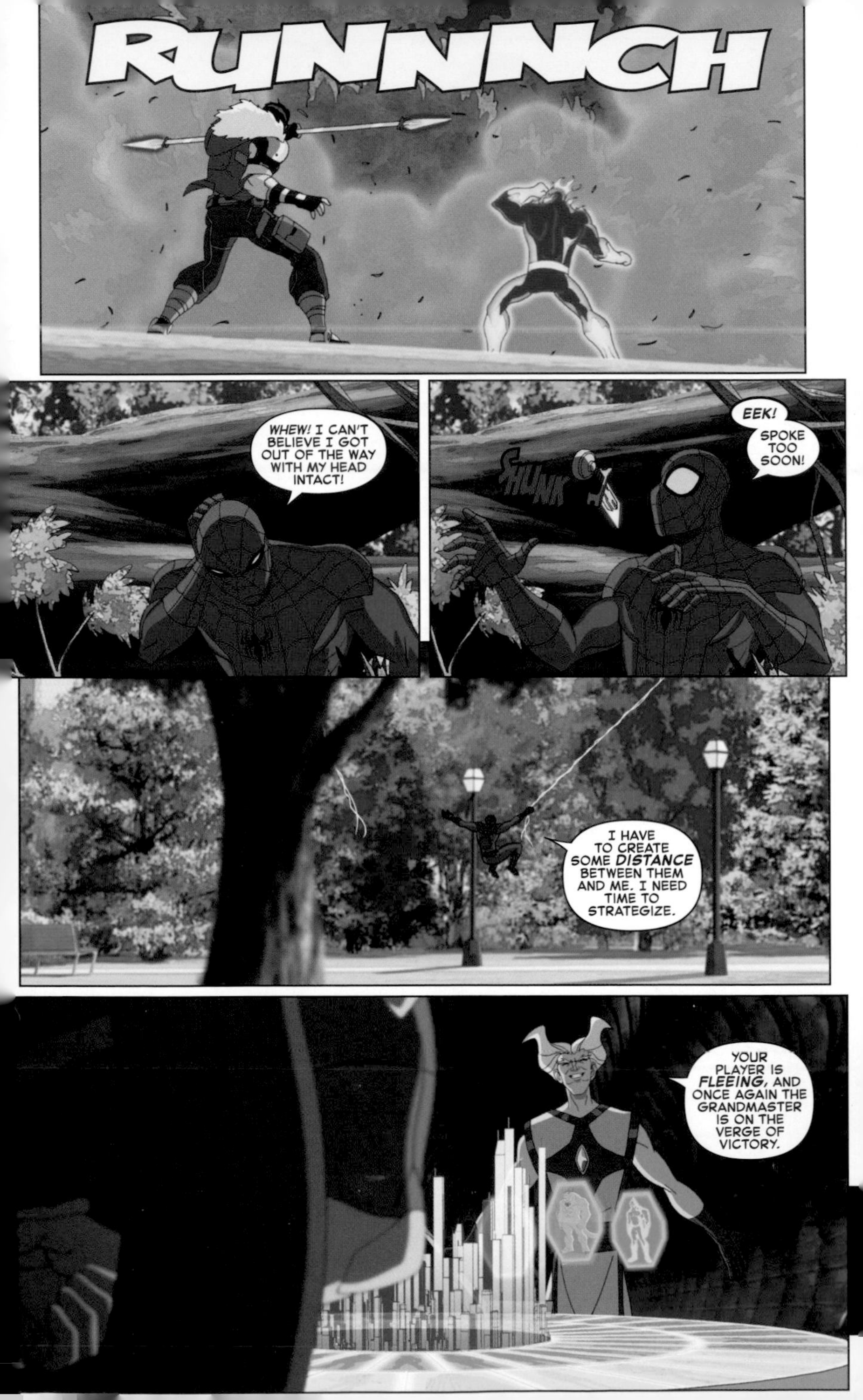
RUNNNCH
WHEW! I CAN'T BELIEVE I GOT OUT OF THE WAY WITH MY HEAD INTACT!
SHUNK
EEK!
SPOKE TOO SOON!
I HAVE TO CREATE SOME DISTANCE BETWEEN THEM AND ME. I NEED TIME TO STRATEGIZE.
YOUR PLAYER IS FLEEING, AND ONCE AGAIN THE GRANDMASTER IS ON THE VERGE OF VICTORY.

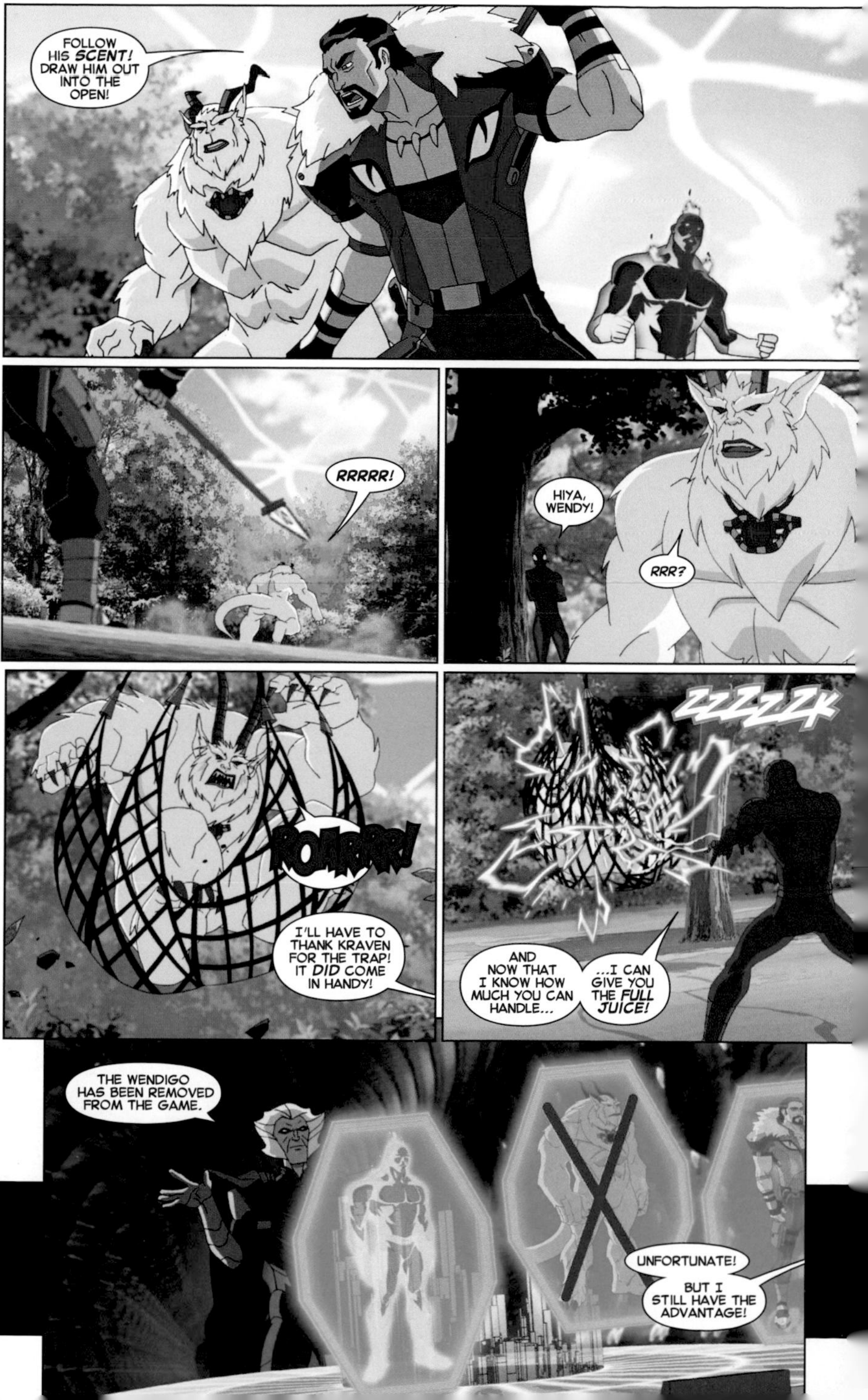
FOLLOW HIS SCENT! DRAW HIM OUT INTO THE OPEN!
RRRRR!
HIYA, WENDY!
RRR?
ROARRR!
I'LL HAVE TO THANK KRAVEN FOR THE TRAP! IT DID COME IN HANDY!
ZZZZZZK
AND NOW THAT I KNOW HOW MUCH YOU CAN HANDLE...
...I CAN GIVE YOU THE FULL JUICE!
THE WENDIGO HAS BEEN REMOVED FROM THE GAME.
UNFORTUNATE!
BUT I STILL HAVE THE ADVANTAGE!

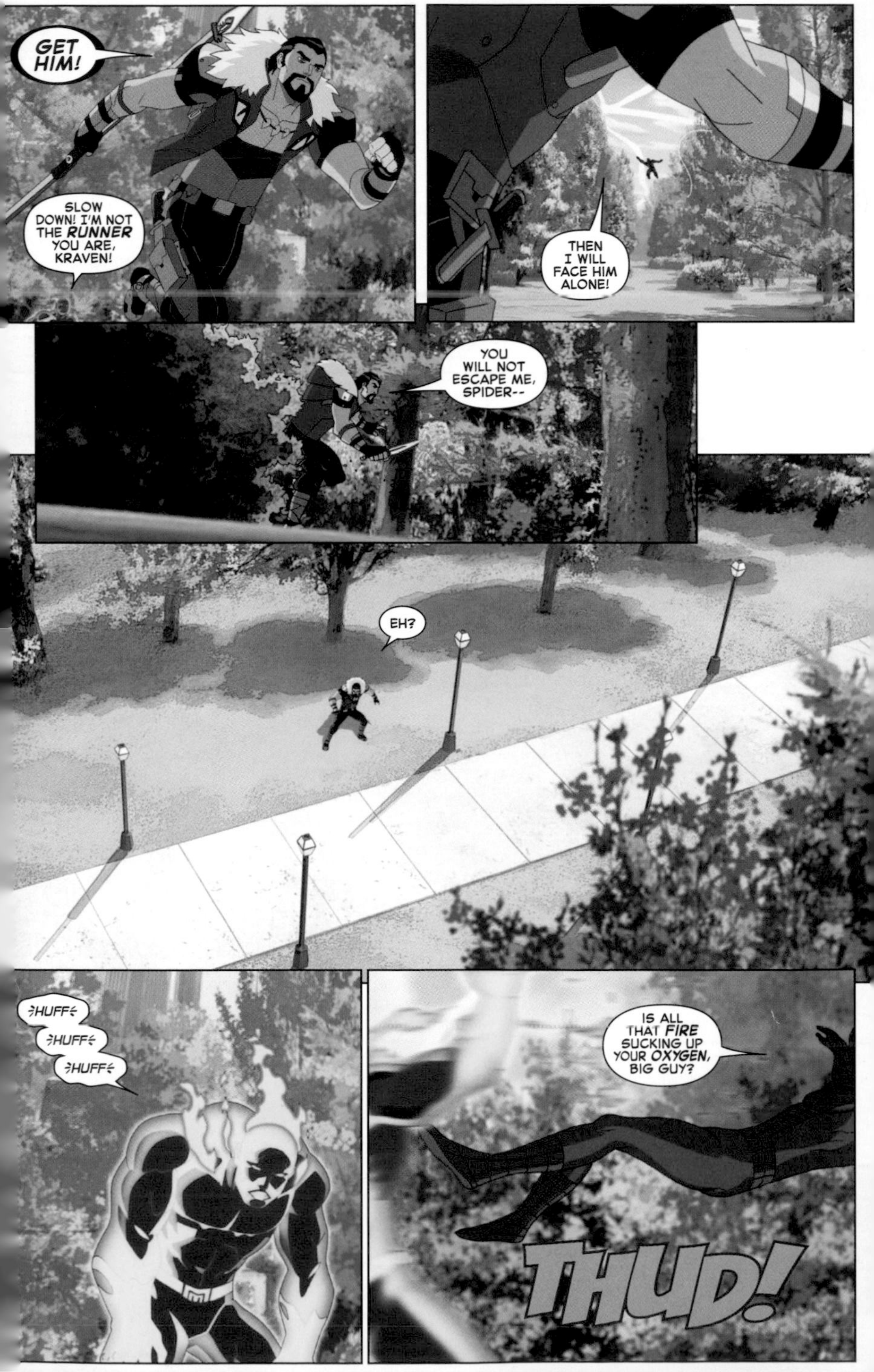
GET HIM!
SLOW DOWN! I'M NOT THE RUNNER YOU ARE, KRAVEN!
THEN I WILL FACE HIM ALONE!
YOU WILL NOT ESCAPE ME, SPIDER--
EH?
HUFF
HUFF
HUFF
IS ALL THAT FIRE SUCKING UP YOUR OXYGEN, BIG GUY?
THUD!

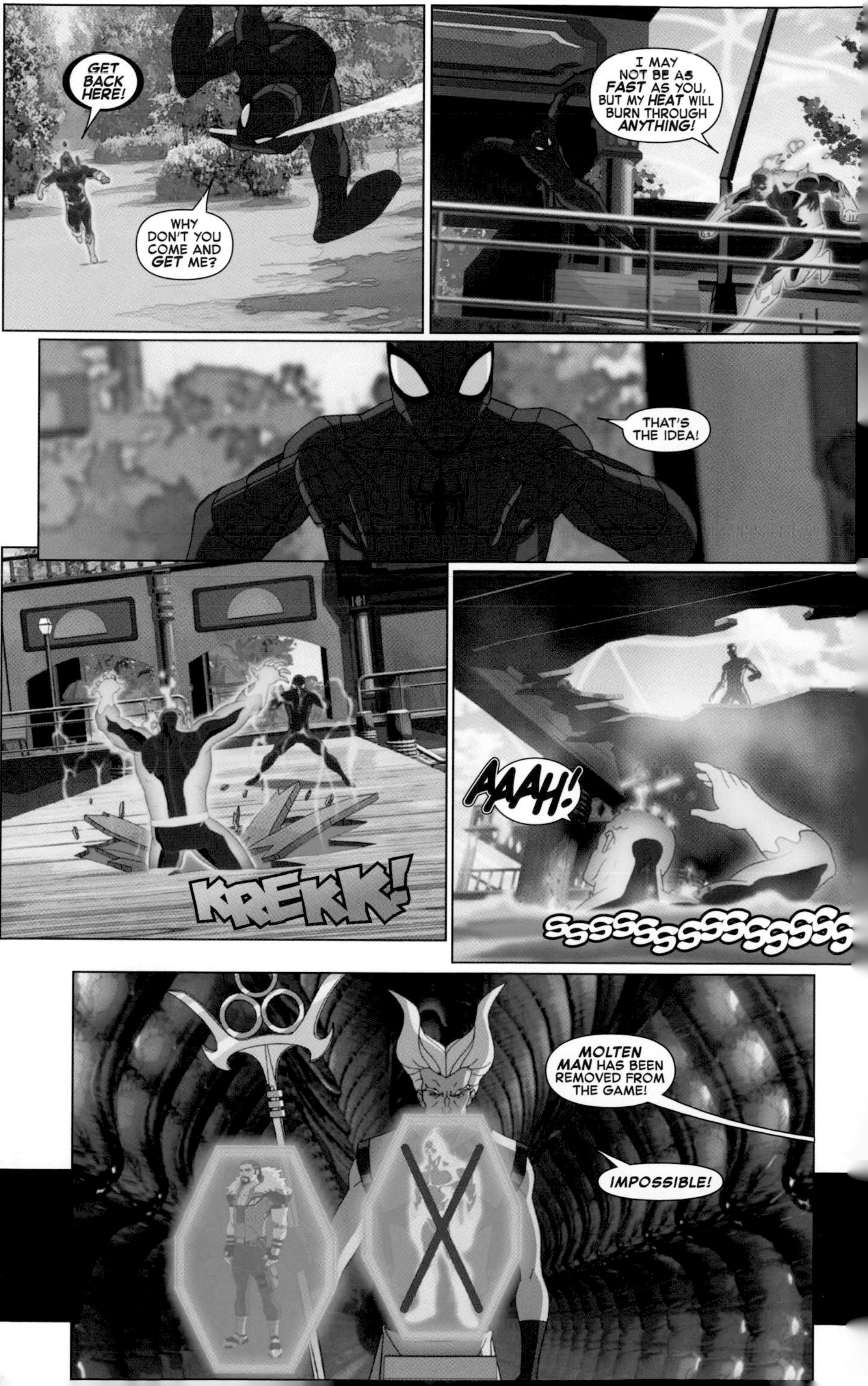
GET BACK HERE!
WHY DON'T YOU COME AND GET ME?
I MAY NOT BE AS FAST AS YOU, BUT MY HEAT WILL BURN THROUGH ANYTHING!
THAT'S THE IDEA!
KREKK!
AAAH!
SSSSSSSSSSSSSSS
MOLTEN MAN HAS BEEN REMOVED FROM THE GAME!
IMPOSSIBLE!

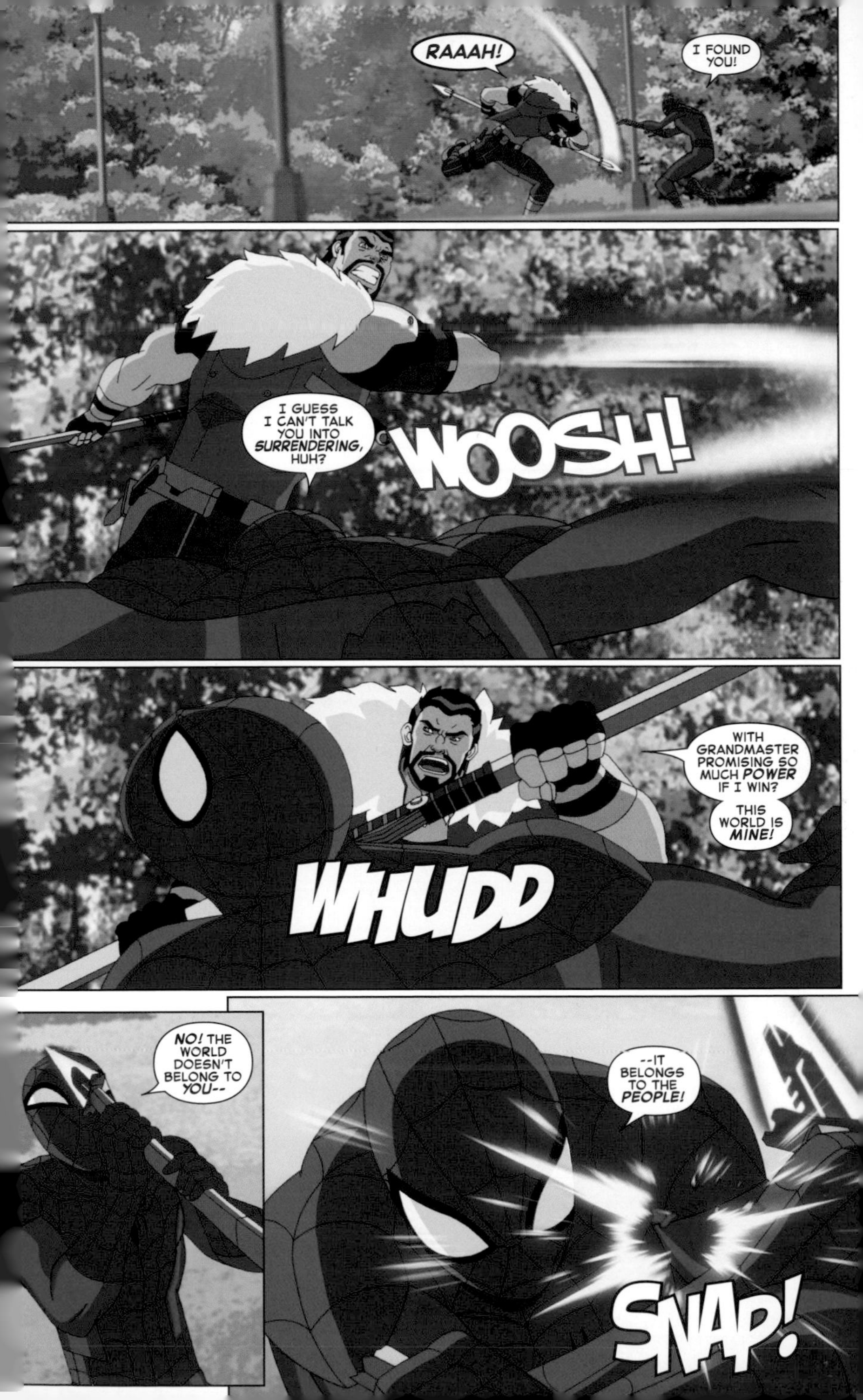
RAAAH!
I FOUND YOU!
I GUESS I CAN'T TALK YOU INTO SURRENDERING, HUH?
WOOSH!
WITH GRANDMASTER PROMISING SO MUCH POWER IF I WIN?
THIS WORLD IS MINE!
WHUDD
NO! THE WORLD DOESN'T BELONG TO YOU--
--IT BELONGS TO THE PEOPLE!
SNAP!

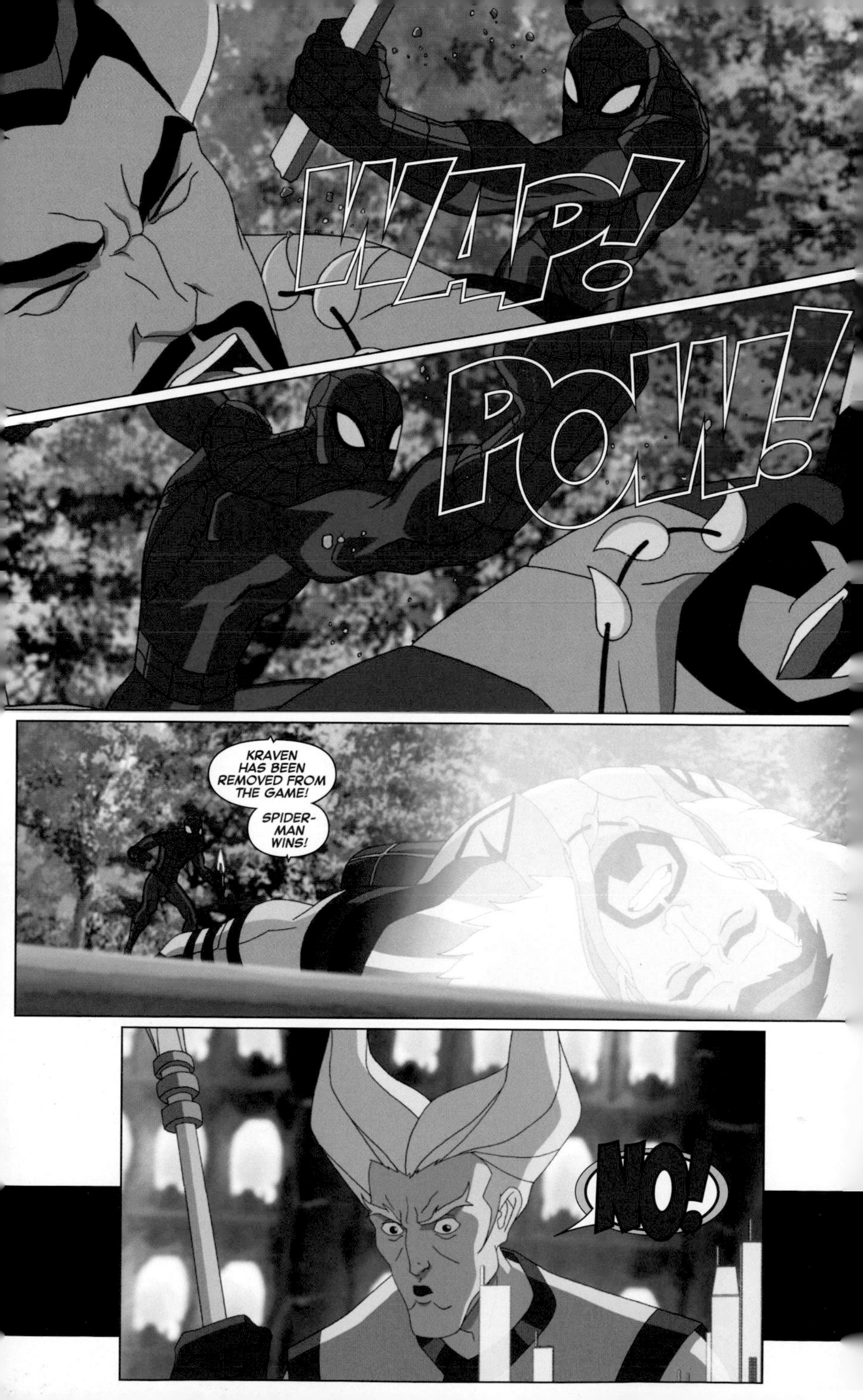
WAP!
POW!
KRAVEN HAS BEEN REMOVED FROM THE GAME!
SPIDER-MAN WINS!
NO!

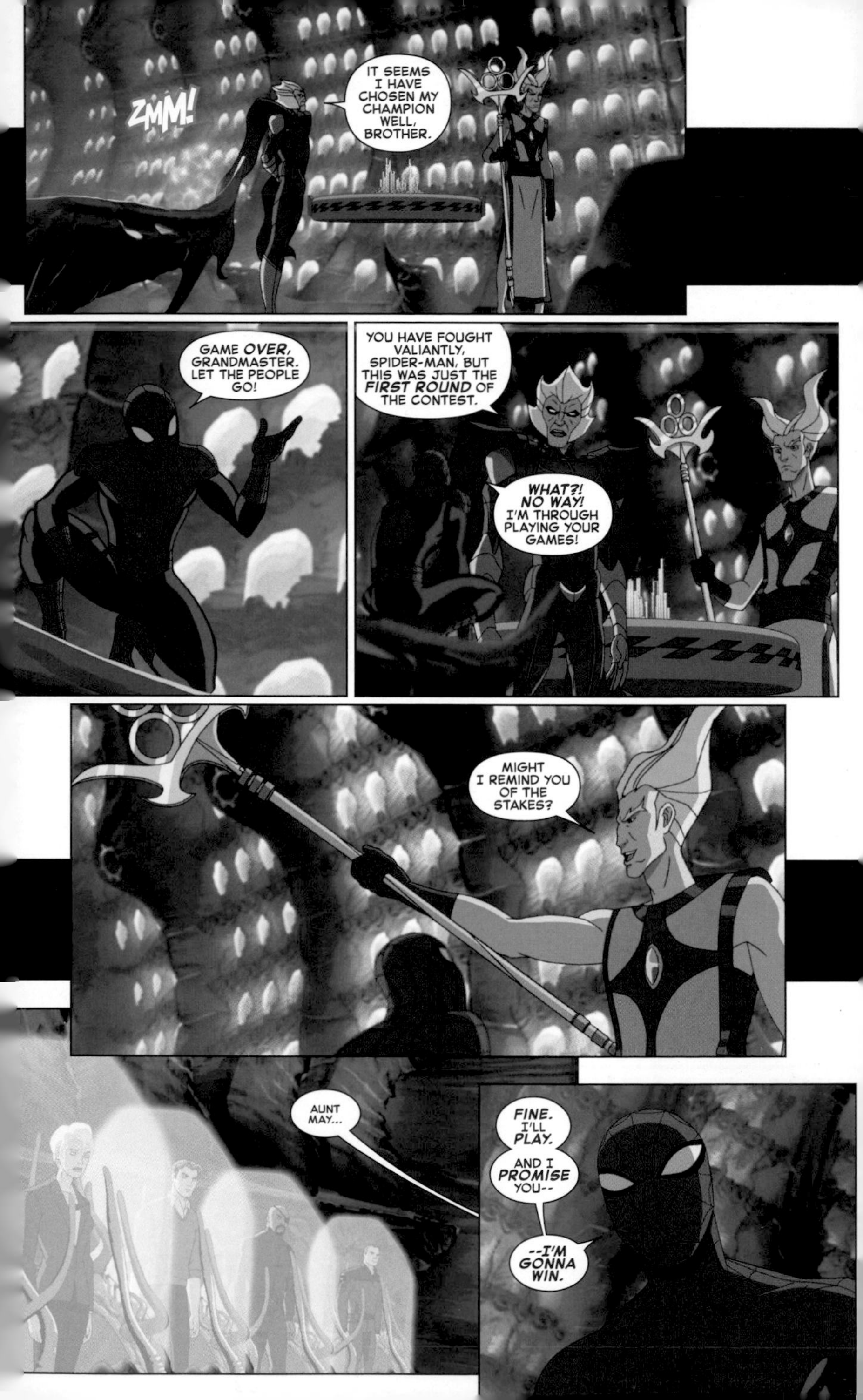
ZMM!
IT SEEMS I HAVE CHOSEN MY CHAMPION WELL, BROTHER.
GAME OVER, GRANDMASTER. LET THE PEOPLE GO!
YOU HAVE FOUGHT VALIANTLY, SPIDER-MAN, BUT THIS WAS JUST THE FIRST ROUND OF THE CONTEST.
WHAT?! NO WAY! I'M THROUGH PLAYING YOUR GAMES!
MIGHT I REMIND YOU OF THE STAKES?
AUNT MAY...
FINE. I'LL PLAY.
AND I PROMISE YOU--
--I'M GONNA WIN.

MARVEL

ULTIMATE SPIDER-MAN WEB-WARRIORS

CONTEST OF CHAMPIONS

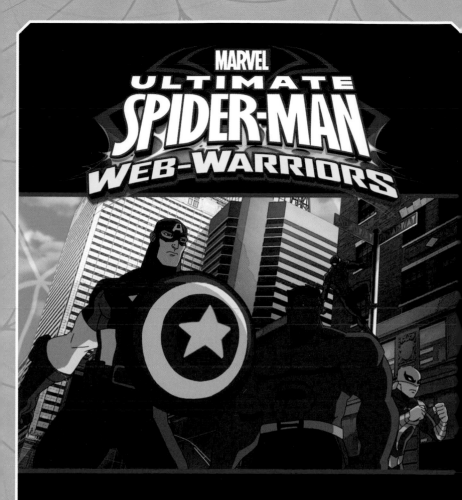

2

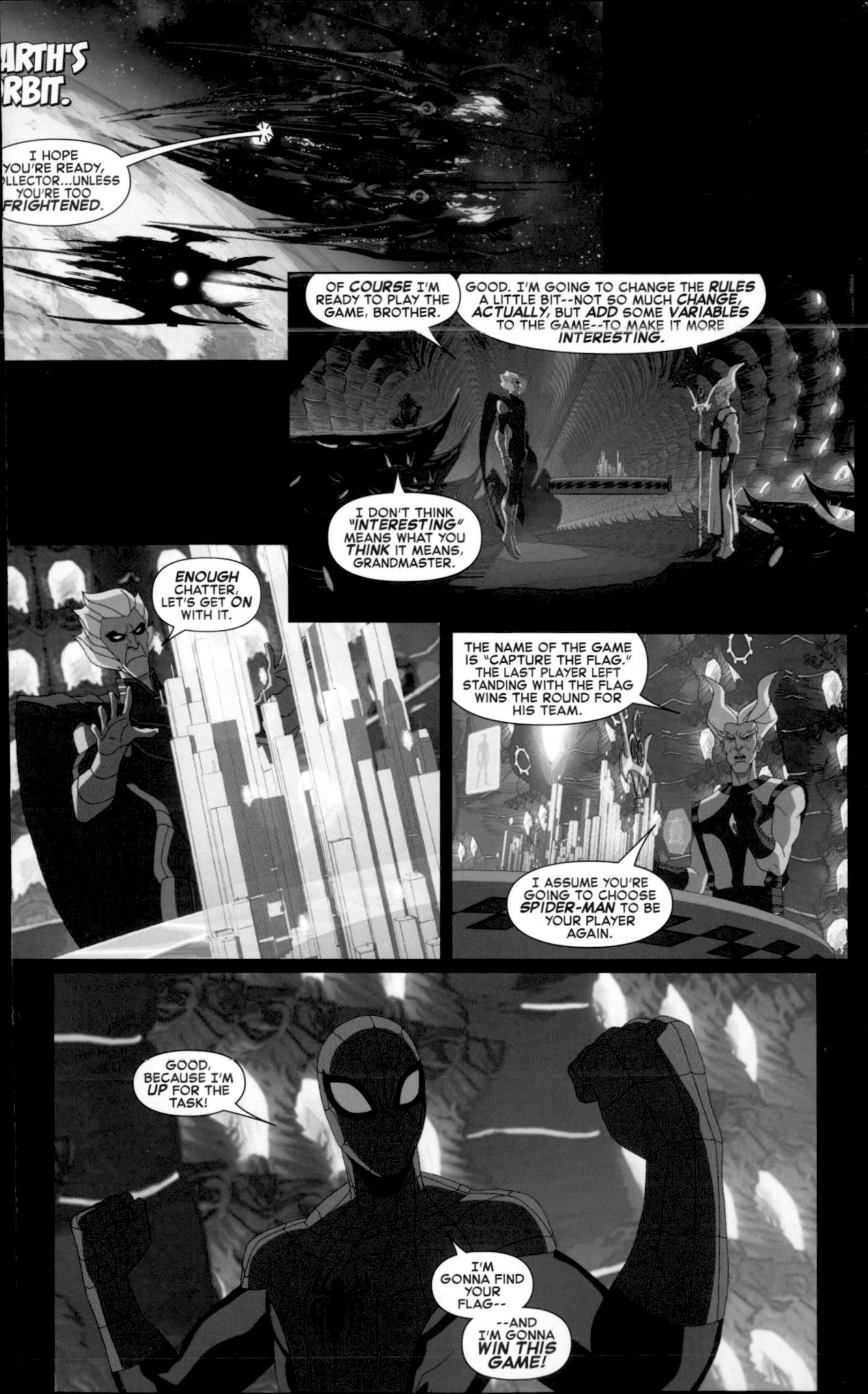

ARTH'S ORBIT.
I HOPE YOU'RE READY, OLLECTOR...UNLESS YOU'RE TOO FRIGHTENED.
OF COURSE I'M READY TO PLAY THE GAME, BROTHER.
GOOD. I'M GOING TO CHANGE THE RULES A LITTLE BIT--NOT SO MUCH CHANGE, ACTUALLY, BUT ADD SOME VARIABLES TO THE GAME--TO MAKE IT MORE INTERESTING.
I DON'T THINK "INTERESTING" MEANS WHAT YOU THINK IT MEANS, GRANDMASTER.
ENOUGH CHATTER, LET'S GET ON WITH IT.
THE NAME OF THE GAME IS "CAPTURE THE FLAG." THE LAST PLAYER LEFT STANDING WITH THE FLAG WINS THE ROUND FOR HIS TEAM.
I ASSUME YOU'RE GOING TO CHOOSE SPIDER-MAN TO BE YOUR PLAYER AGAIN.
GOOD, BECAUSE I'M UP FOR THE TASK!
I'M GONNA FIND YOUR FLAG--
--AND I'M GONNA WIN THIS GAME!

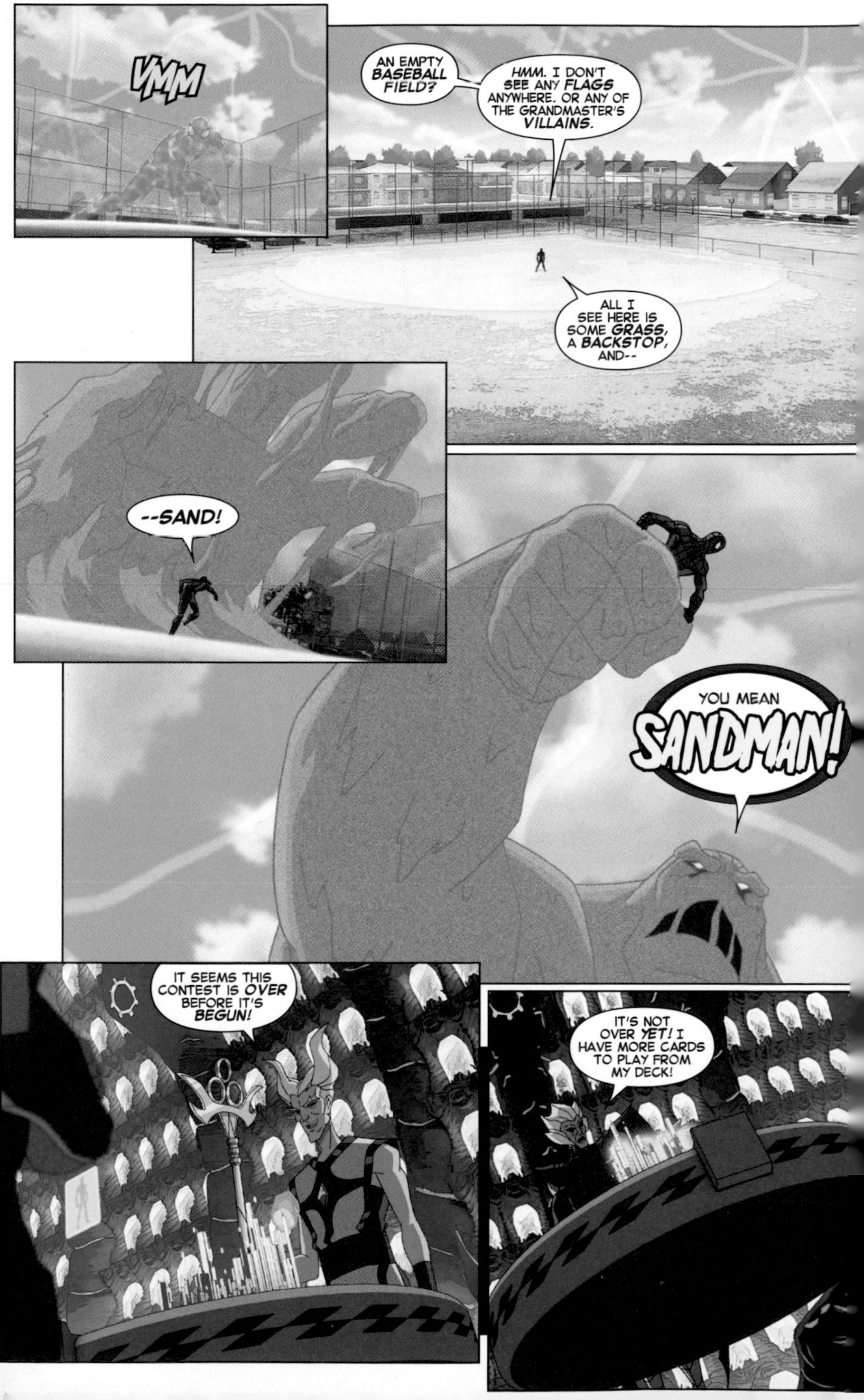
VMM
AN EMPTY BASEBALL FIELD?
HMM. I DON'T SEE ANY FLAGS ANYWHERE. OR ANY OF THE GRANDMASTER'S VILLAINS.
ALL I SEE HERE IS SOME GRASS, A BACKSTOP, AND--
--SAND!
YOU MEAN SANDMAN!
IT SEEMS THIS CONTEST IS OVER BEFORE IT'S BEGUN!
IT'S NOT OVER YET! I HAVE MORE CARDS TO PLAY FROM MY DECK!

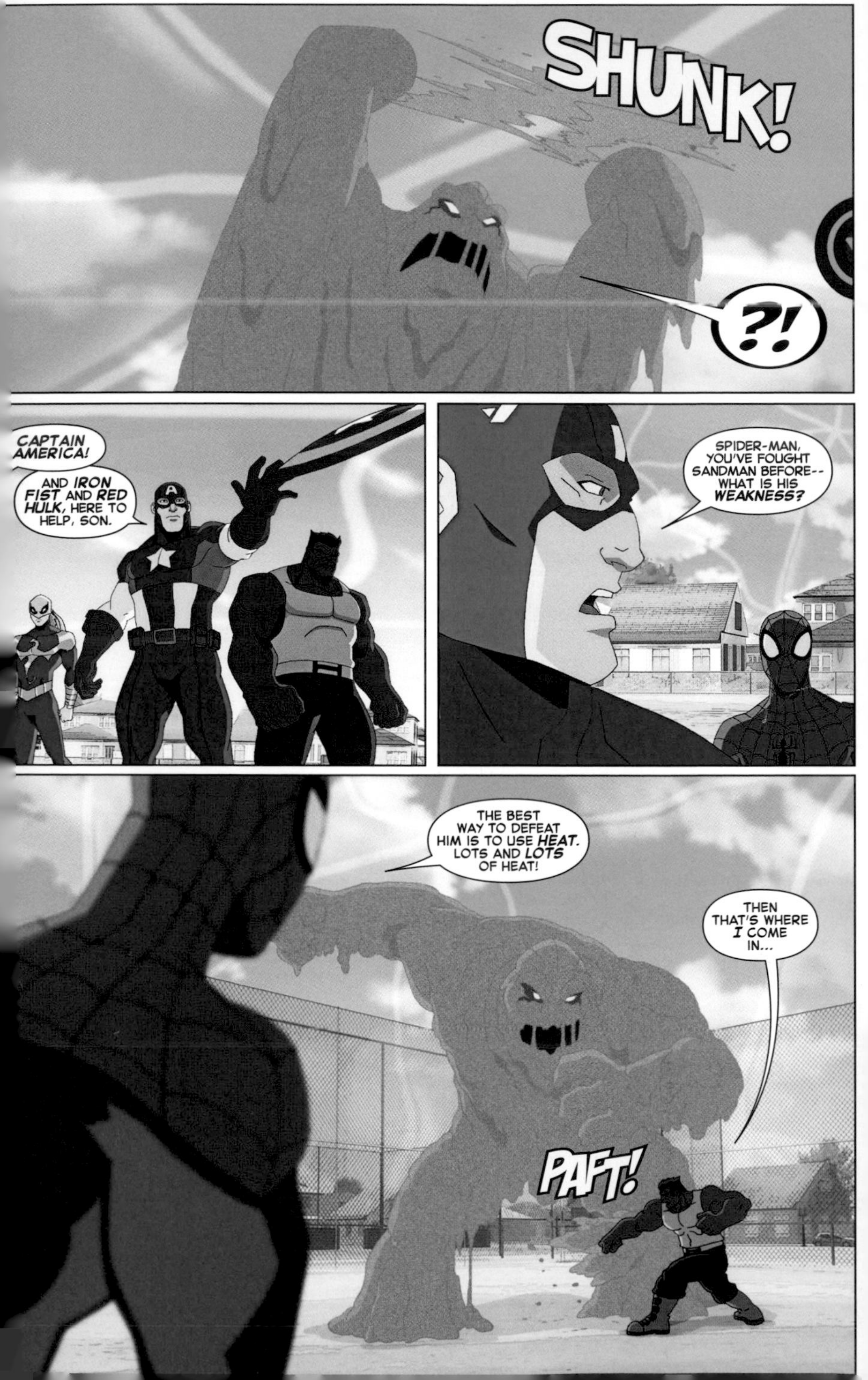
SHUNK!
?!
CAPTAIN AMERICA!
AND IRON FIST AND RED HULK, HERE TO HELP, SON.
SPIDER-MAN, YOU'VE FOUGHT SANDMAN BEFORE--WHAT IS HIS WEAKNESS?
THE BEST WAY TO DEFEAT HIM IS TO USE HEAT. LOTS AND LOTS OF HEAT!
THEN THAT'S WHERE I COME IN...
PAFT!

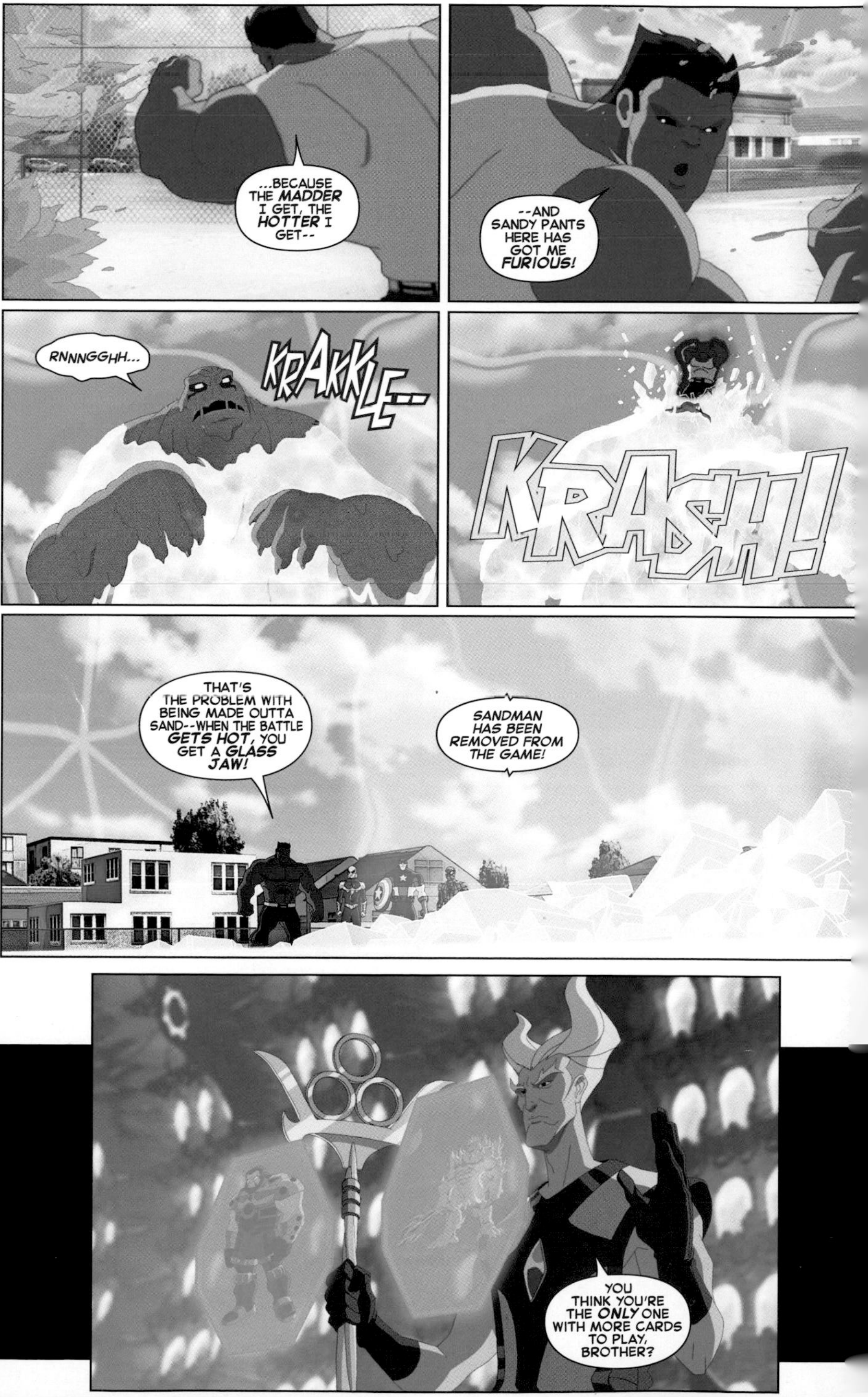
...BECAUSE THE MADDER I GET, THE HOTTER I GET--
--AND SANDY PANTS HERE HAS GOT ME FURIOUS!
RNNNGGHH...
KRAKKLE--
KRASH!
THAT'S THE PROBLEM WITH BEING MADE OUTTA SAND--WHEN THE BATTLE GETS HOT, YOU GET A GLASS JAW!
SANDMAN HAS BEEN REMOVED FROM THE GAME!
YOU THINK YOU'RE THE ONLY ONE WITH MORE CARDS TO PLAY, BROTHER?

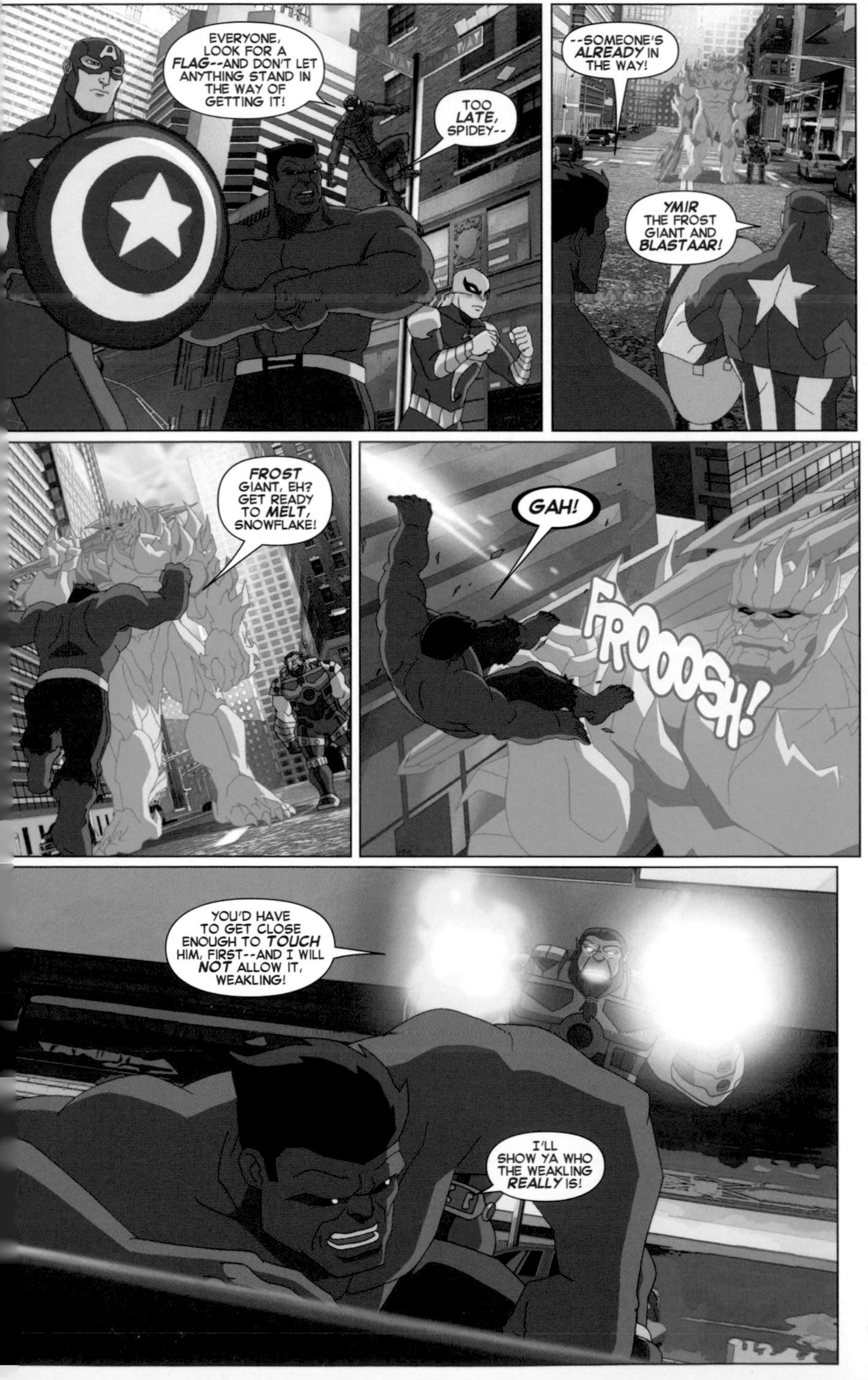
EVERYONE, LOOK FOR A FLAG--AND DON'T LET ANYTHING STAND IN THE WAY OF GETTING IT!
TOO LATE, SPIDEY--
--SOMEONE'S ALREADY IN THE WAY!
YMIR THE FROST GIANT AND BLASTAAR!
FROST GIANT, EH? GET READY TO MELT, SNOWFLAKE!
GAH!
FROOOSH!
YOU'D HAVE TO GET CLOSE ENOUGH TO TOUCH HIM, FIRST--AND I WILL NOT ALLOW IT, WEAKLING!
I'LL SHOW YA WHO THE WEAKLING REALLY IS!

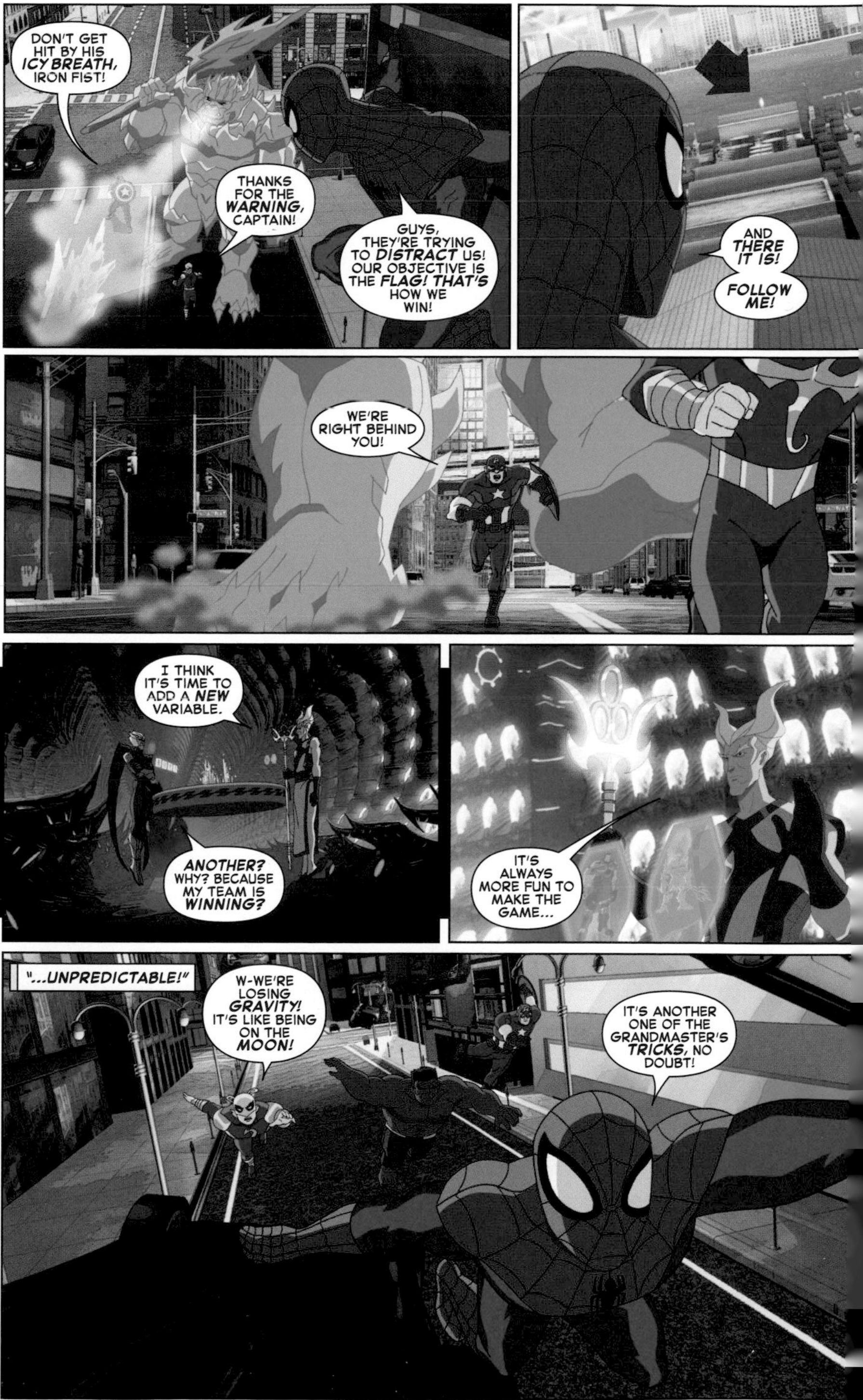
DON'T GET HIT BY HIS *ICY BREATH,* IRON FIST!
THANKS FOR THE *WARNING,* CAPTAIN!
GUYS, THEY'RE TRYING TO *DISTRACT* US! OUR OBJECTIVE IS THE *FLAG! THAT'S* HOW WE WIN!
AND *THERE IT IS!*
FOLLOW ME!
WE'RE RIGHT BEHIND YOU!
I THINK IT'S TIME TO ADD A *NEW* VARIABLE.
ANOTHER? WHY? BECAUSE MY TEAM IS *WINNING?*
IT'S ALWAYS MORE FUN TO MAKE THE GAME...
"...UNPREDICTABLE!"
W-WE'RE LOSING *GRAVITY!* IT'S LIKE BEING ON THE *MOON!*
IT'S ANOTHER ONE OF THE GRANDMASTER'S *TRICKS,* NO DOUBT!

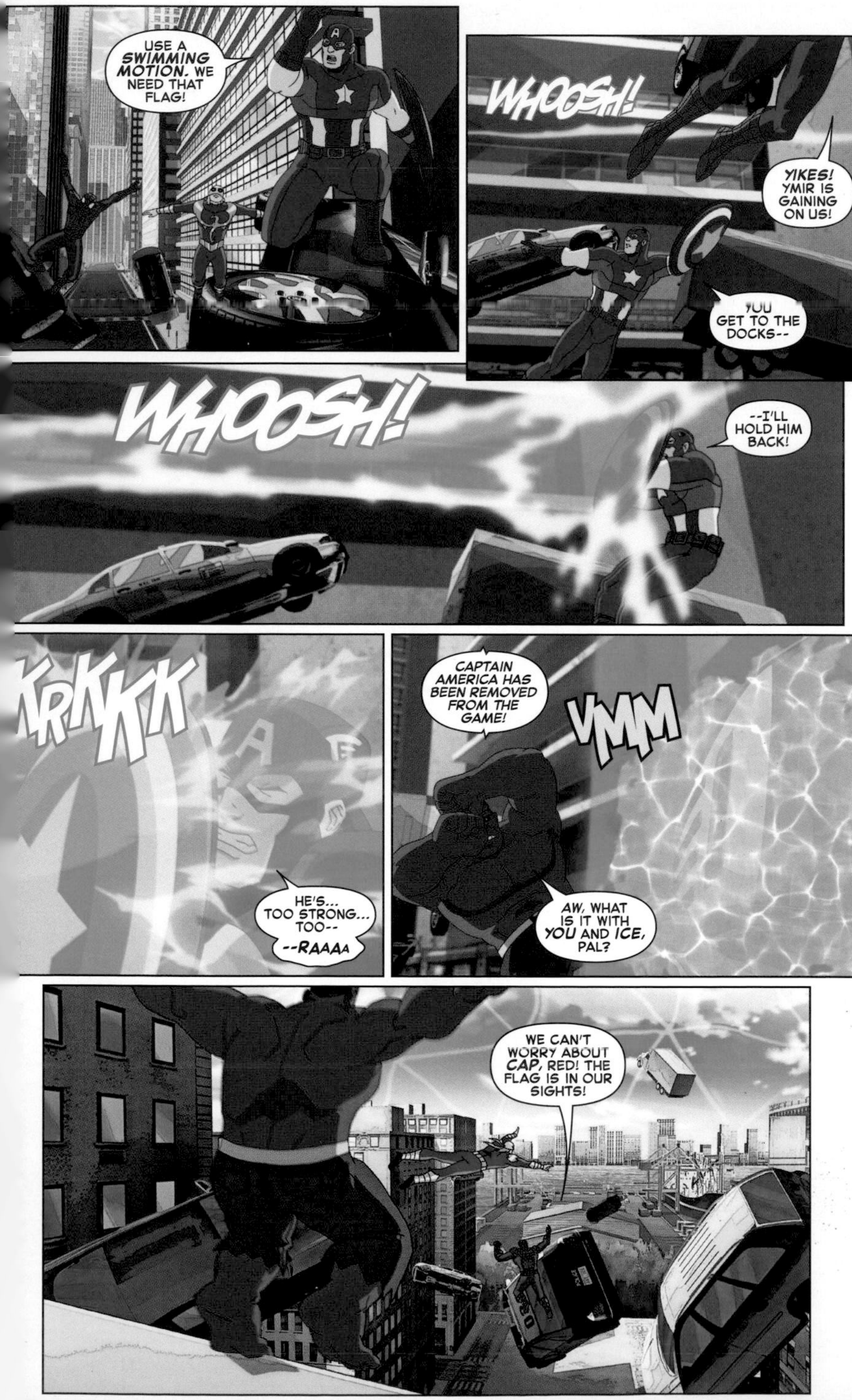

USE A SWIMMING MOTION. WE NEED THAT FLAG!
WHOOSH!
YIKES! YMIR IS GAINING ON US!
YOU GET TO THE DOCKS--
WHOOSH!
--I'LL HOLD HIM BACK!
KRKKK
HE'S... TOO STRONG... TOO--
--RAAAA
CAPTAIN AMERICA HAS BEEN REMOVED FROM THE GAME!
VMM
AW, WHAT IS IT WITH YOU AND ICE, PAL?
WE CAN'T WORRY ABOUT CAP, RED! THE FLAG IS IN OUR SIGHTS!

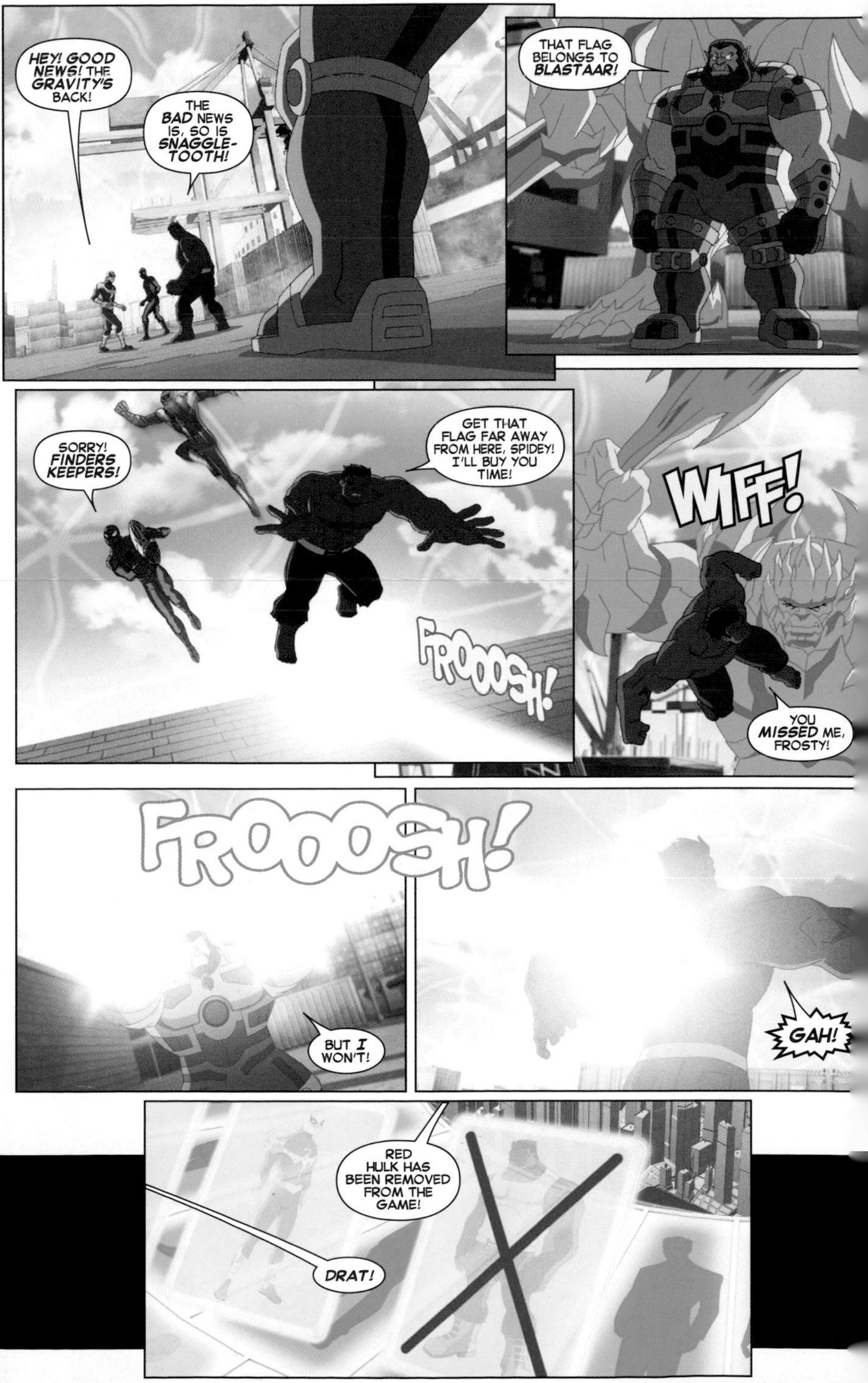
HEY! GOOD NEWS! THE GRAVITY'S BACK!
THE BAD NEWS IS, SO IS SNAGGLE-TOOTH!
THAT FLAG BELONGS TO BLASTAAR!
SORRY! FINDERS KEEPERS!
GET THAT FLAG FAR AWAY FROM HERE, SPIDEY! I'LL BUY YOU TIME!
FROOOSH!
WIFF!
YOU MISSED ME, FROSTY!
FROOOSH!
BUT I WON'T!
GAH!
RED HULK HAS BEEN REMOVED FROM THE GAME!
DRAT!

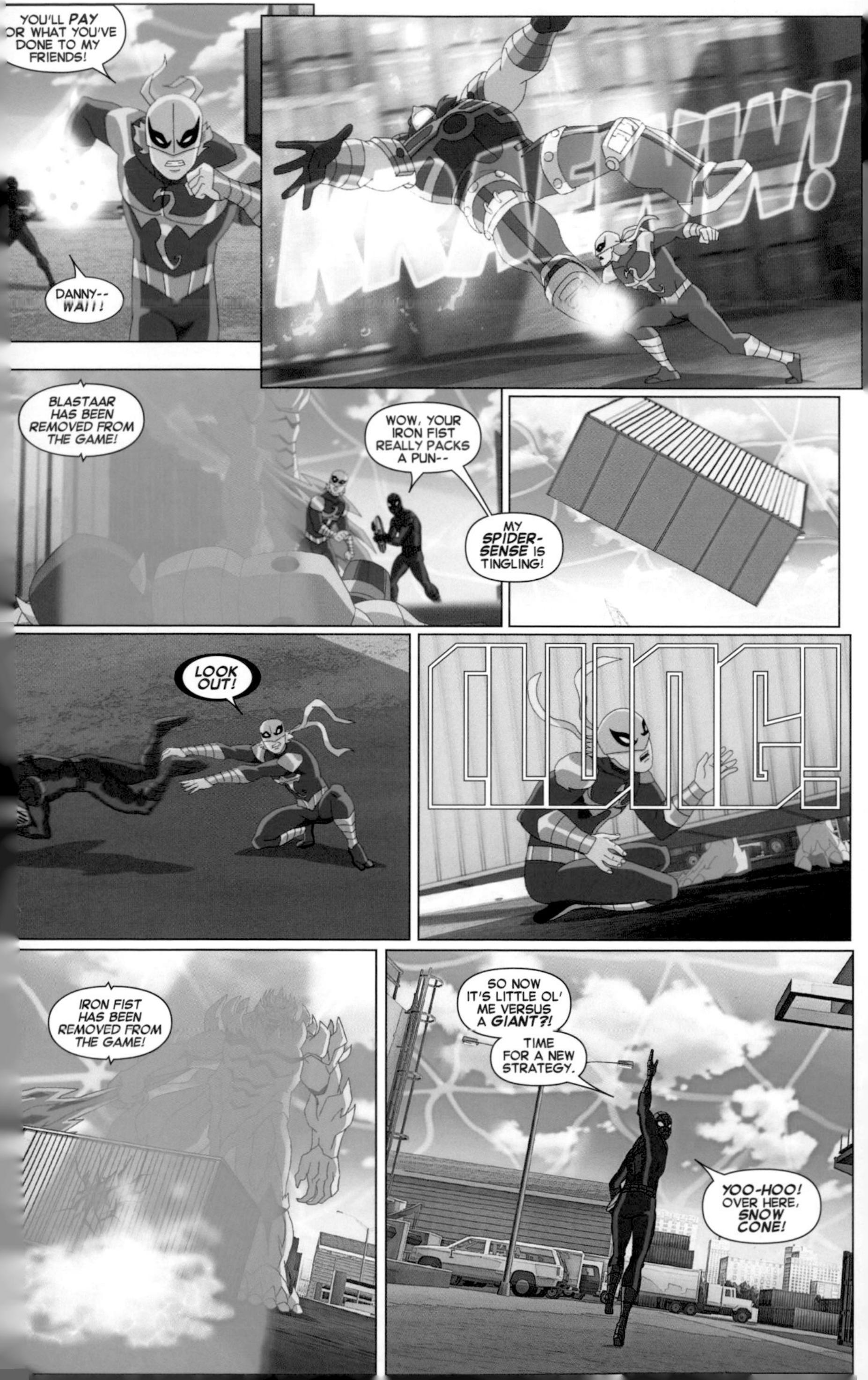

YOU'LL PAY OR WHAT YOU'VE DONE TO MY FRIENDS!
DANNY-- WAIT!
BLASTAAR HAS BEEN REMOVED FROM THE GAME!
WOW, YOUR IRON FIST REALLY PACKS A PUN--
MY SPIDER-SENSE IS TINGLING!
LOOK OUT!
CLUNG!
IRON FIST HAS BEEN REMOVED FROM THE GAME!
SO NOW IT'S LITTLE OL' ME VERSUS A GIANT?!
TIME FOR A NEW STRATEGY.
YOO-HOO! OVER HERE, SNOW CONE!

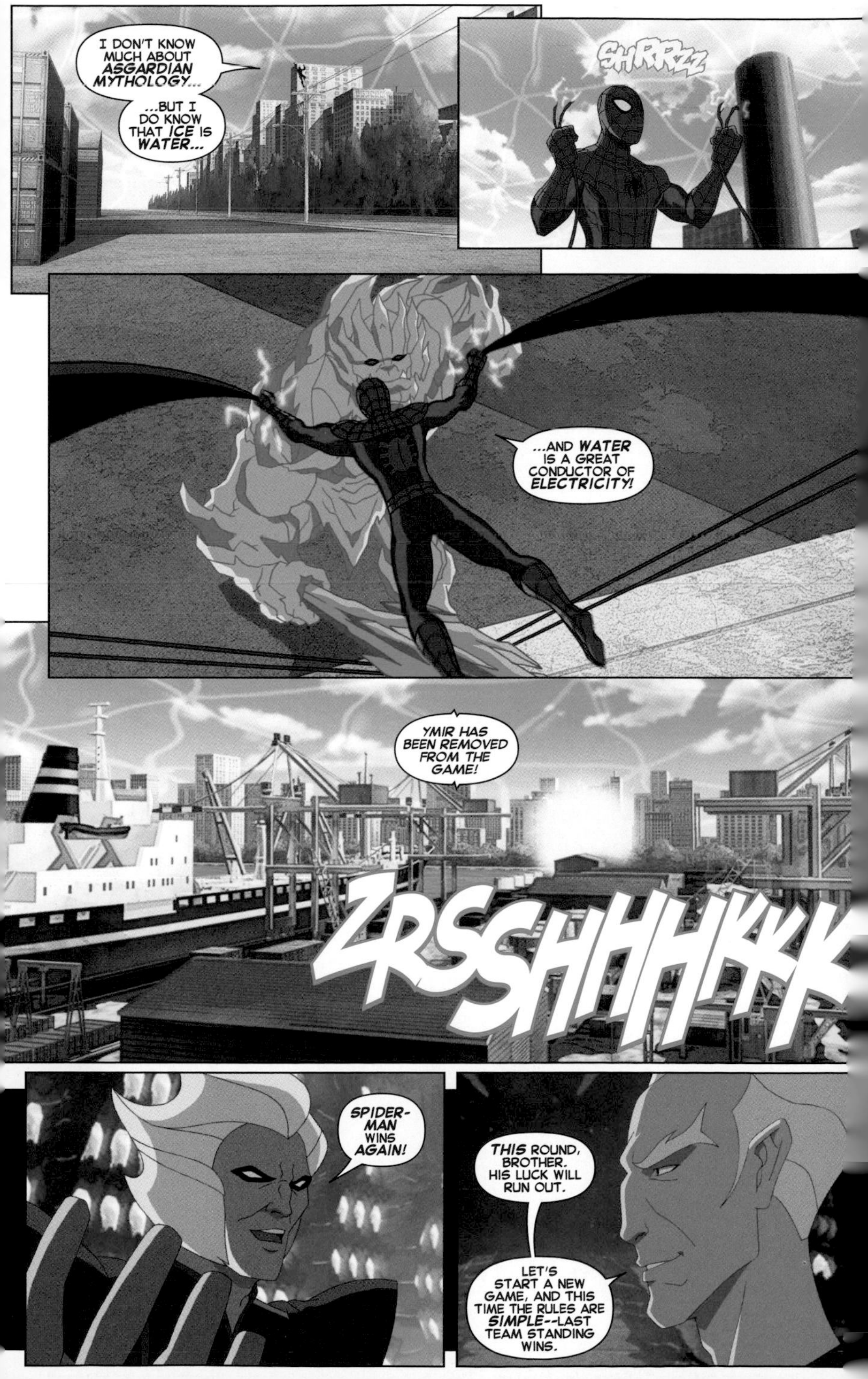

I DON'T KNOW MUCH ABOUT ASGARDIAN MYTHOLOGY...
...BUT I DO KNOW THAT ICE IS WATER...
SHRRZZ
...AND WATER IS A GREAT CONDUCTOR OF ELECTRICITY!
YMIR HAS BEEN REMOVED FROM THE GAME!
ZRSSHHHKKK
SPIDER-MAN WINS AGAIN!
THIS ROUND, BROTHER. HIS LUCK WILL RUN OUT.
LET'S START A NEW GAME, AND THIS TIME THE RULES ARE SIMPLE--LAST TEAM STANDING WINS.

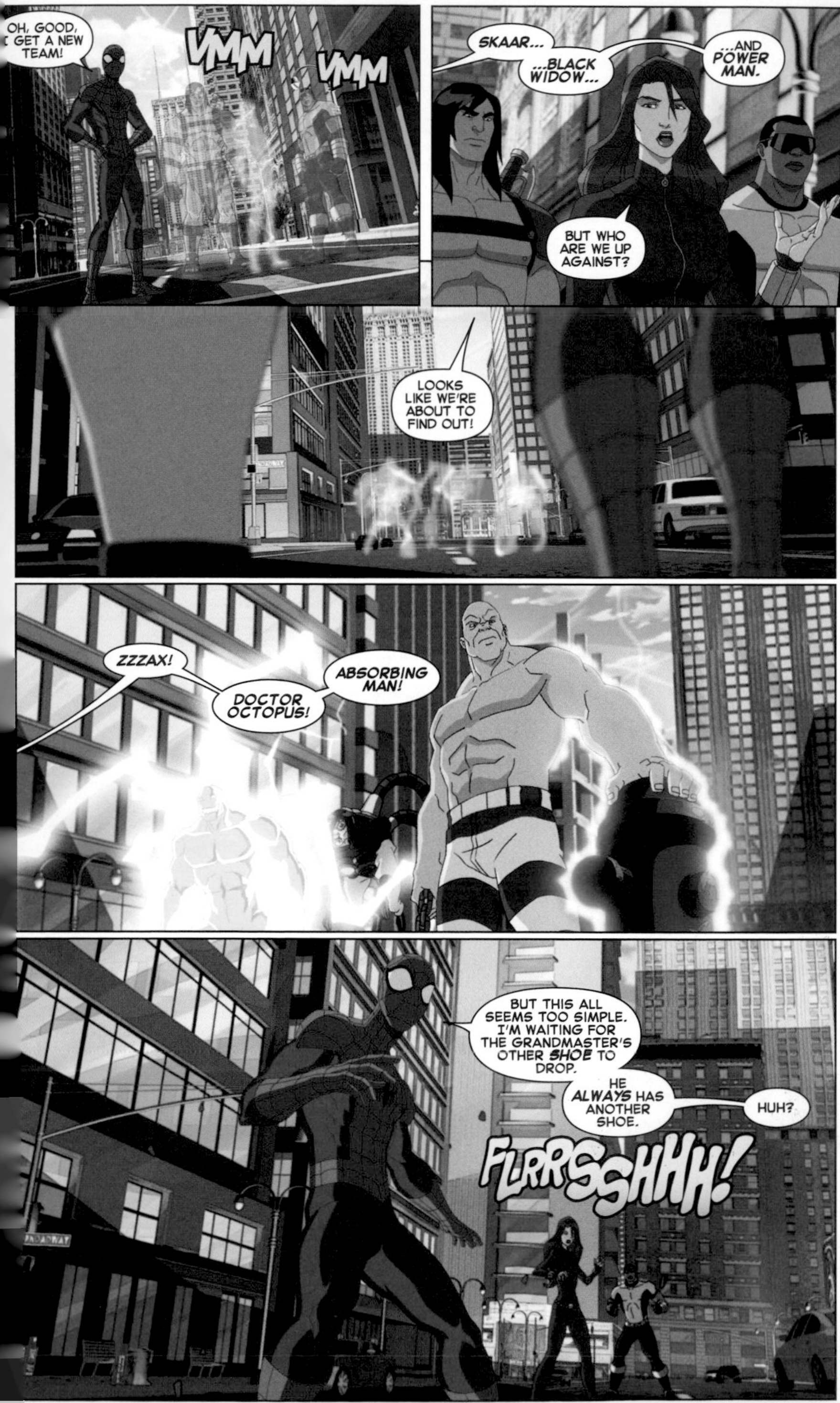
OH, GOOD, I GET A NEW TEAM!
VMM
VMM
SKAAR...
...BLACK WIDOW...
...AND POWER MAN.
BUT WHO ARE WE UP AGAINST?
LOOKS LIKE WE'RE ABOUT TO FIND OUT!
ZZZAX!
DOCTOR OCTOPUS!
ABSORBING MAN!
BUT THIS ALL SEEMS TOO SIMPLE. I'M WAITING FOR THE GRANDMASTER'S OTHER *SHOE* TO DROP.
HE *ALWAYS* HAS ANOTHER SHOE.
HUH?
FLRRSSHHH!

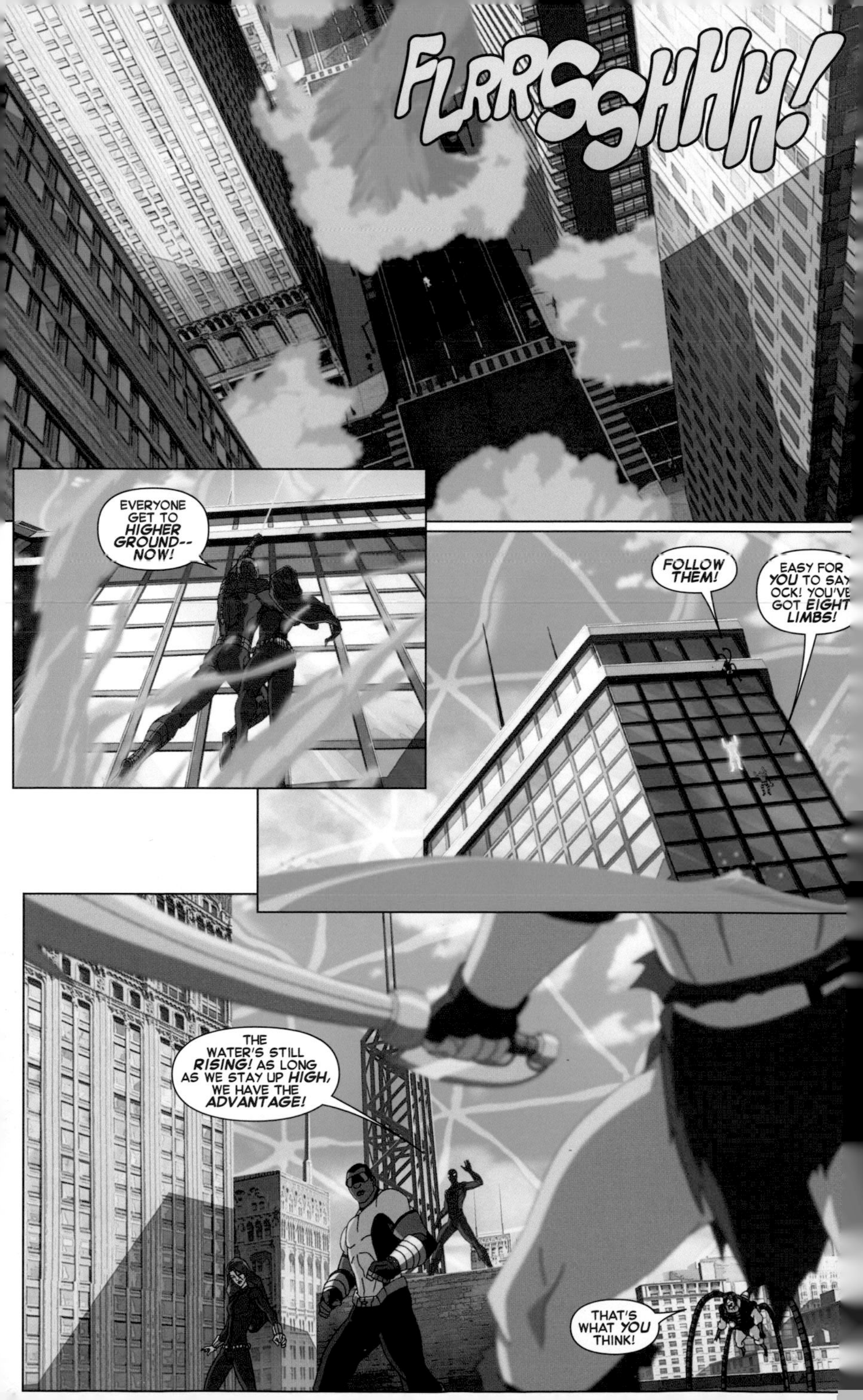
FLRRSSHHHH!
EVERYONE GET TO HIGHER GROUND-- NOW!
FOLLOW THEM!
EASY FOR YOU TO SAY OCK! YOU'VE GOT EIGHT LIMBS!
THE WATER'S STILL RISING! AS LONG AS WE STAY UP HIGH, WE HAVE THE ADVANTAGE!
THAT'S WHAT YOU THINK!

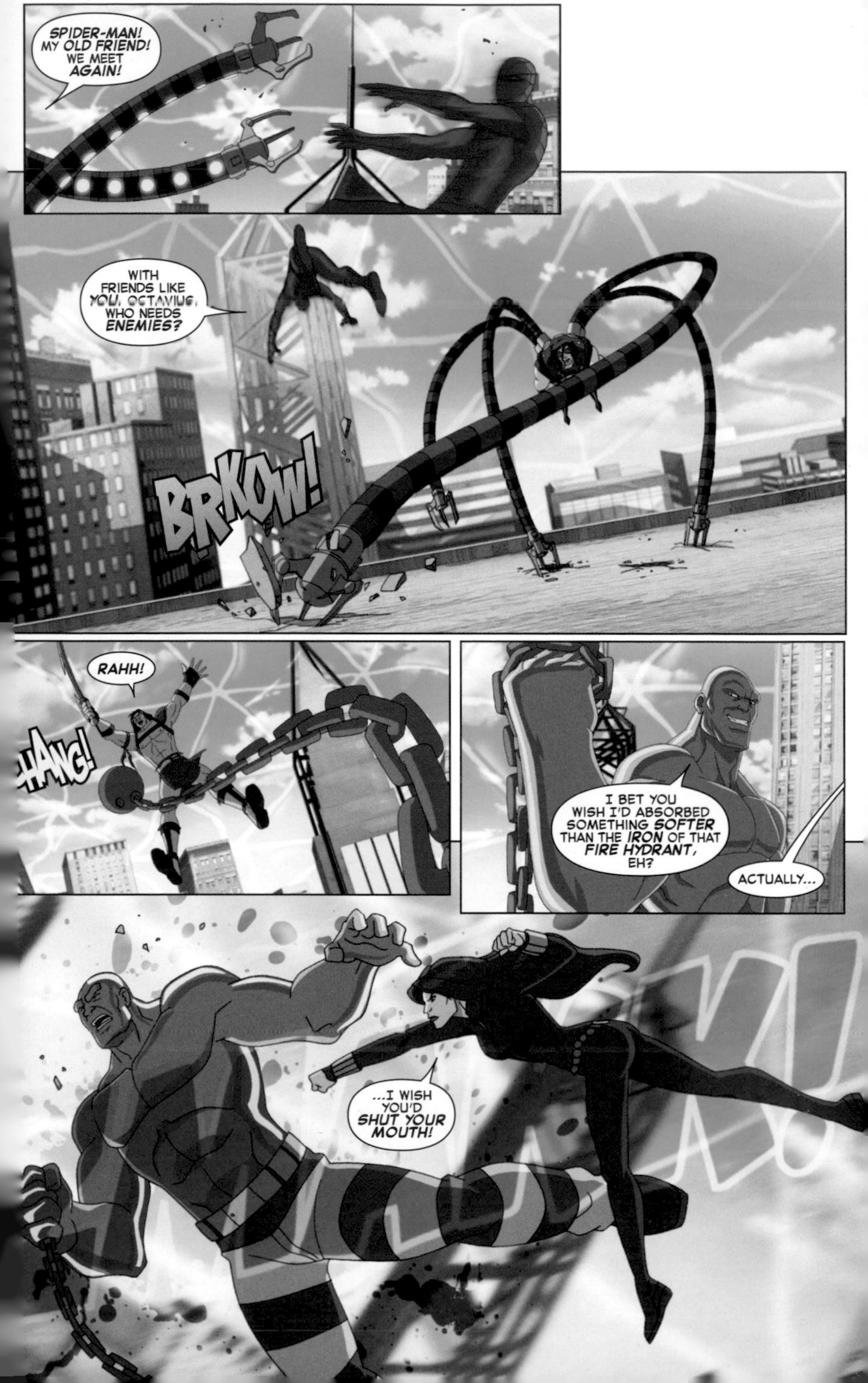
SPIDER-MAN! MY OLD FRIEND! WE MEET AGAIN!
WITH FRIENDS LIKE YOU, OCTAVIUS, WHO NEEDS ENEMIES?
BRKOW!
RAHH!
I BET YOU WISH I'D ABSORBED SOMETHING SOFTER THAN THE IRON OF THAT FIRE HYDRANT, EH?
ACTUALLY...
...I WISH YOU'D SHUT YOUR MOUTH!

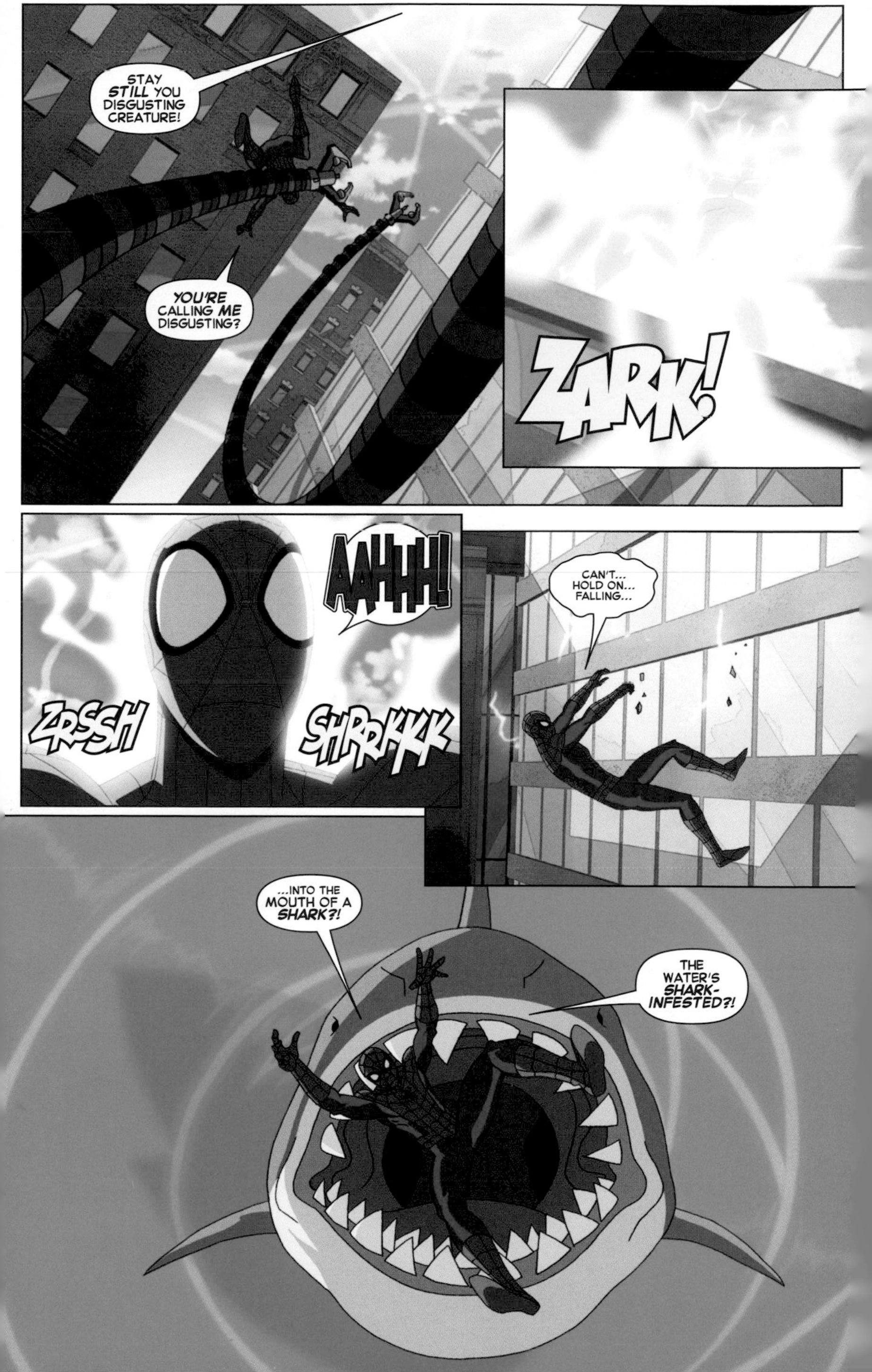
STAY STILL YOU DISGUSTING CREATURE!
YOU'RE CALLING ME DISGUSTING?
ZARK!
AAHHH!
ZRSSH
SHRRKKK
CAN'T... HOLD ON... FALLING...
...INTO THE MOUTH OF A SHARK?!
THE WATER'S SHARK-INFESTED?!

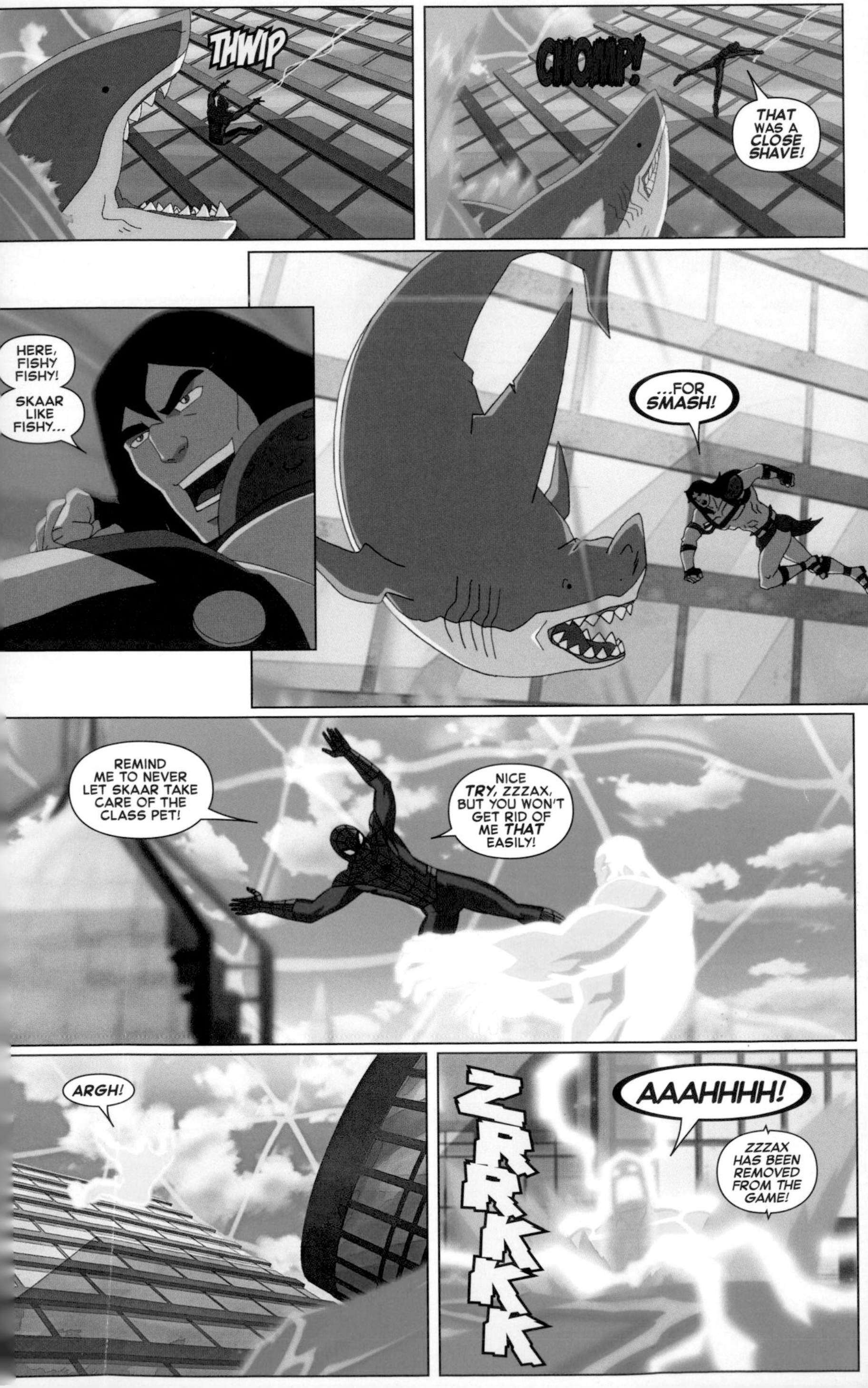
THWIP
CHOMP!
THAT WAS A CLOSE SHAVE!
HERE, FISHY FISHY!
SKAAR LIKE FISHY...
...FOR SMASH!
REMIND ME TO NEVER LET SKAAR TAKE CARE OF THE CLASS PET!
NICE TRY, ZZZAX, BUT YOU WON'T GET RID OF ME THAT EASILY!
ARGH!
ZRRKKK
AAAHHHH!
ZZZAX HAS BEEN REMOVED FROM THE GAME!

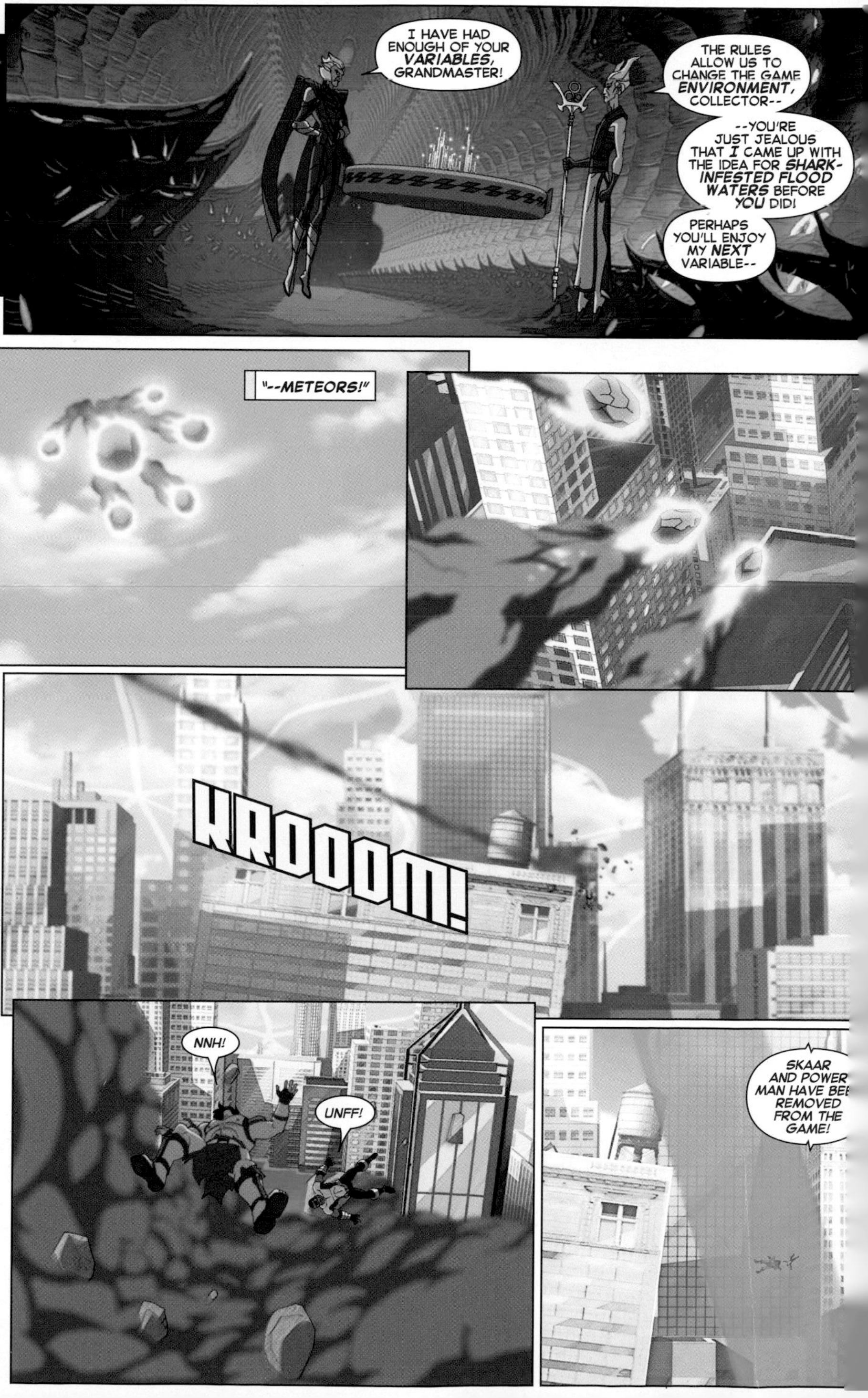
I HAVE HAD ENOUGH OF YOUR VARIABLES, GRANDMASTER!
THE RULES ALLOW US TO CHANGE THE GAME ENVIRONMENT, COLLECTOR--
--YOU'RE JUST JEALOUS THAT I CAME UP WITH THE IDEA FOR SHARK-INFESTED FLOOD WATERS BEFORE YOU DID!
PERHAPS YOU'LL ENJOY MY NEXT VARIABLE--
"--METEORS!"
KROOOM!
NNH!
UNFF!
SKAAR AND POWER MAN HAVE BEE REMOVED FROM THE GAME!

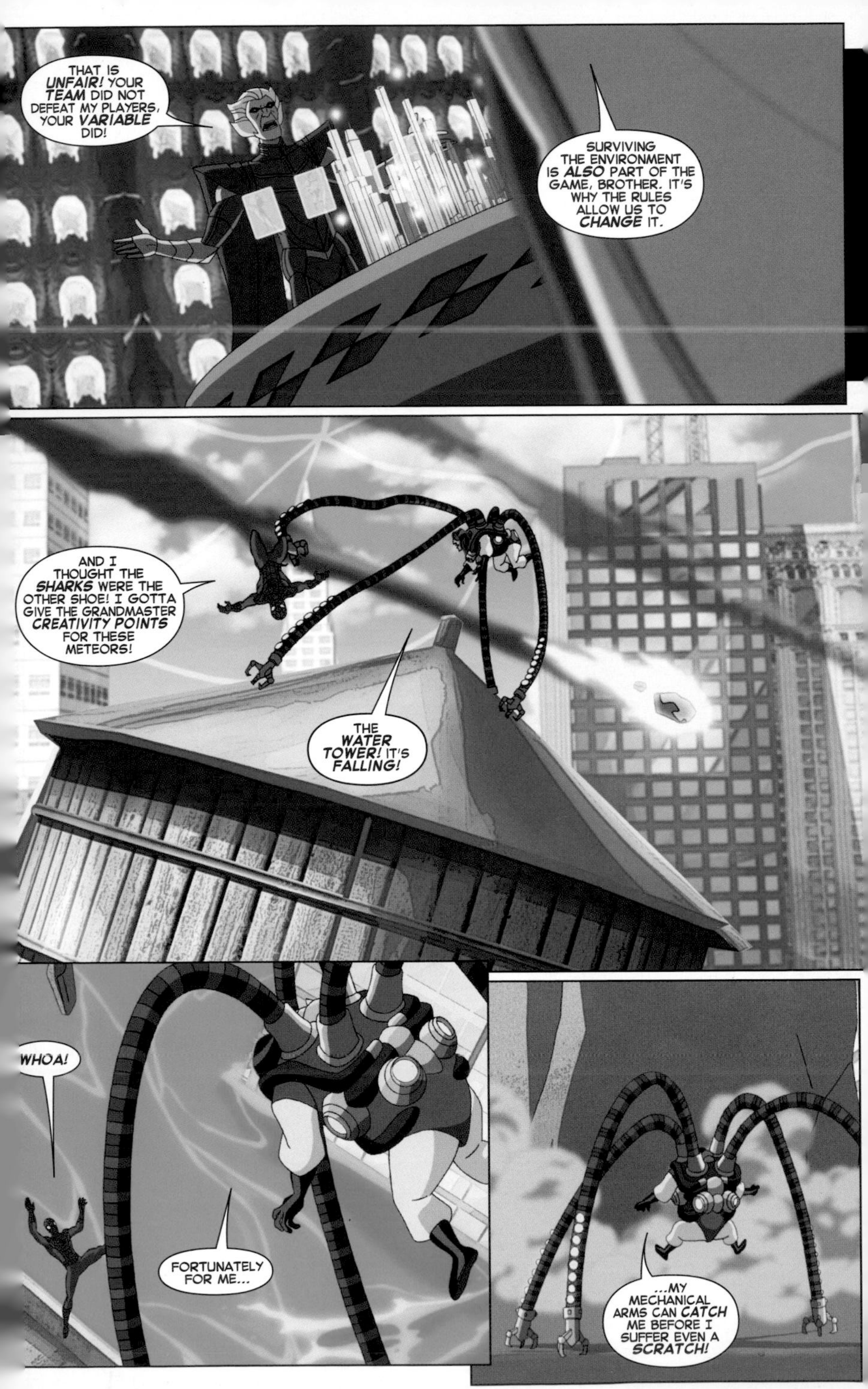
THAT IS UNFAIR! YOUR TEAM DID NOT DEFEAT MY PLAYERS, YOUR VARIABLE DID!
SURVIVING THE ENVIRONMENT IS ALSO PART OF THE GAME, BROTHER. IT'S WHY THE RULES ALLOW US TO CHANGE IT.
AND I THOUGHT THE SHARKS WERE THE OTHER SHOE! I GOTTA GIVE THE GRANDMASTER CREATIVITY POINTS FOR THESE METEORS!
THE WATER TOWER! IT'S FALLING!
WHOA!
FORTUNATELY FOR ME...
...MY MECHANICAL ARMS CAN CATCH ME BEFORE I SUFFER EVEN A SCRATCH!

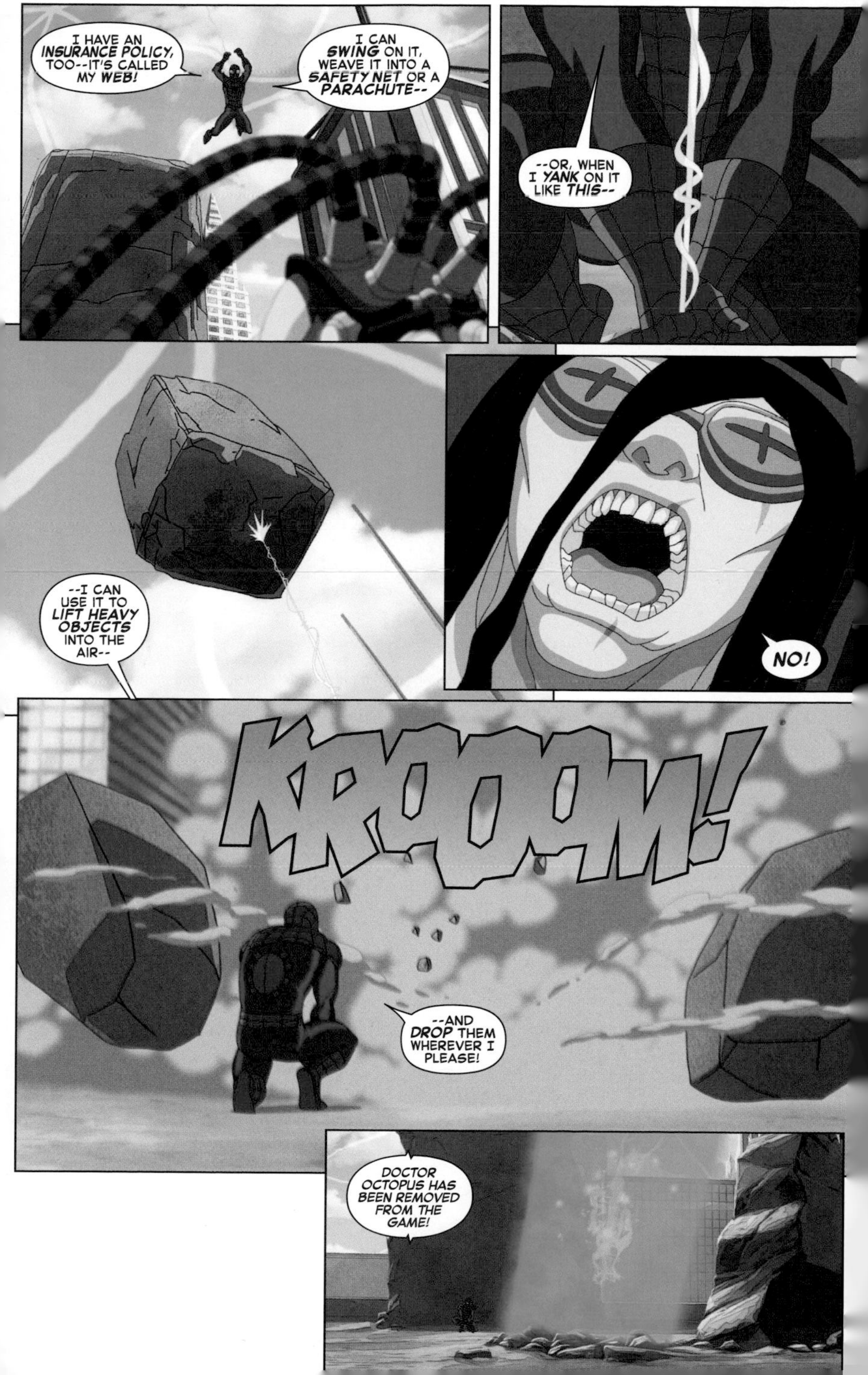
I HAVE AN INSURANCE POLICY, TOO--IT'S CALLED MY WEB!
I CAN SWING ON IT, WEAVE IT INTO A SAFETY NET OR A PARACHUTE--
--OR, WHEN I YANK ON IT LIKE THIS--
--I CAN USE IT TO LIFT HEAVY OBJECTS INTO THE AIR--
NO!
KROOOM!
--AND DROP THEM WHEREVER I PLEASE!
DOCTOR OCTOPUS HAS BEEN REMOVED FROM THE GAME!

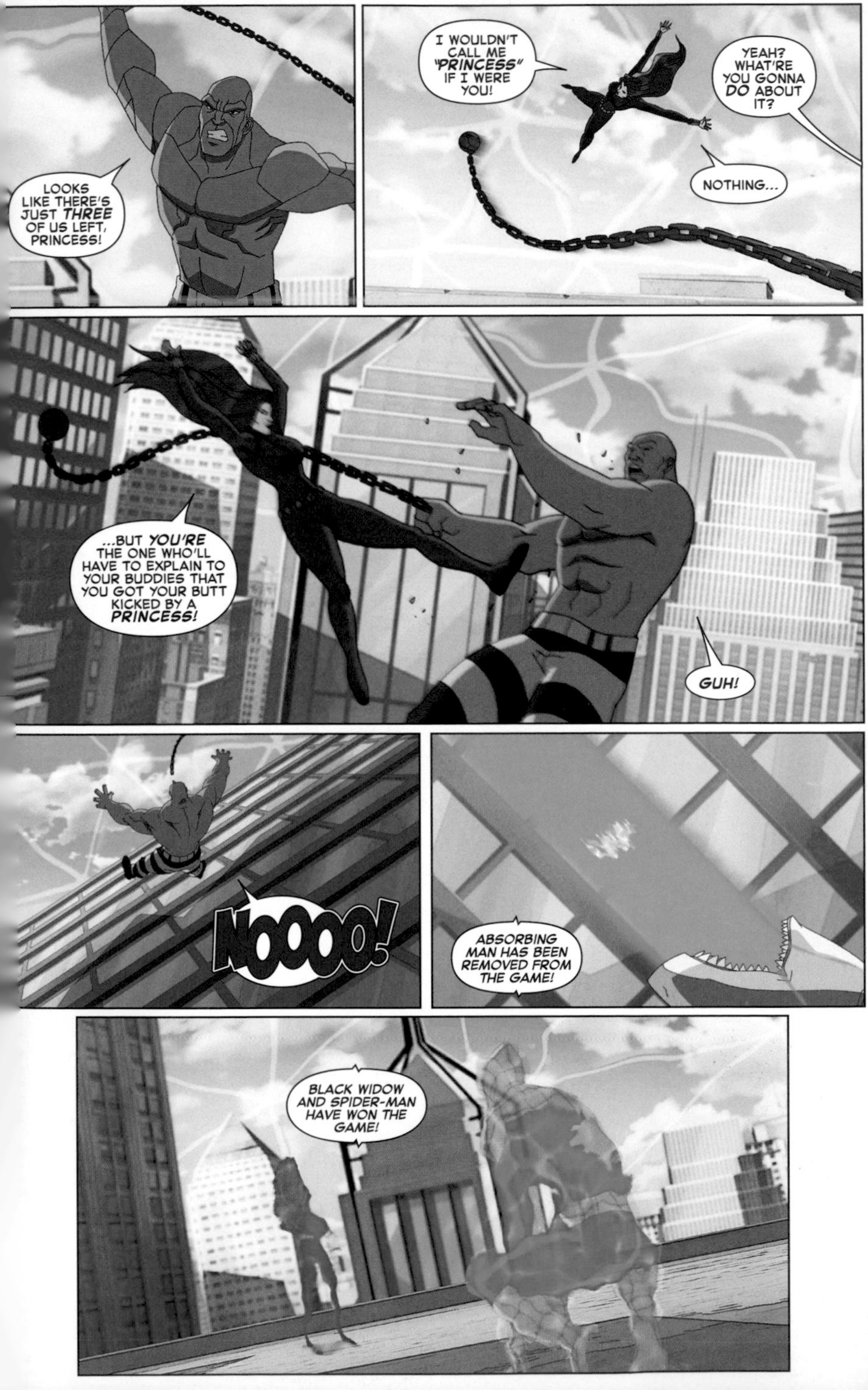
LOOKS LIKE THERE'S JUST THREE OF US LEFT, PRINCESS!
I WOULDN'T CALL ME "PRINCESS" IF I WERE YOU!
YEAH? WHAT'RE YOU GONNA DO ABOUT IT?
NOTHING...
...BUT YOU'RE THE ONE WHO'LL HAVE TO EXPLAIN TO YOUR BUDDIES THAT YOU GOT YOUR BUTT KICKED BY A PRINCESS!
GUH!
NOOOO!
ABSORBING MAN HAS BEEN REMOVED FROM THE GAME!
BLACK WIDOW AND SPIDER-MAN HAVE WON THE GAME!

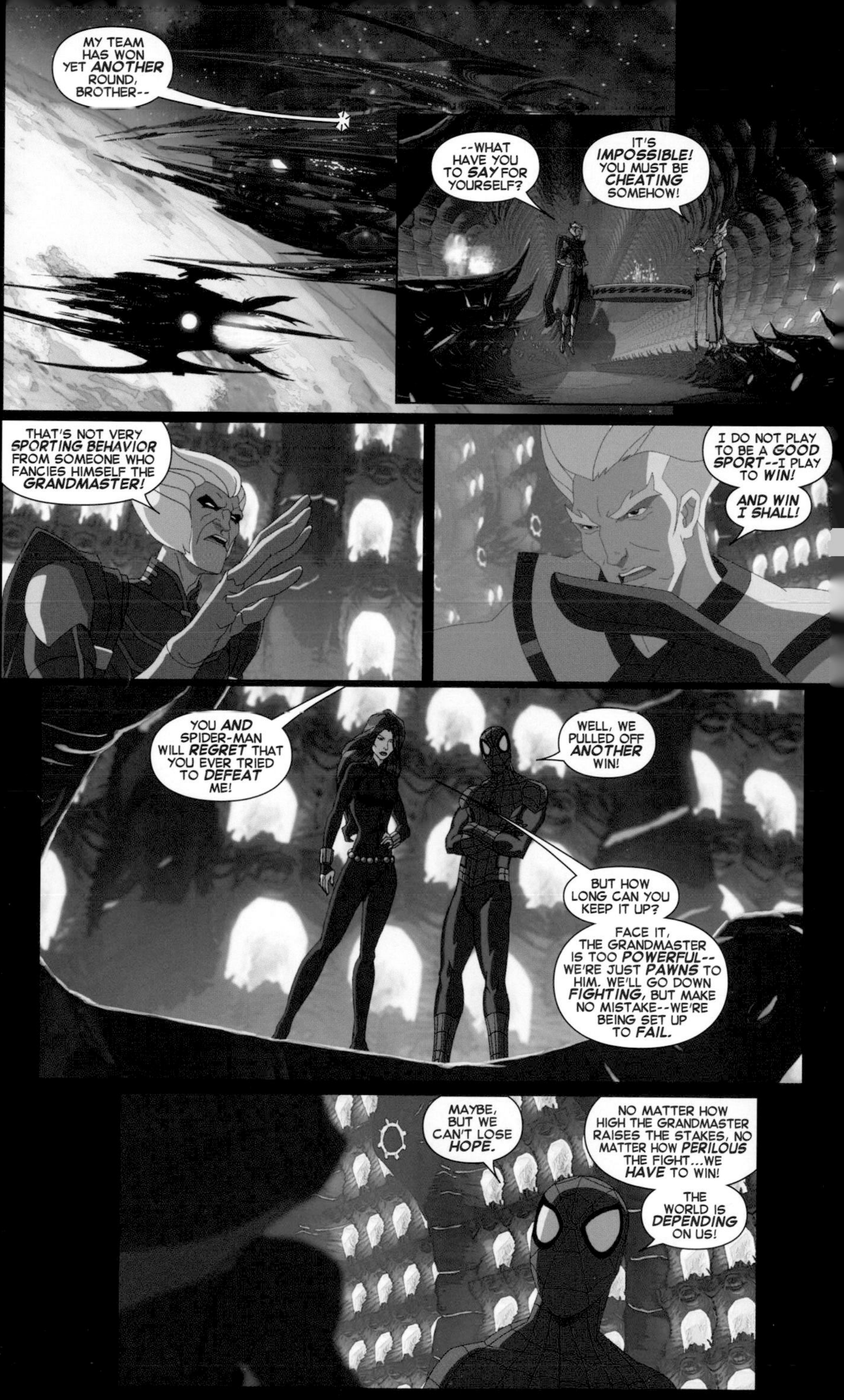
MY TEAM HAS WON YET ANOTHER ROUND, BROTHER--
--WHAT HAVE YOU TO SAY FOR YOURSELF?
IT'S IMPOSSIBLE! YOU MUST BE CHEATING SOMEHOW!
THAT'S NOT VERY SPORTING BEHAVIOR FROM SOMEONE WHO FANCIES HIMSELF THE GRANDMASTER!
I DO NOT PLAY TO BE A GOOD SPORT--I PLAY TO WIN!
AND WIN I SHALL!
YOU AND SPIDER-MAN WILL REGRET THAT YOU EVER TRIED TO DEFEAT ME!
WELL, WE PULLED OFF ANOTHER WIN!
BUT HOW LONG CAN YOU KEEP IT UP?
FACE IT, THE GRANDMASTER IS TOO POWERFUL--WE'RE JUST PAWNS TO HIM. WE'LL GO DOWN FIGHTING, BUT MAKE NO MISTAKE--WE'RE BEING SET UP TO FAIL.
MAYBE, BUT WE CAN'T LOSE HOPE.
NO MATTER HOW HIGH THE GRANDMASTER RAISES THE STAKES, NO MATTER HOW PERILOUS THE FIGHT...WE HAVE TO WIN!
THE WORLD IS DEPENDING ON US!

MARVEL

ULTIMATE SPIDER-MAN WEB-WARRIORS

CONTEST OF CHAMPIONS

3

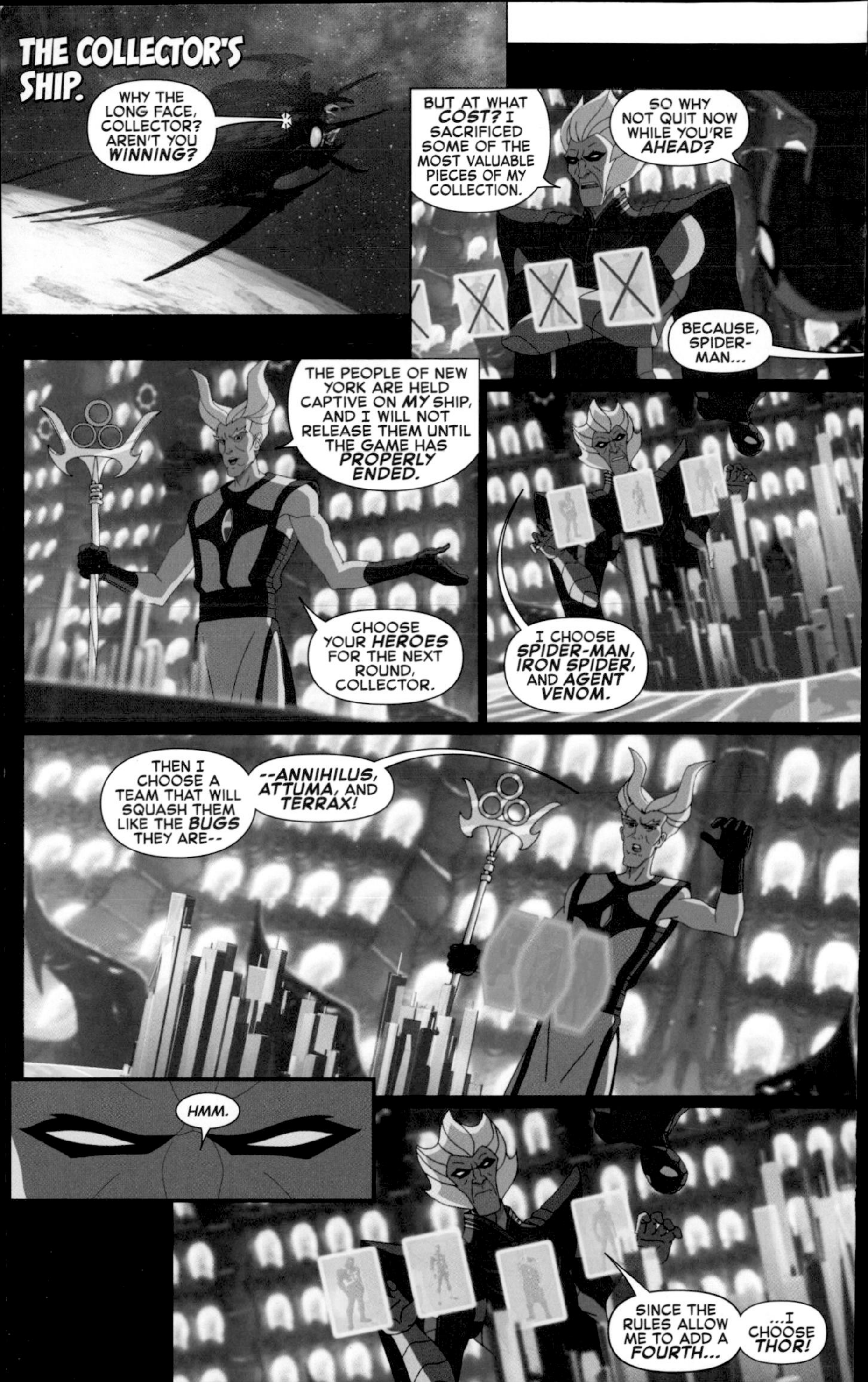
THE COLLECTOR'S SHIP.
WHY THE LONG FACE, COLLECTOR? AREN'T YOU WINNING?
BUT AT WHAT COST? I SACRIFICED SOME OF THE MOST VALUABLE PIECES OF MY COLLECTION.
SO WHY NOT QUIT NOW WHILE YOU'RE AHEAD?
BECAUSE, SPIDER-MAN...
THE PEOPLE OF NEW YORK ARE HELD CAPTIVE ON MY SHIP, AND I WILL NOT RELEASE THEM UNTIL THE GAME HAS PROPERLY ENDED.
CHOOSE YOUR HEROES FOR THE NEXT ROUND, COLLECTOR.
I CHOOSE SPIDER-MAN, IRON SPIDER, AND AGENT VENOM.
THEN I CHOOSE A TEAM THAT WILL SQUASH THEM LIKE THE BUGS THEY ARE--
--ANNIHILUS, ATTUMA, AND TERRAX!
HMM.
SINCE THE RULES ALLOW ME TO ADD A FOURTH...
...I CHOOSE THOR!

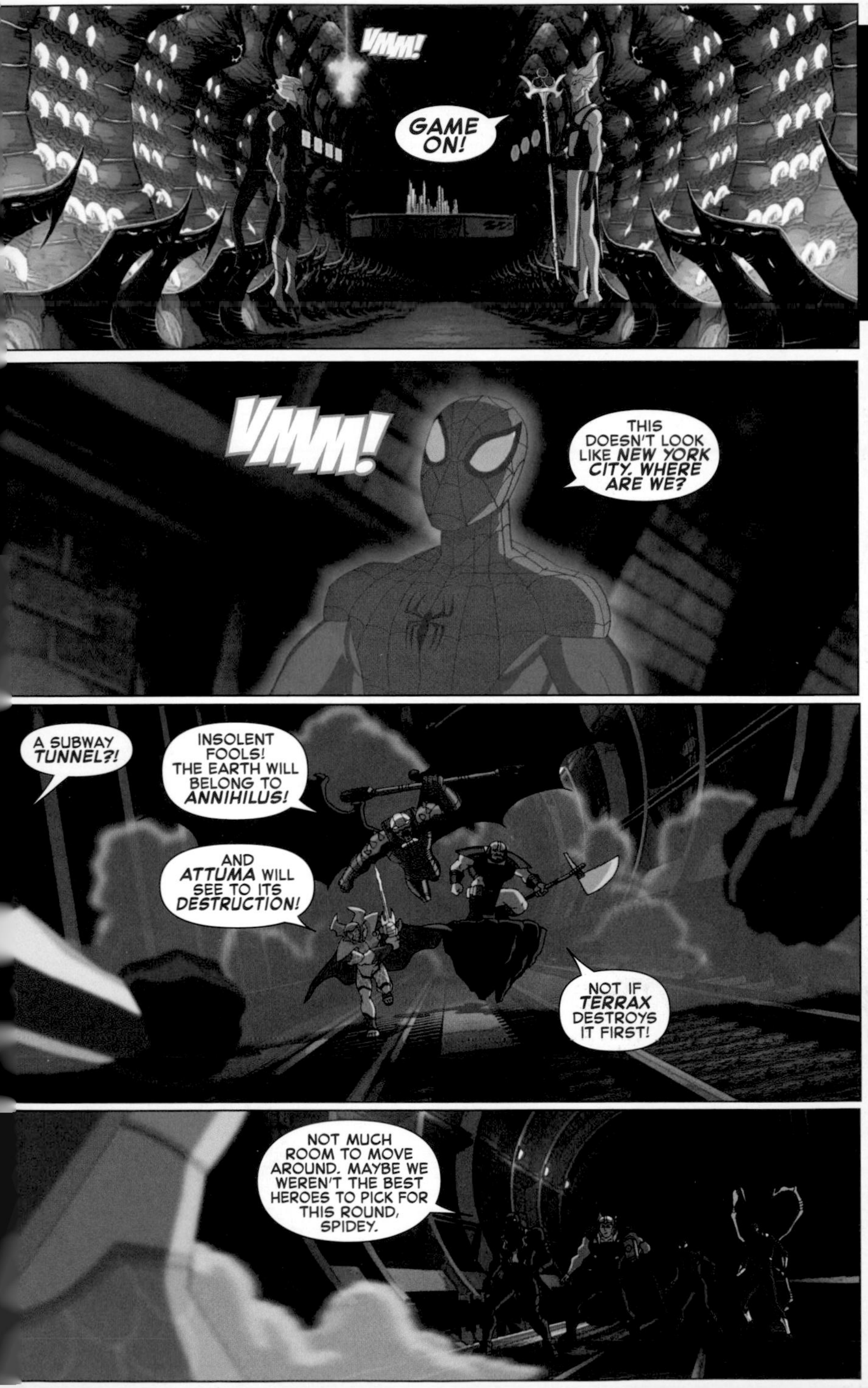
VMM!
GAME ON!
VMM!
THIS DOESN'T LOOK LIKE NEW YORK CITY. WHERE ARE WE?
A SUBWAY TUNNEL?!
INSOLENT FOOLS! THE EARTH WILL BELONG TO ANNIHILUS!
AND ATTUMA WILL SEE TO ITS DESTRUCTION!
NOT IF TERRAX DESTROYS IT FIRST!
NOT MUCH ROOM TO MOVE AROUND. MAYBE WE WEREN'T THE BEST HEROES TO PICK FOR THIS ROUND, SPIDEY.

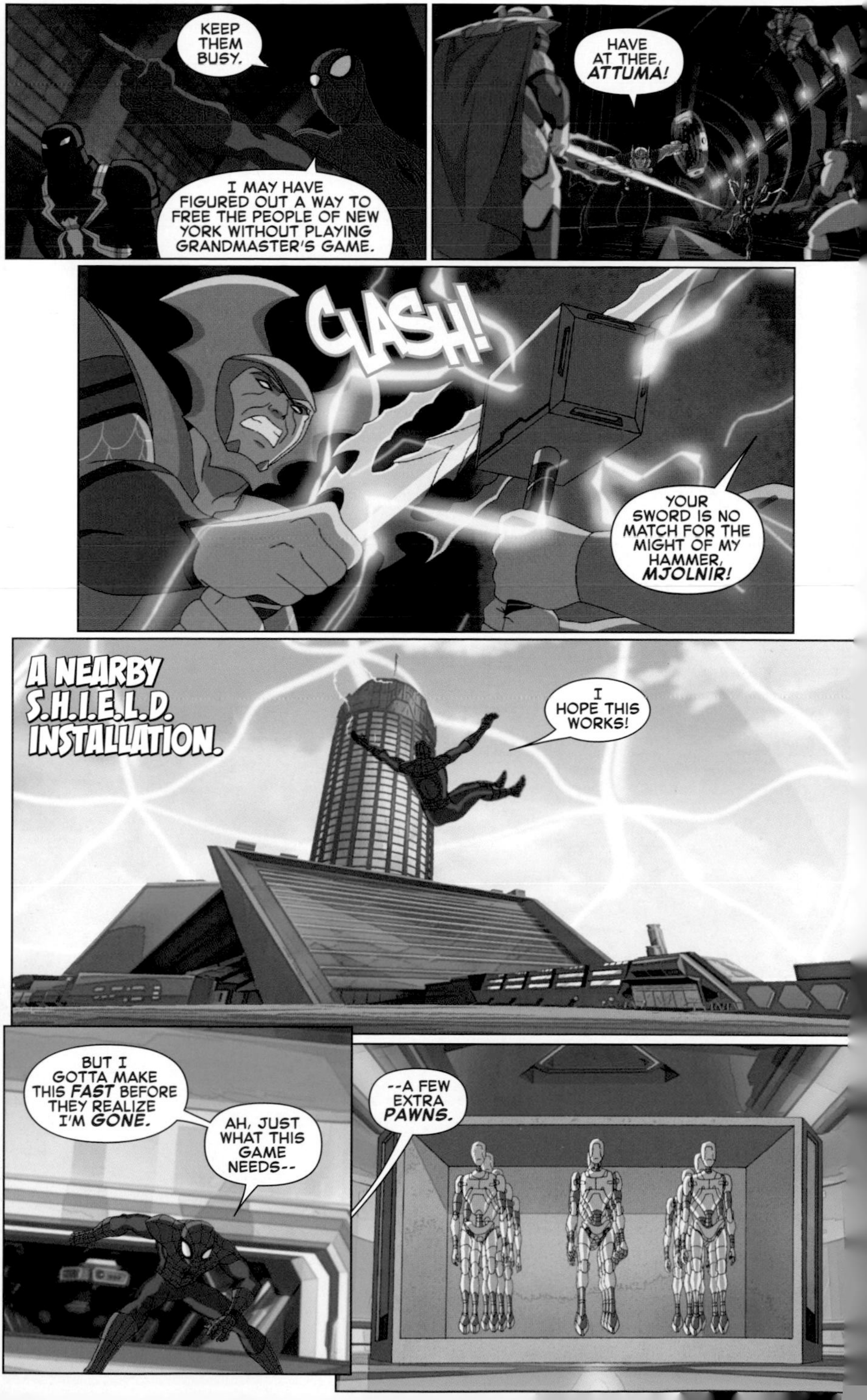
KEEP THEM BUSY.
I MAY HAVE FIGURED OUT A WAY TO FREE THE PEOPLE OF NEW YORK WITHOUT PLAYING GRANDMASTER'S GAME.
HAVE AT THEE, ATTUMA!
CLASH!
YOUR SWORD IS NO MATCH FOR THE MIGHT OF MY HAMMER, MJOLNIR!
A NEARBY S.H.I.E.L.D. INSTALLATION.
I HOPE THIS WORKS!
BUT I GOTTA MAKE THIS FAST BEFORE THEY REALIZE I'M GONE.
AH, JUST WHAT THIS GAME NEEDS--
--A FEW EXTRA PAWNS.

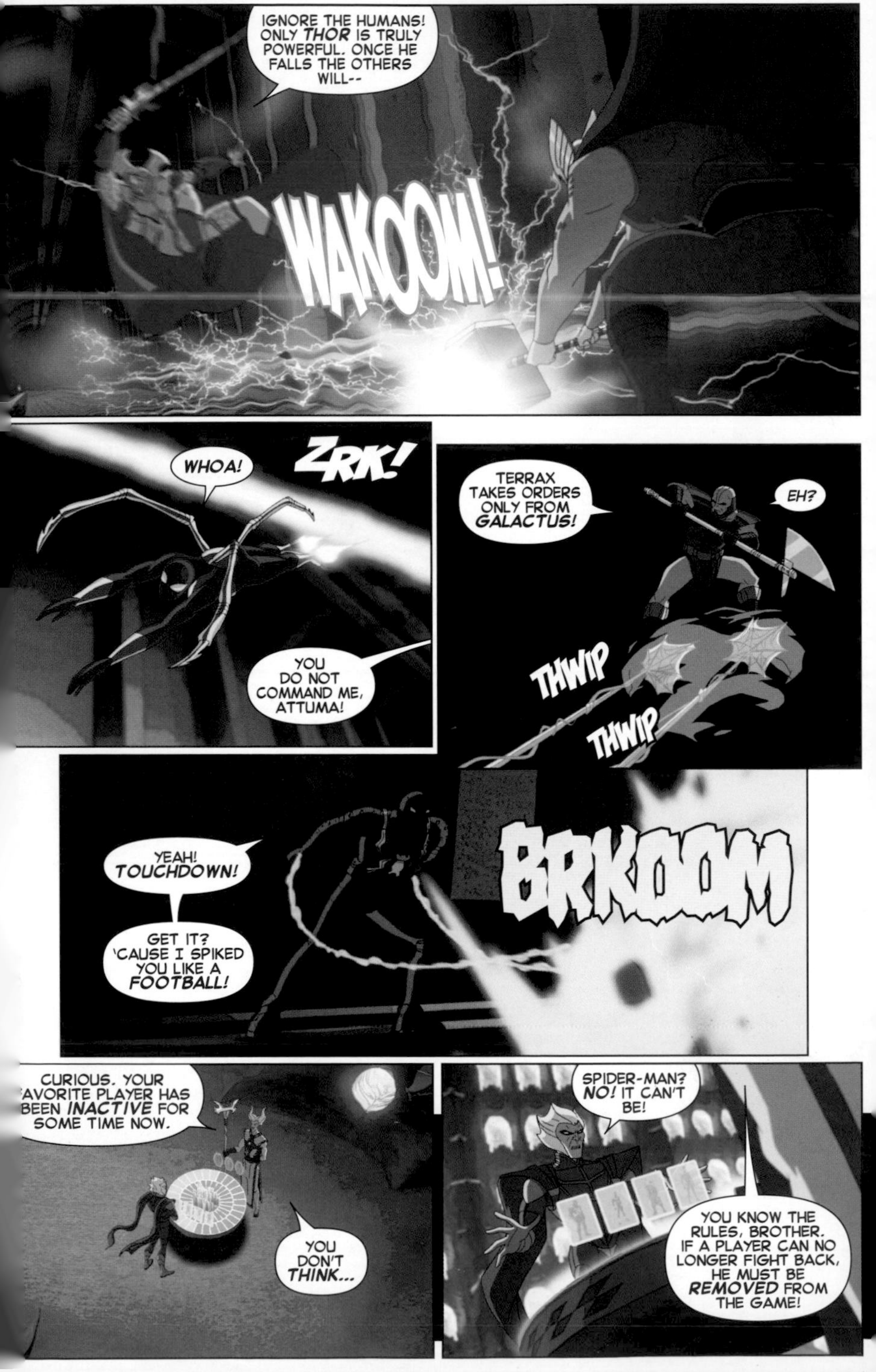
IGNORE THE HUMANS! ONLY THOR IS TRULY POWERFUL. ONCE HE FALLS THE OTHERS WILL--
WAKOOM!
WHOA!
ZRK!
YOU DO NOT COMMAND ME, ATTUMA!
TERRAX TAKES ORDERS ONLY FROM GALACTUS!
EH?
THWIP
THWIP
YEAH! TOUCHDOWN!
GET IT? 'CAUSE I SPIKED YOU LIKE A FOOTBALL!
BRKOOM
CURIOUS. YOUR FAVORITE PLAYER HAS BEEN INACTIVE FOR SOME TIME NOW.
YOU DON'T THINK...
SPIDER-MAN? NO! IT CAN'T BE!
YOU KNOW THE RULES, BROTHER. IF A PLAYER CAN NO LONGER FIGHT BACK, HE MUST BE REMOVED FROM THE GAME!

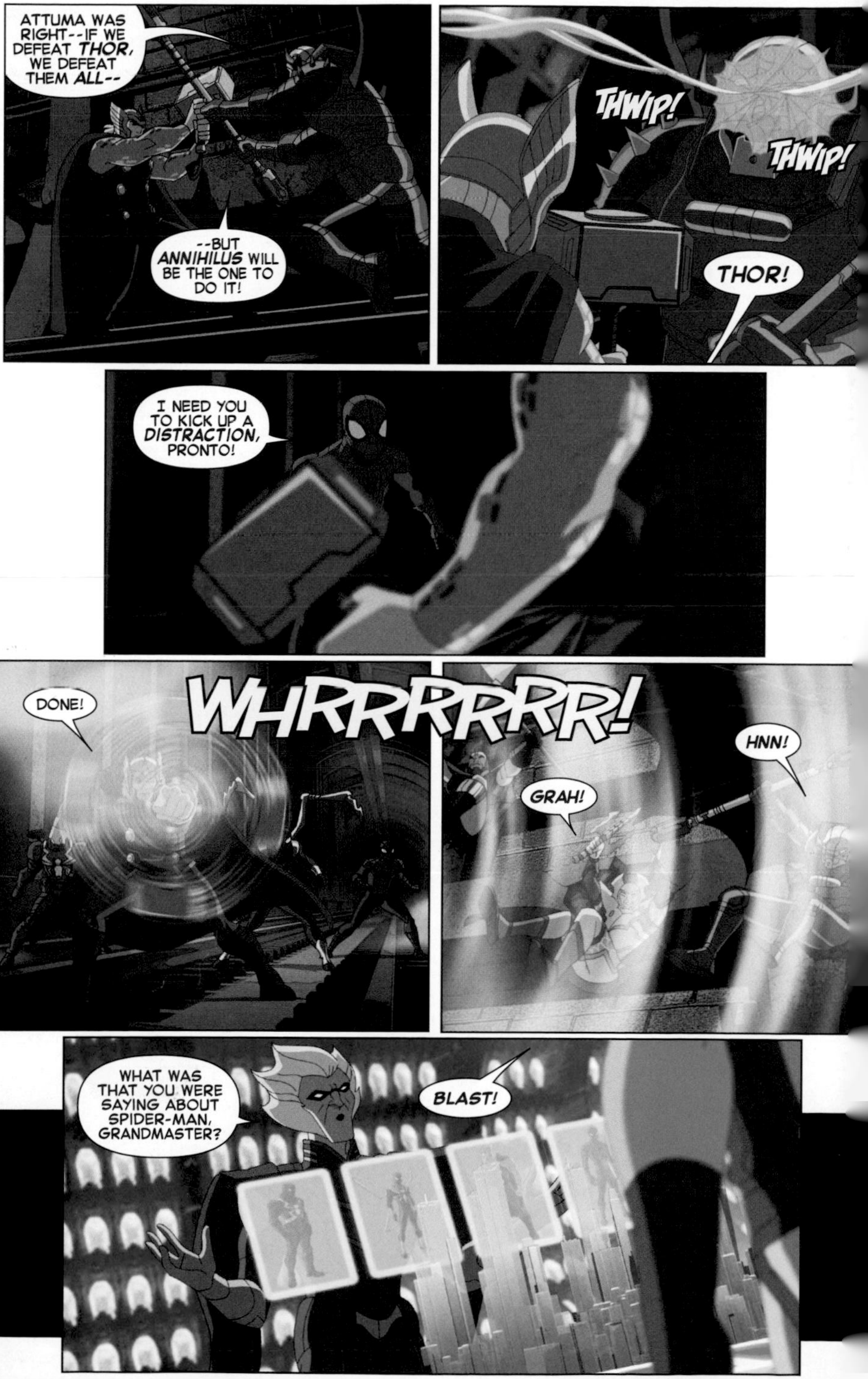
ATTUMA WAS RIGHT--IF WE DEFEAT THOR, WE DEFEAT THEM ALL--
--BUT ANNIHILUS WILL BE THE ONE TO DO IT!
THWIP!
THWIP!
THOR!
I NEED YOU TO KICK UP A DISTRACTION, PRONTO!
DONE!
WHRRRRRR!
HNN!
GRAH!
WHAT WAS THAT YOU WERE SAYING ABOUT SPIDER-MAN, GRANDMASTER?
BLAST!

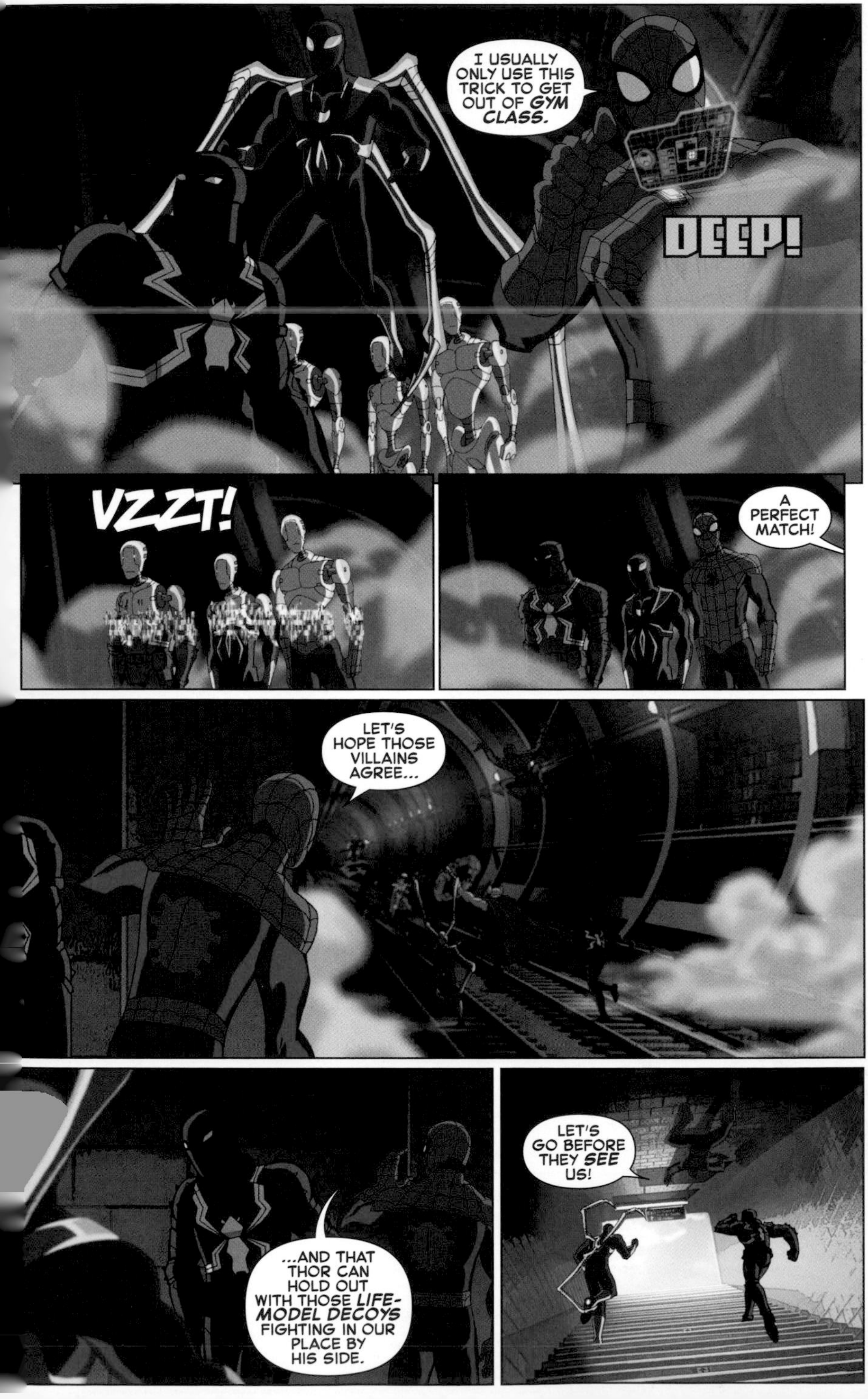
I USUALLY ONLY USE THIS TRICK TO GET OUT OF *GYM CLASS.*
DEEP!
VZZT!
A PERFECT MATCH!
LET'S HOPE THOSE VILLAINS AGREE...
...AND THAT THOR CAN HOLD OUT WITH THOSE *LIFE-MODEL DECOYS* FIGHTING IN OUR PLACE BY HIS SIDE.
LET'S GO BEFORE THEY *SEE* US!

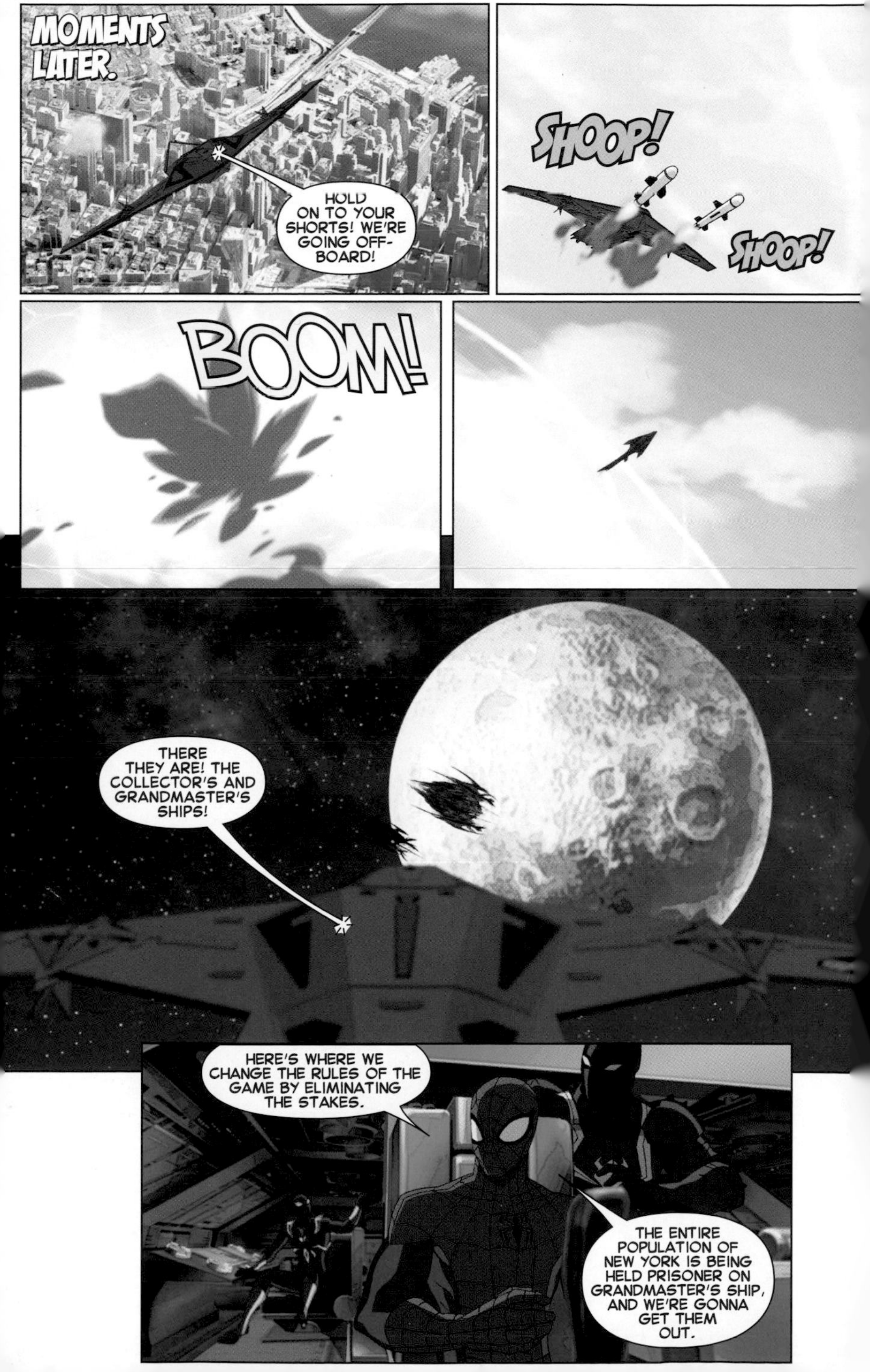
MOMENTS LATER.
HOLD ON TO YOUR SHORTS! WE'RE GOING OFF-BOARD!
SHOOP!
SHOOP!
BOOM!
THERE THEY ARE! THE COLLECTOR'S AND GRANDMASTER'S SHIPS!
HERE'S WHERE WE CHANGE THE RULES OF THE GAME BY ELIMINATING THE STAKES.
THE ENTIRE POPULATION OF NEW YORK IS BEING HELD PRISONER ON GRANDMASTER'S SHIP, AND WE'RE GONNA GET THEM OUT.

FIRST, WE TAKE OUT HIS COMMUNICATIONS ARRAY.

SINCE HE'S BUSY PLAYING GAMES ON THE *COLLECTOR'S* SHIP, HE'LL NEVER KNOW WE'RE HERE.

AND THE PEOPLE OF NEW YORK ARE *GOING HOME!*

COURTESY OF *SPIDER-MAN* AND HIS *ULTIMATE* FRIENDS!

EHH... WE'LL HAVE TO WORK ON THE NAME.

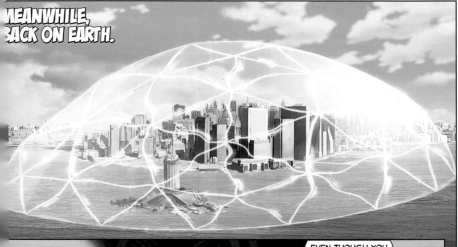

MEANWHILE, BACK ON EARTH.

EVEN THOUGH YOU *DEFY* ME, THOR, YOUR COHORTS GROW *WEAK.*

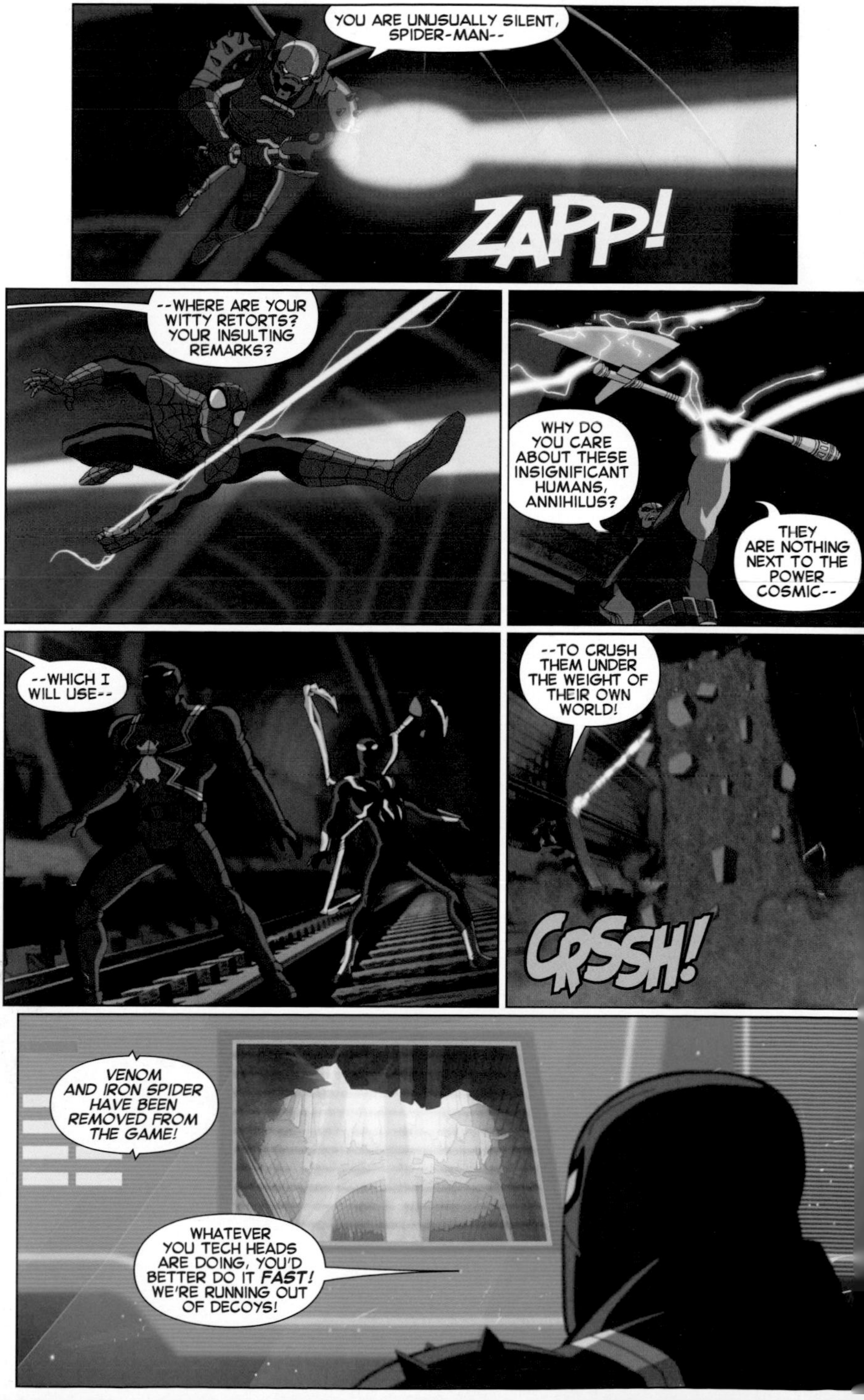
YOU ARE UNUSUALLY SILENT, SPIDER-MAN--
ZAPP!
--WHERE ARE YOUR WITTY RETORTS? YOUR INSULTING REMARKS?
WHY DO YOU CARE ABOUT THESE INSIGNIFICANT HUMANS, ANNIHILUS?
THEY ARE NOTHING NEXT TO THE POWER COSMIC--
--WHICH I WILL USE--
--TO CRUSH THEM UNDER THE WEIGHT OF THEIR OWN WORLD!
CRSSH!
VENOM AND IRON SPIDER HAVE BEEN REMOVED FROM THE GAME!
WHATEVER YOU TECH HEADS ARE DOING, YOU'D BETTER DO IT FAST! WE'RE RUNNING OUT OF DECOYS!

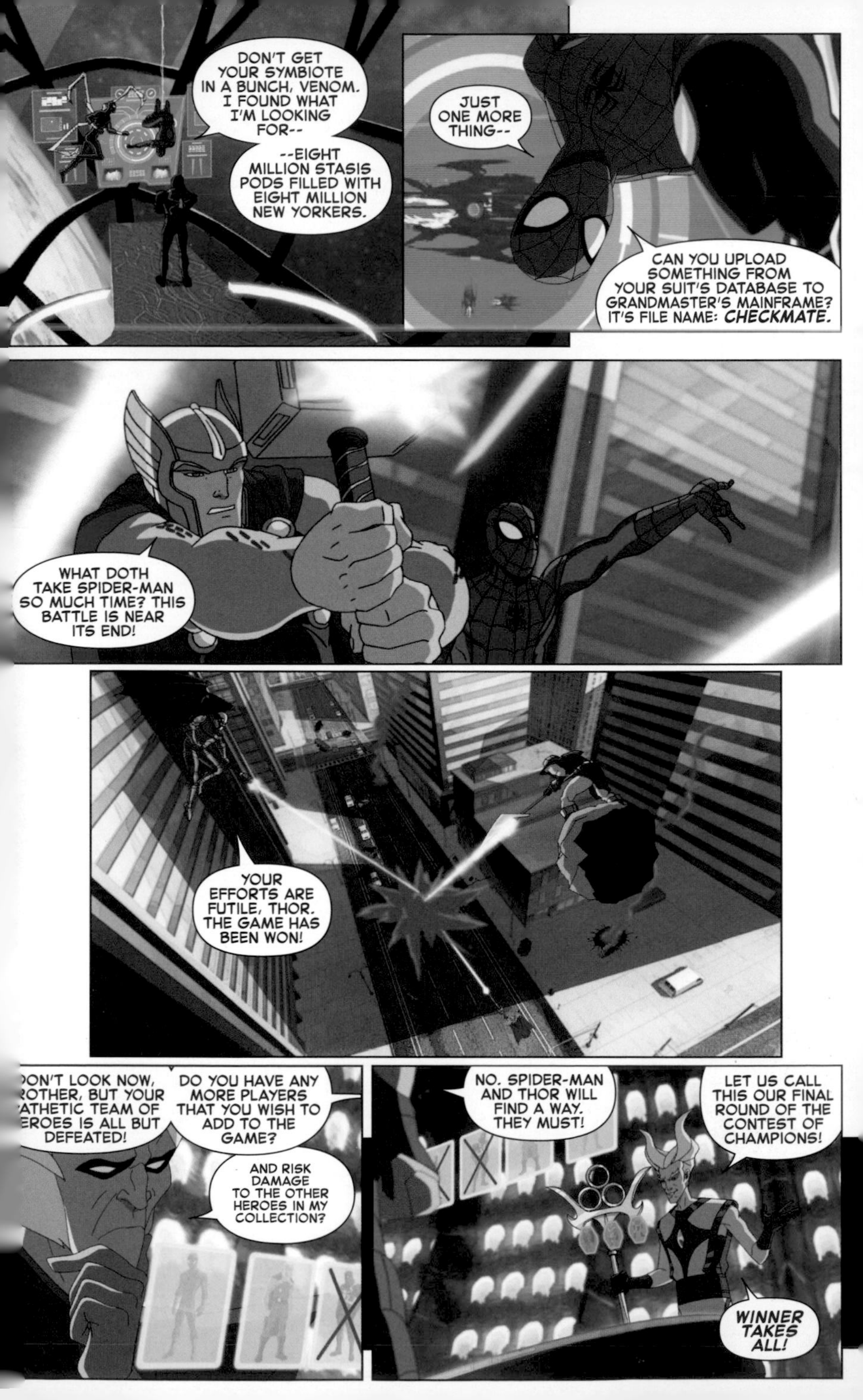
DON'T GET YOUR SYMBIOTE IN A BUNCH, VENOM. I FOUND WHAT I'M LOOKING FOR--
--EIGHT MILLION STASIS PODS FILLED WITH EIGHT MILLION NEW YORKERS.
JUST ONE MORE THING--
CAN YOU UPLOAD SOMETHING FROM YOUR SUIT'S DATABASE TO GRANDMASTER'S MAINFRAME? IT'S FILE NAME: CHECKMATE.
WHAT DOTH TAKE SPIDER-MAN SO MUCH TIME? THIS BATTLE IS NEAR ITS END!
YOUR EFFORTS ARE FUTILE, THOR. THE GAME HAS BEEN WON!
DON'T LOOK NOW, BROTHER, BUT YOUR PATHETIC TEAM OF HEROES IS ALL BUT DEFEATED!
DO YOU HAVE ANY MORE PLAYERS THAT YOU WISH TO ADD TO THE GAME?
AND RISK DAMAGE TO THE OTHER HEROES IN MY COLLECTION?
NO. SPIDER-MAN AND THOR WILL FIND A WAY. THEY MUST!
LET US CALL THIS OUR FINAL ROUND OF THE CONTEST OF CHAMPIONS!
WINNER TAKES ALL!

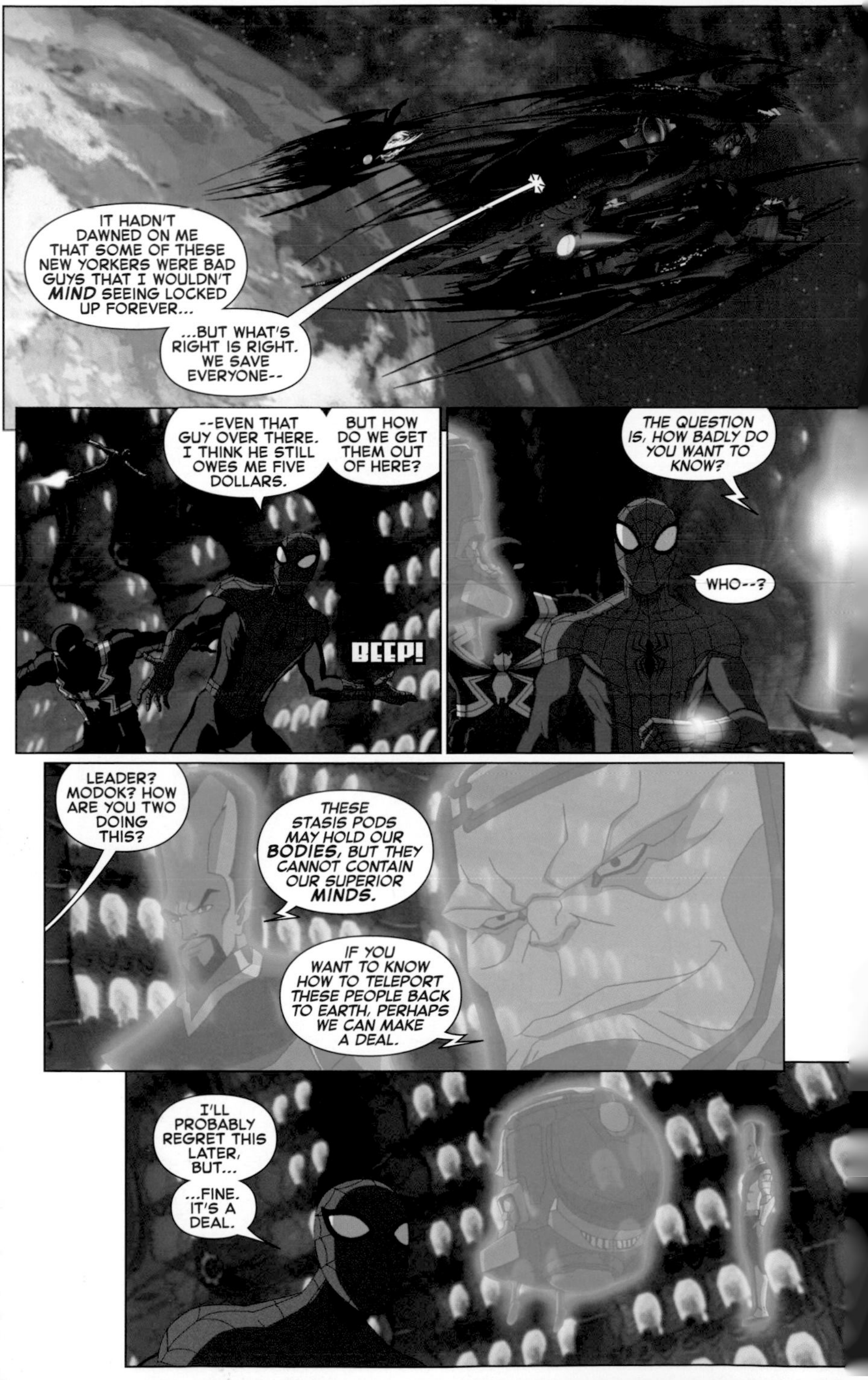

IT HADN'T DAWNED ON ME THAT SOME OF THESE NEW YORKERS WERE BAD GUYS THAT I WOULDN'T *MIND* SEEING LOCKED UP FOREVER...
...BUT WHAT'S RIGHT IS RIGHT. WE SAVE EVERYONE--
--EVEN THAT GUY OVER THERE. I THINK HE STILL OWES ME FIVE DOLLARS.
BUT HOW DO WE GET THEM OUT OF HERE?
BEEP!
THE QUESTION IS, HOW BADLY DO YOU WANT TO KNOW?
WHO--?
LEADER? MODOK? HOW ARE YOU TWO DOING THIS?
THESE STASIS PODS MAY HOLD OUR **BODIES**, BUT THEY CANNOT CONTAIN OUR SUPERIOR **MINDS.**
IF YOU WANT TO KNOW HOW TO TELEPORT THESE PEOPLE BACK TO EARTH, PERHAPS WE CAN MAKE A DEAL.
I'LL PROBABLY REGRET THIS LATER, BUT...
...FINE. IT'S A DEAL.

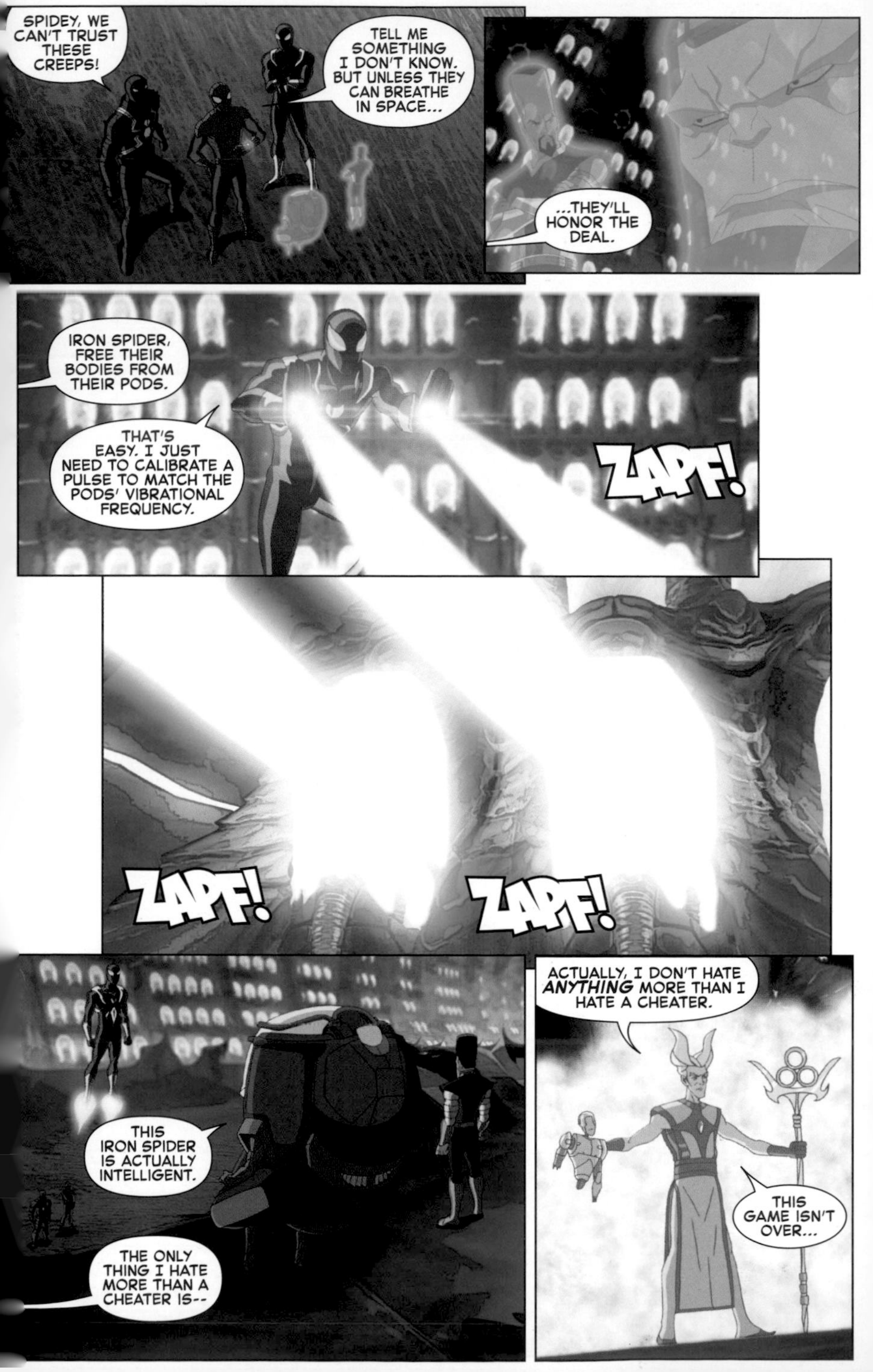
SPIDEY, WE CAN'T TRUST THESE CREEPS!
TELL ME SOMETHING I DON'T KNOW. BUT UNLESS THEY CAN BREATHE IN SPACE...
...THEY'LL HONOR THE DEAL.
IRON SPIDER, FREE THEIR BODIES FROM THEIR PODS.
THAT'S EASY. I JUST NEED TO CALIBRATE A PULSE TO MATCH THE PODS' VIBRATIONAL FREQUENCY.
ZAPF!
ZAPF!
ZAPF!
THIS IRON SPIDER IS ACTUALLY INTELLIGENT.
THE ONLY THING I HATE MORE THAN A CHEATER IS--
ACTUALLY, I DON'T HATE *ANYTHING* MORE THAN I HATE A CHEATER.
THIS GAME ISN'T OVER...

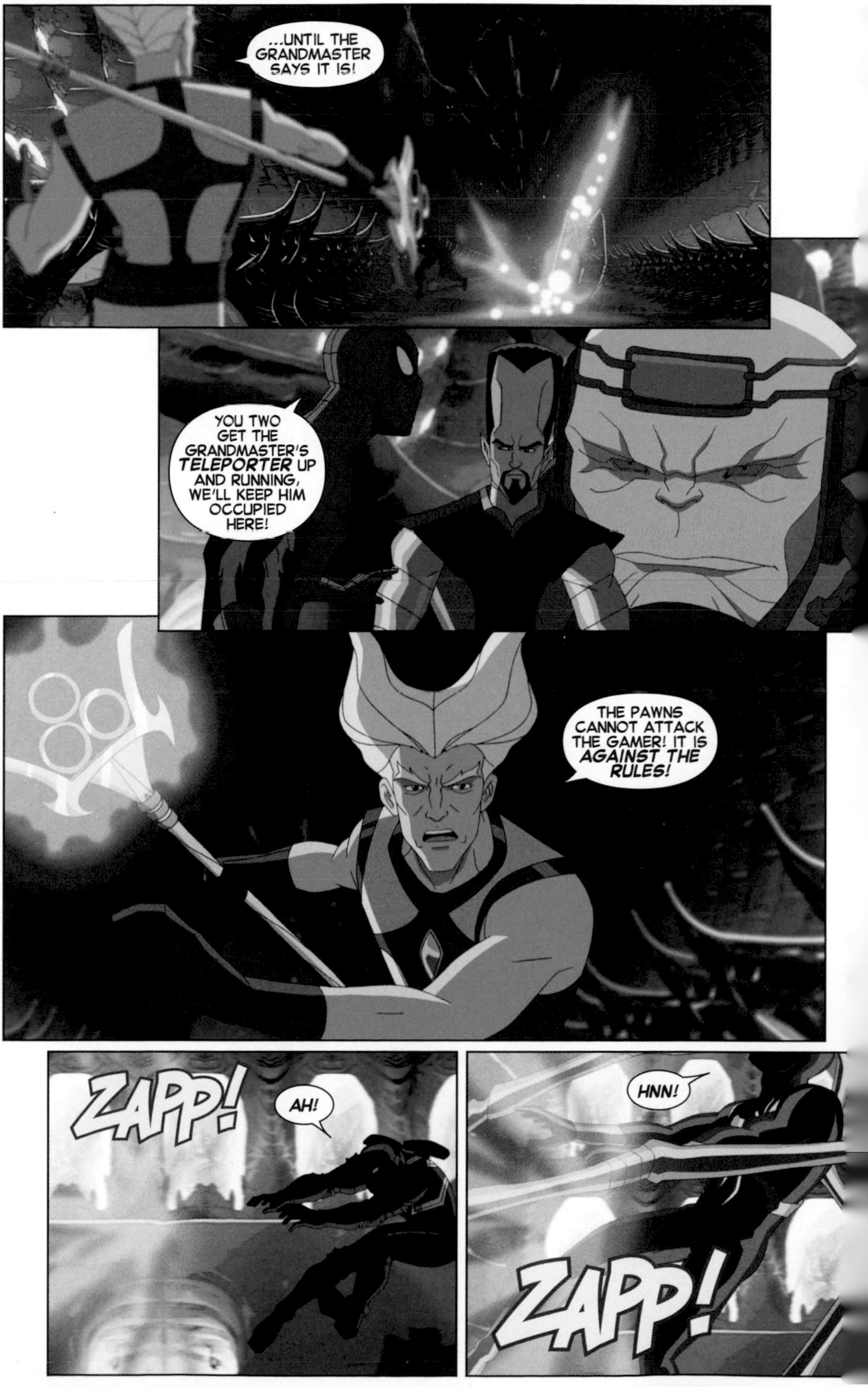
...UNTIL THE GRANDMASTER SAYS IT IS!
YOU TWO GET THE GRANDMASTER'S TELEPORTER UP AND RUNNING, WE'LL KEEP HIM OCCUPIED HERE!
THE PAWNS CANNOT ATTACK THE GAMER! IT IS AGAINST THE RULES!
ZAPP!
AH!
HNN!
ZAPP!

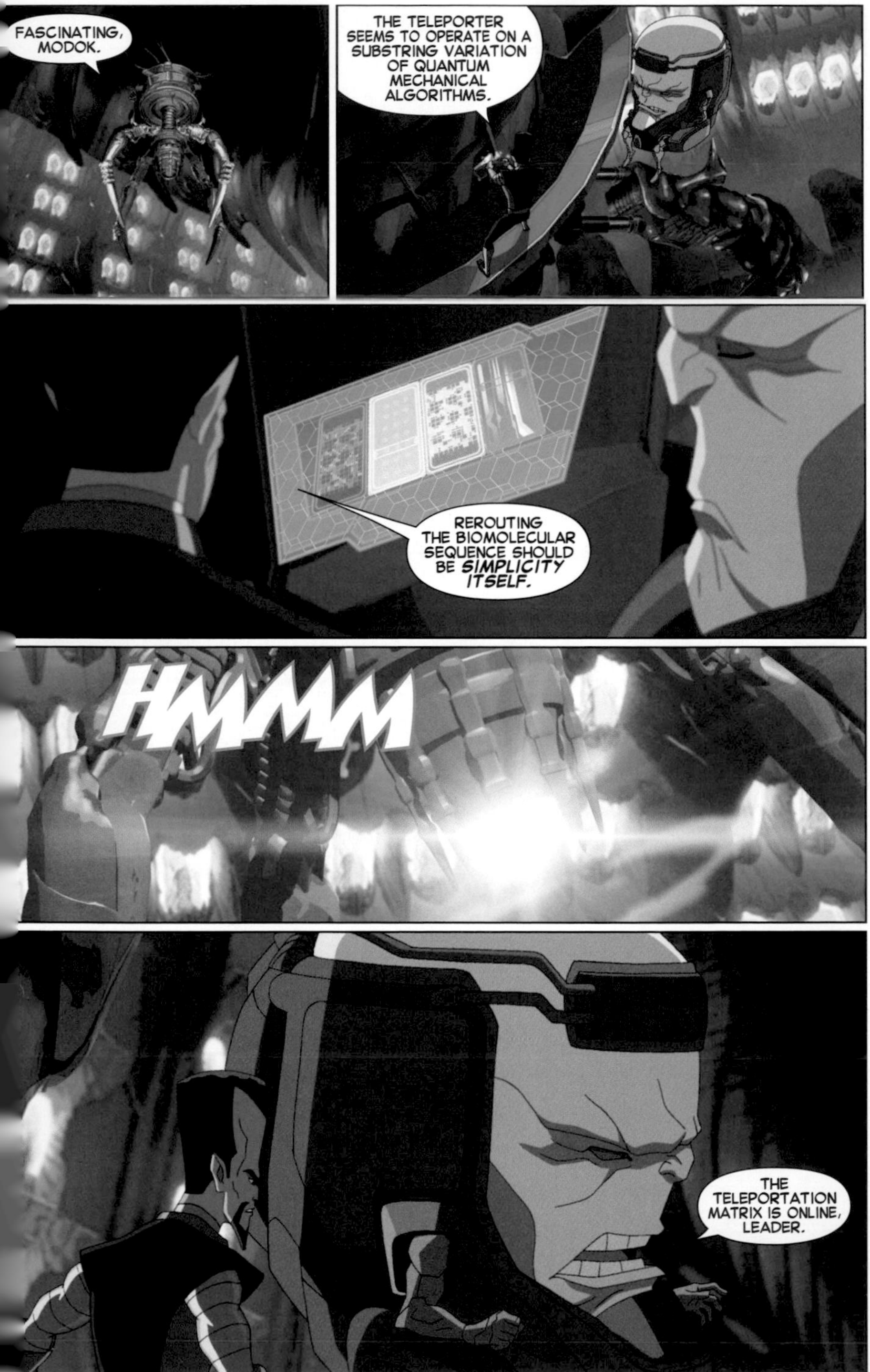
FASCINATING, MODOK.
THE TELEPORTER SEEMS TO OPERATE ON A SUBSTRING VARIATION OF QUANTUM MECHANICAL ALGORITHMS.
REROUTING THE BIOMOLECULAR SEQUENCE SHOULD BE *SIMPLICITY ITSELF.*
HMMM
THE TELEPORTATION MATRIX IS ONLINE, LEADER.

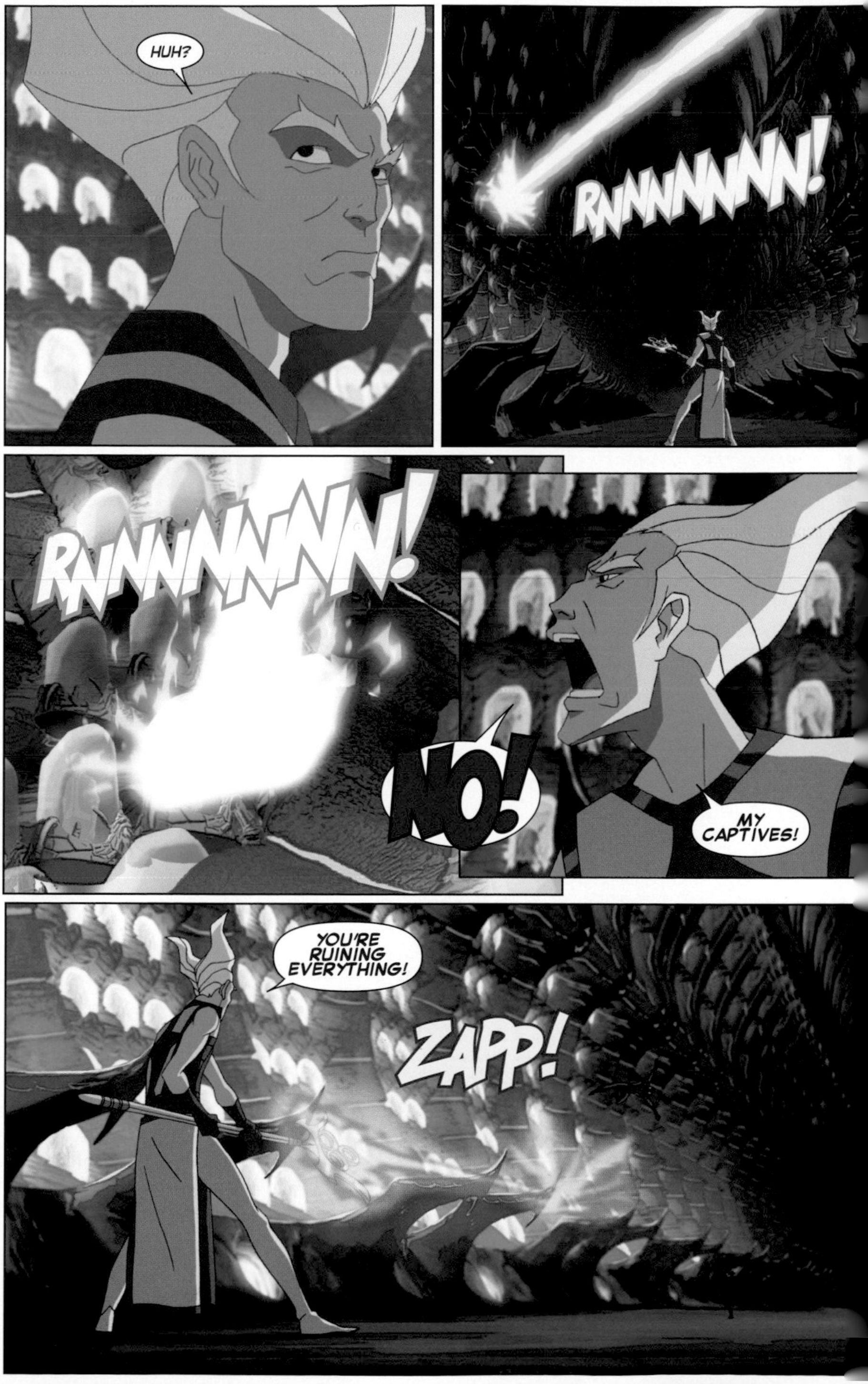
HUH?
RNNNNNNN!
RNNNNNNNN!
NO!
MY CAPTIVES!
YOU'RE RUINING EVERYTHING!
ZAPP!

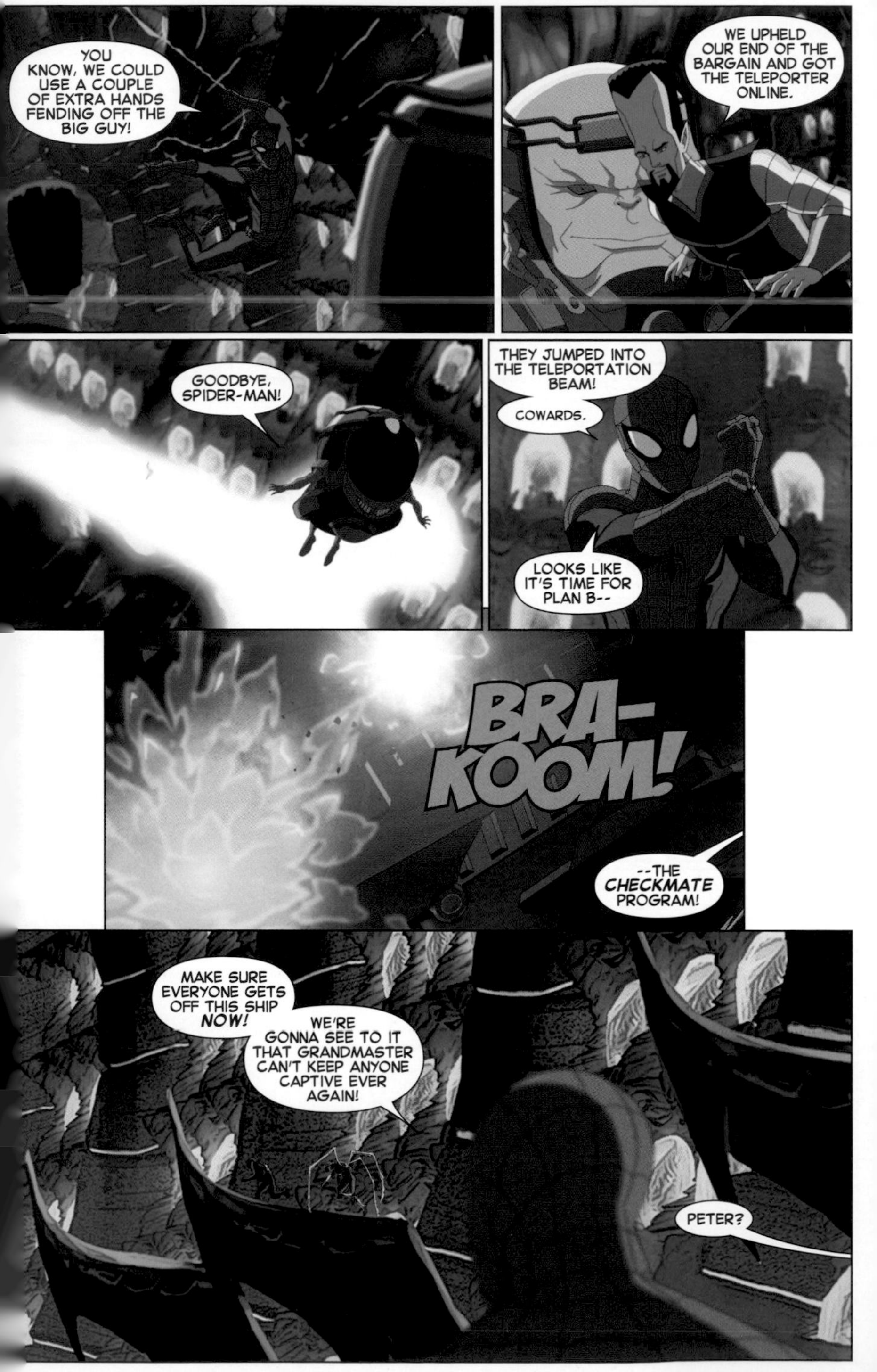
YOU KNOW, WE COULD USE A COUPLE OF EXTRA HANDS FENDING OFF THE BIG GUY!
WE UPHELD OUR END OF THE BARGAIN AND GOT THE TELEPORTER ONLINE.
GOODBYE, SPIDER-MAN!
THEY JUMPED INTO THE TELEPORTATION BEAM!
COWARDS.
LOOKS LIKE IT'S TIME FOR PLAN B--
BRA-KOOM!
--THE CHECKMATE PROGRAM!
MAKE SURE EVERYONE GETS OFF THIS SHIP NOW!
WE'RE GONNA SEE TO IT THAT GRANDMASTER CAN'T KEEP ANYONE CAPTIVE EVER AGAIN!
PETER?

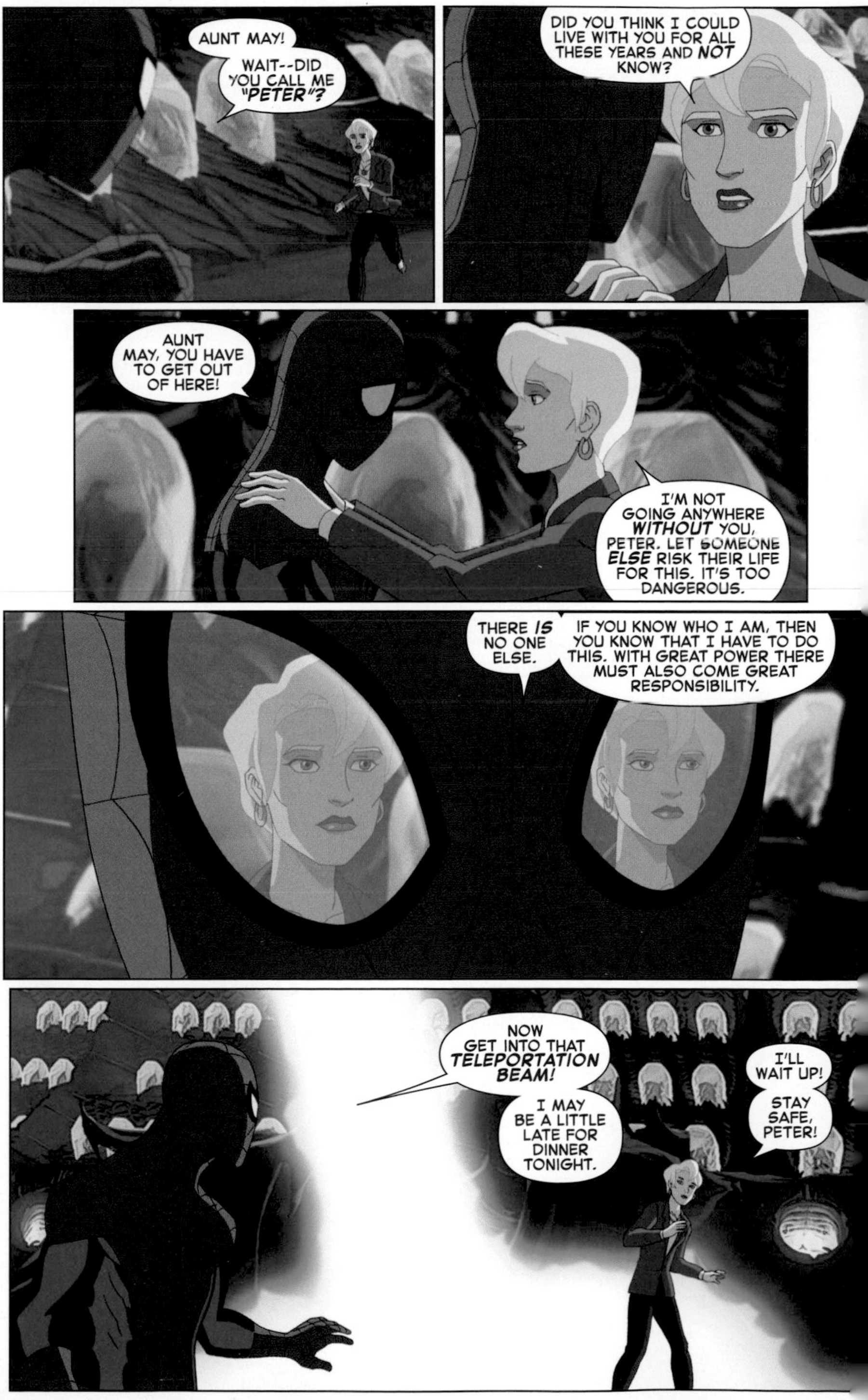
AUNT MAY!
WAIT--DID YOU CALL ME "PETER"?
DID YOU THINK I COULD LIVE WITH YOU FOR ALL THESE YEARS AND NOT KNOW?
AUNT MAY, YOU HAVE TO GET OUT OF HERE!
I'M NOT GOING ANYWHERE WITHOUT YOU, PETER. LET SOMEONE ELSE RISK THEIR LIFE FOR THIS. IT'S TOO DANGEROUS.
IF YOU KNOW WHO I AM, THEN YOU KNOW THAT I HAVE TO DO THIS. WITH GREAT POWER THERE MUST ALSO COME GREAT RESPONSIBILITY.
THERE IS NO ONE ELSE.
NOW GET INTO THAT TELEPORTATION BEAM!
I MAY BE A LITTLE LATE FOR DINNER TONIGHT.
I'LL WAIT UP!
STAY SAFE, PETER!

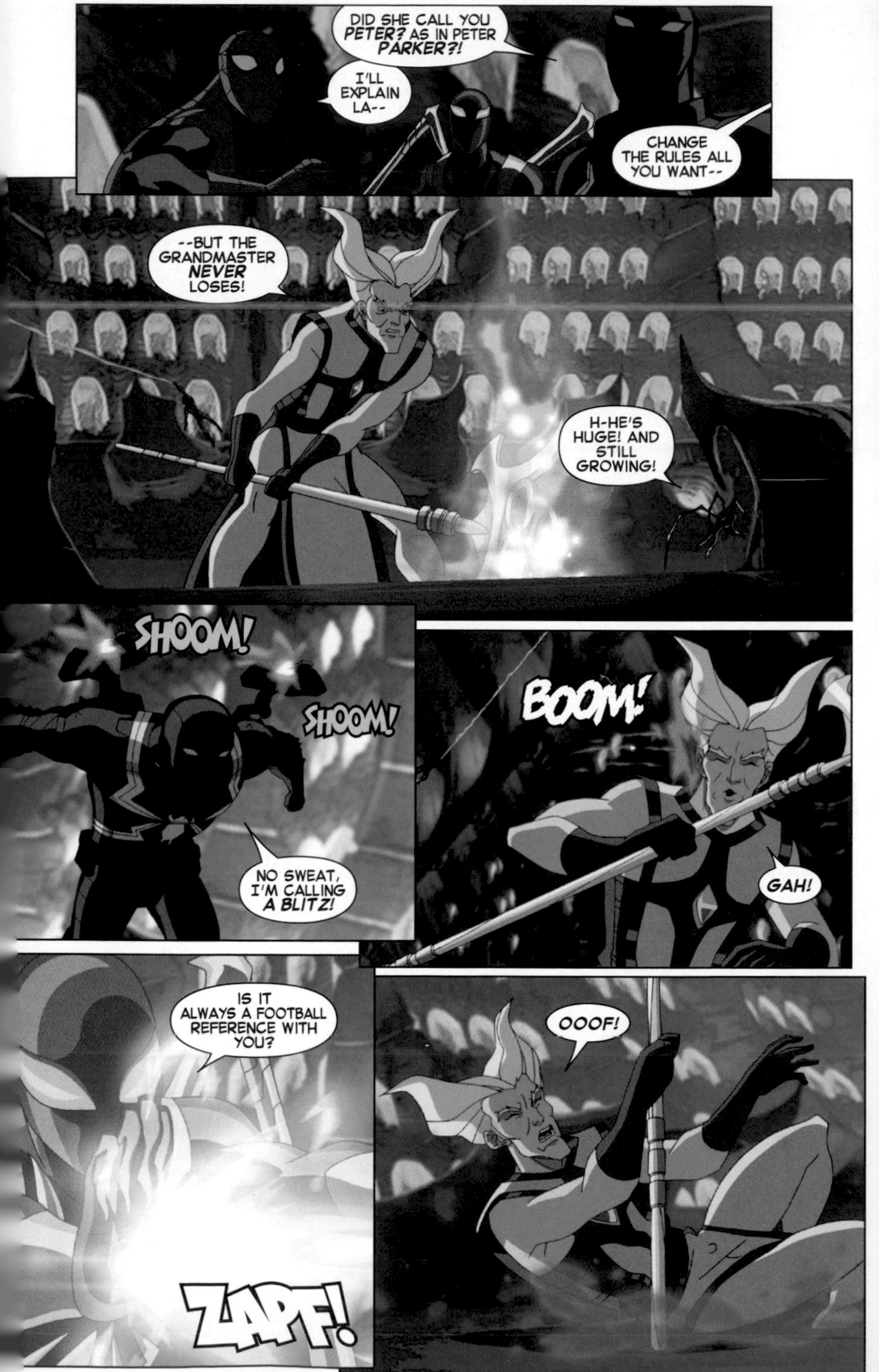
DID SHE CALL YOU PETER? AS IN PETER PARKER?!
I'LL EXPLAIN LA--
CHANGE THE RULES ALL YOU WANT--
--BUT THE GRANDMASTER NEVER LOSES!
H-HE'S HUGE! AND STILL GROWING!
SHOOM!
SHOOM!
NO SWEAT, I'M CALLING A BLITZ!
BOOM!
GAH!
IS IT ALWAYS A FOOTBALL REFERENCE WITH YOU?
ZAPF!
OOOF!

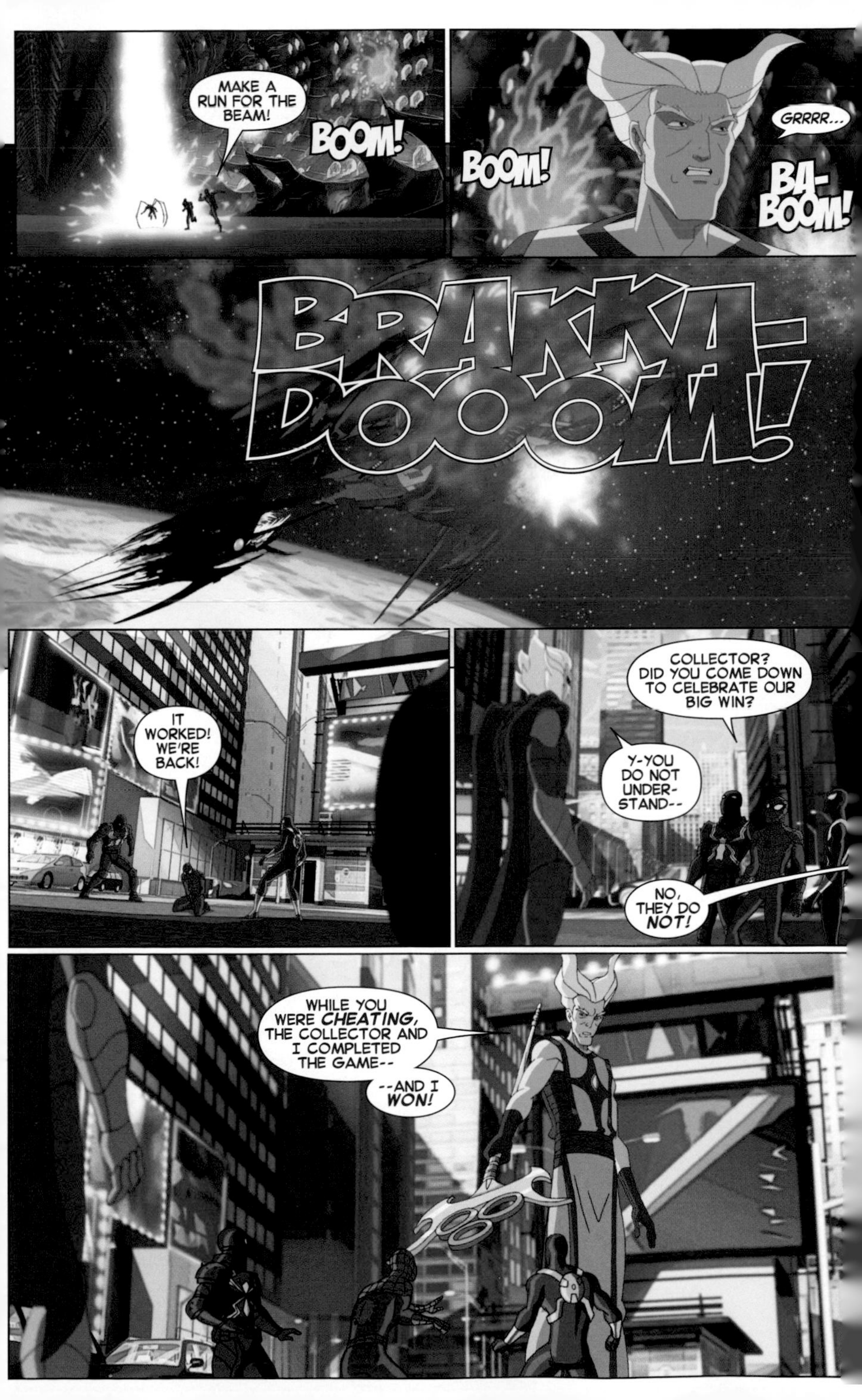
MAKE A RUN FOR THE BEAM!
BOOM!
BOOM!
GRRRR...
BA-BOOM!
BRAKKA-DOOOM!
IT WORKED! WE'RE BACK!
COLLECTOR? DID YOU COME DOWN TO CELEBRATE OUR BIG WIN?
Y-YOU DO NOT UNDER-STAND--
NO, THEY DO NOT!
WHILE YOU WERE CHEATING, THE COLLECTOR AND I COMPLETED THE GAME--
--AND I WON!

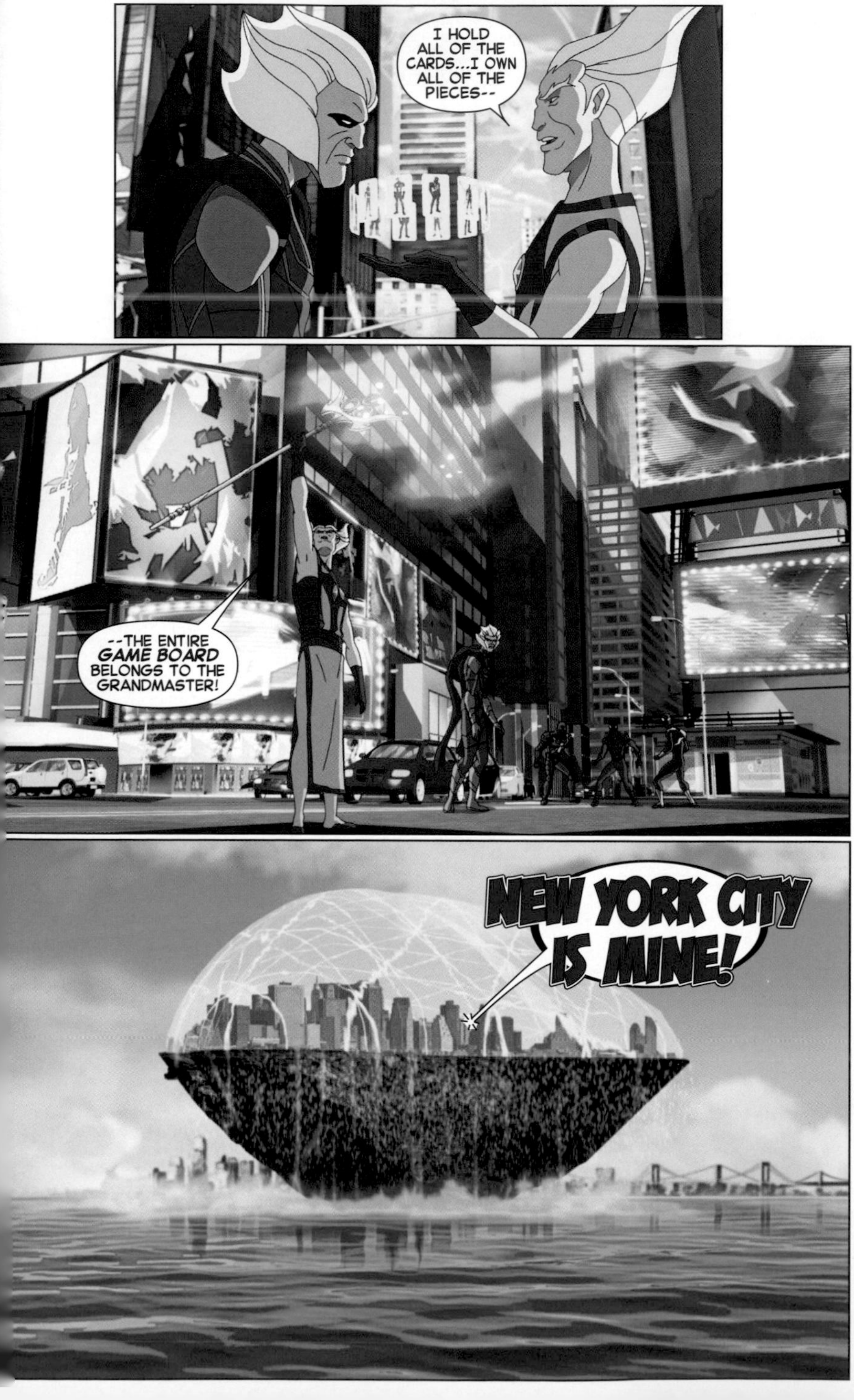
I HOLD ALL OF THE CARDS...I OWN ALL OF THE PIECES--
--THE ENTIRE GAME BOARD BELONGS TO THE GRANDMASTER!
NEW YORK CITY IS MINE!

MARVEL

ULTIMATE SPIDER-MAN WEB-WARRIORS

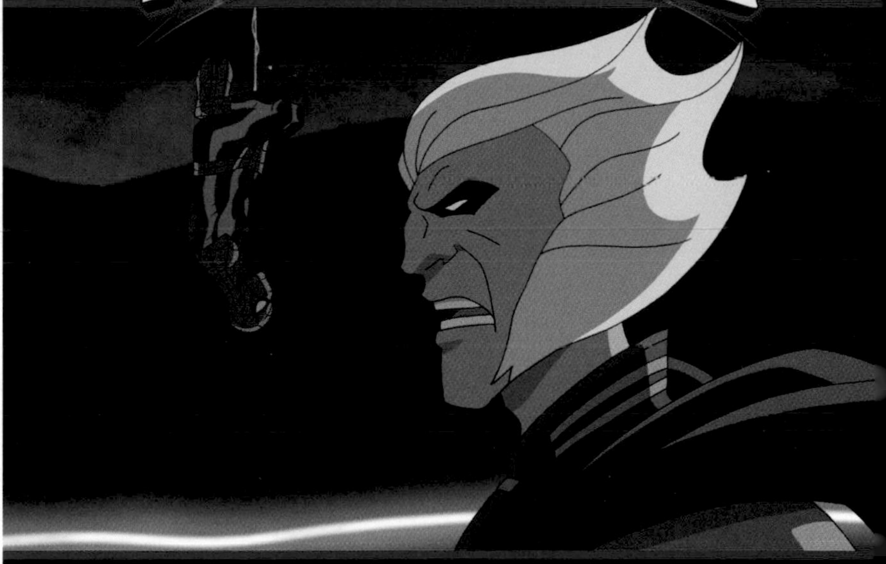

CONTEST OF CHAMPIONS

4

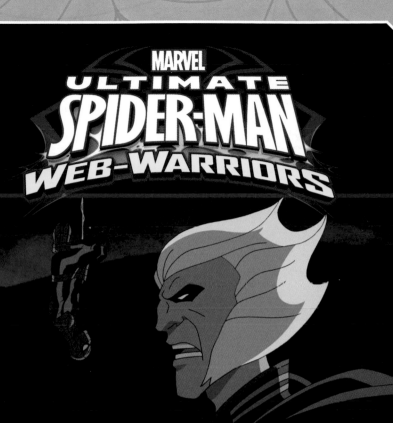

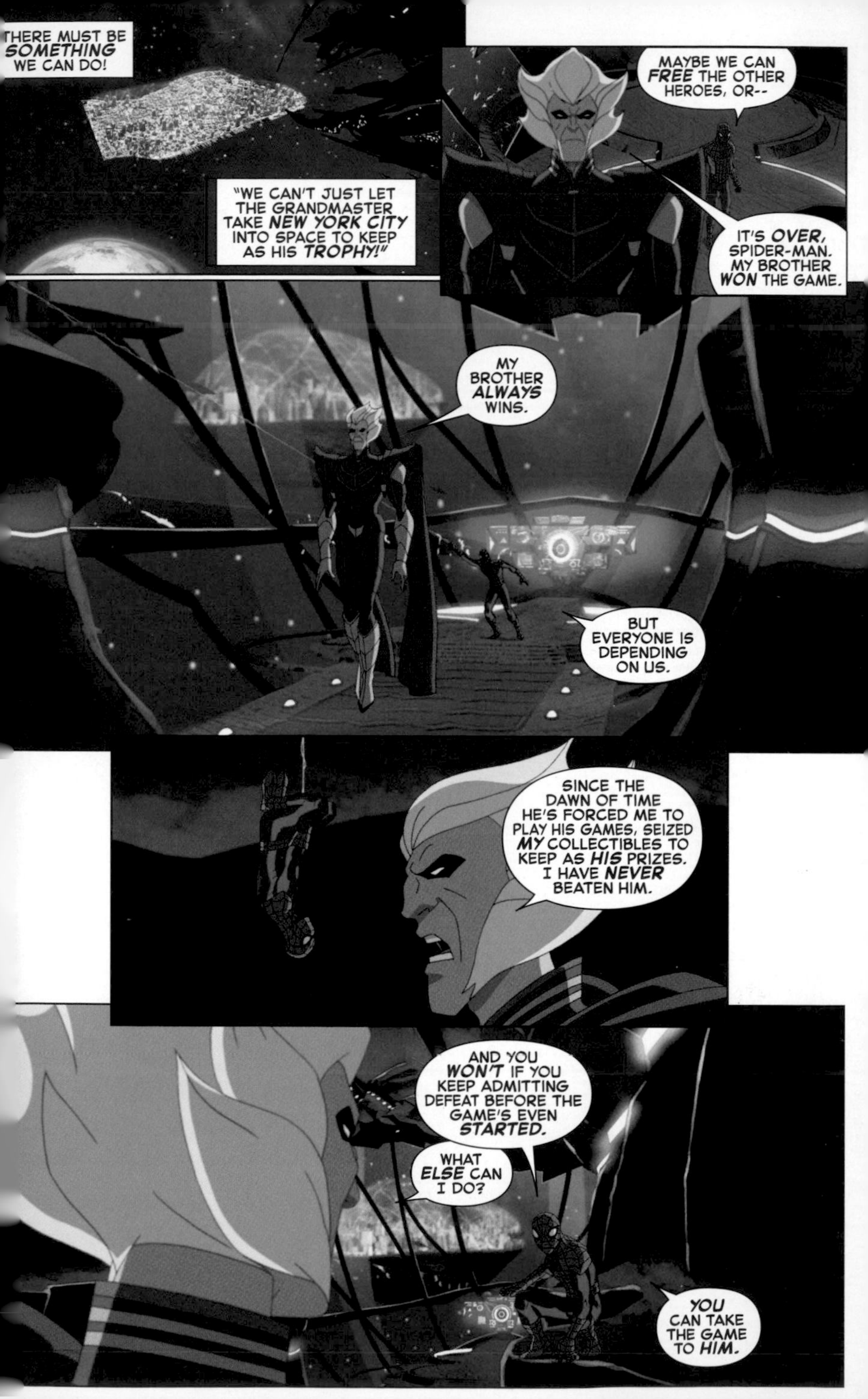
THERE MUST BE SOMETHING WE CAN DO!
"WE CAN'T JUST LET THE GRANDMASTER TAKE NEW YORK CITY INTO SPACE TO KEEP AS HIS TROPHY!"
MAYBE WE CAN FREE THE OTHER HEROES, OR--
IT'S OVER, SPIDER-MAN. MY BROTHER WON THE GAME.
MY BROTHER ALWAYS WINS.
BUT EVERYONE IS DEPENDING ON US.
SINCE THE DAWN OF TIME HE'S FORCED ME TO PLAY HIS GAMES, SEIZED MY COLLECTIBLES TO KEEP AS HIS PRIZES. I HAVE NEVER BEATEN HIM.
AND YOU WON'T IF YOU KEEP ADMITTING DEFEAT BEFORE THE GAME'S EVEN STARTED.
WHAT ELSE CAN I DO?
YOU CAN TAKE THE GAME TO HIM.

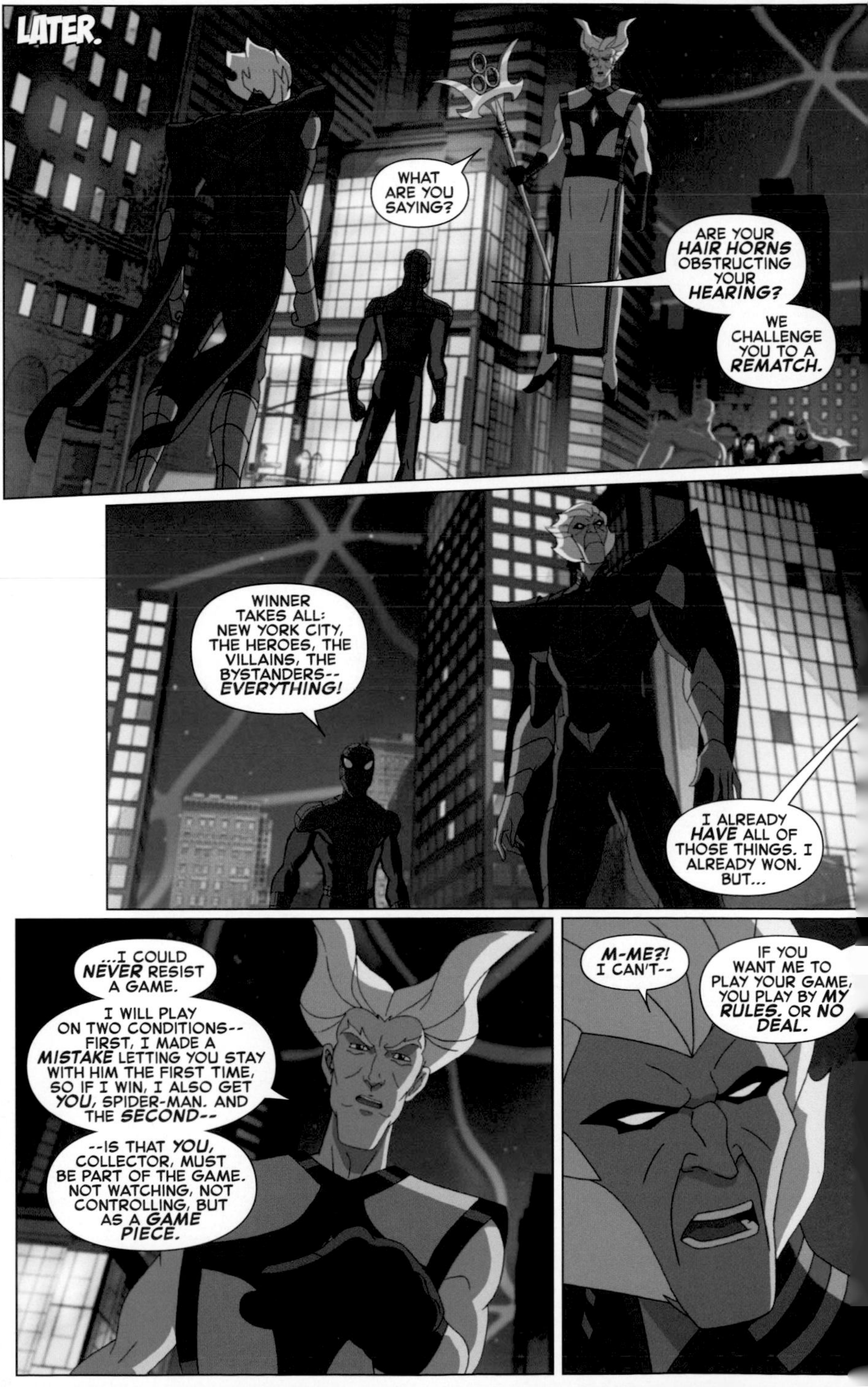
LATER.
WHAT ARE YOU SAYING?
ARE YOUR HAIR HORNS OBSTRUCTING YOUR HEARING?
WE CHALLENGE YOU TO A REMATCH.
WINNER TAKES ALL: NEW YORK CITY, THE HEROES, THE VILLAINS, THE BYSTANDERS-- EVERYTHING!
I ALREADY HAVE ALL OF THOSE THINGS. I ALREADY WON. BUT...
...I COULD NEVER RESIST A GAME.
I WILL PLAY ON TWO CONDITIONS-- FIRST, I MADE A MISTAKE LETTING YOU STAY WITH HIM THE FIRST TIME, SO IF I WIN, I ALSO GET YOU, SPIDER-MAN. AND THE SECOND--
--IS THAT YOU, COLLECTOR, MUST BE PART OF THE GAME. NOT WATCHING, NOT CONTROLLING, BUT AS A GAME PIECE.
M-ME?! I CAN'T--
IF YOU WANT ME TO PLAY YOUR GAME, YOU PLAY BY MY RULES. OR NO DEAL.

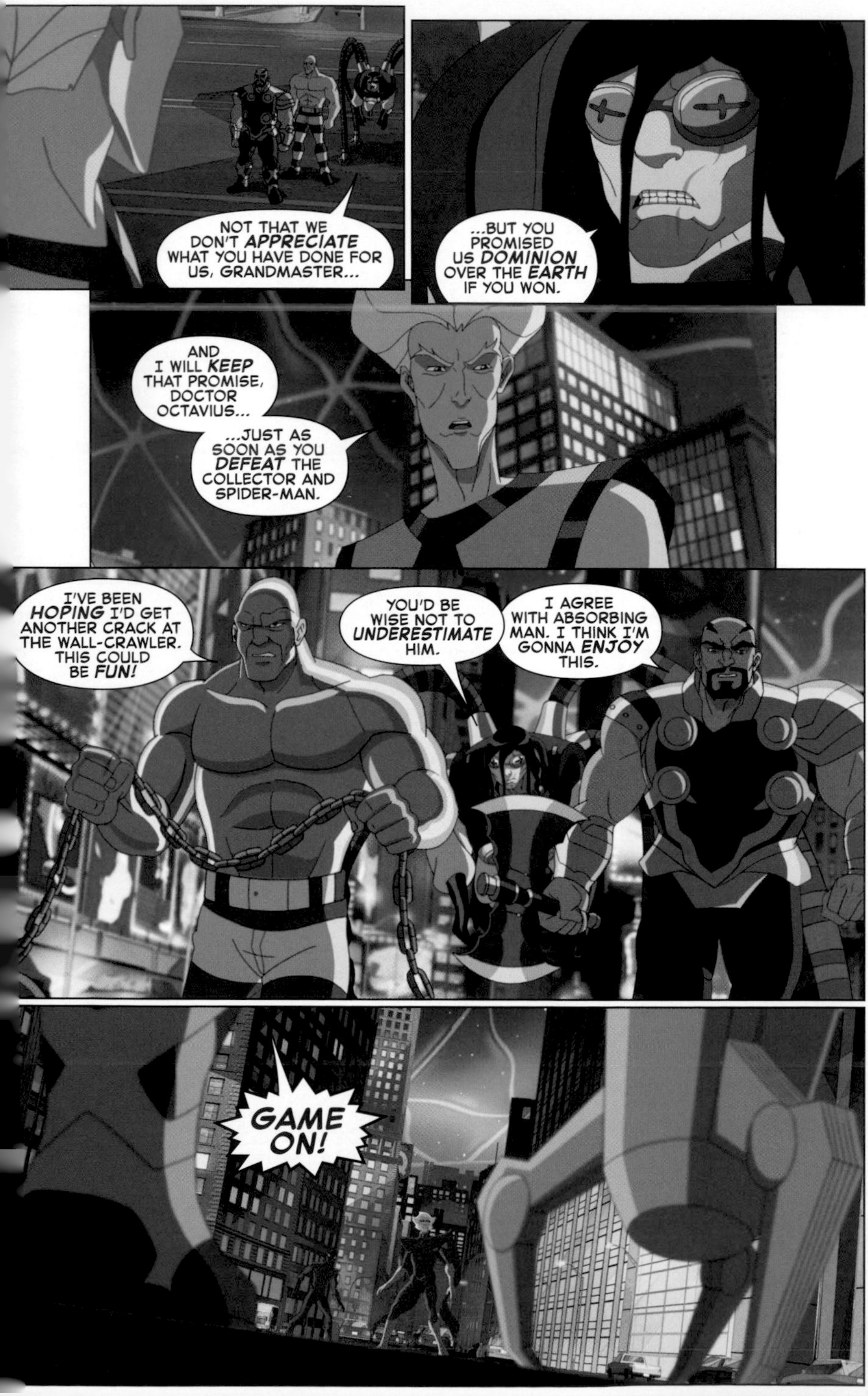
NOT THAT WE DON'T APPRECIATE WHAT YOU HAVE DONE FOR US, GRANDMASTER...
...BUT YOU PROMISED US DOMINION OVER THE EARTH IF YOU WON.
AND I WILL KEEP THAT PROMISE, DOCTOR OCTAVIUS...
...JUST AS SOON AS YOU DEFEAT THE COLLECTOR AND SPIDER-MAN.
I'VE BEEN HOPING I'D GET ANOTHER CRACK AT THE WALL-CRAWLER. THIS COULD BE FUN!
YOU'D BE WISE NOT TO UNDERESTIMATE HIM.
I AGREE WITH ABSORBING MAN. I THINK I'M GONNA ENJOY THIS.
GAME ON!

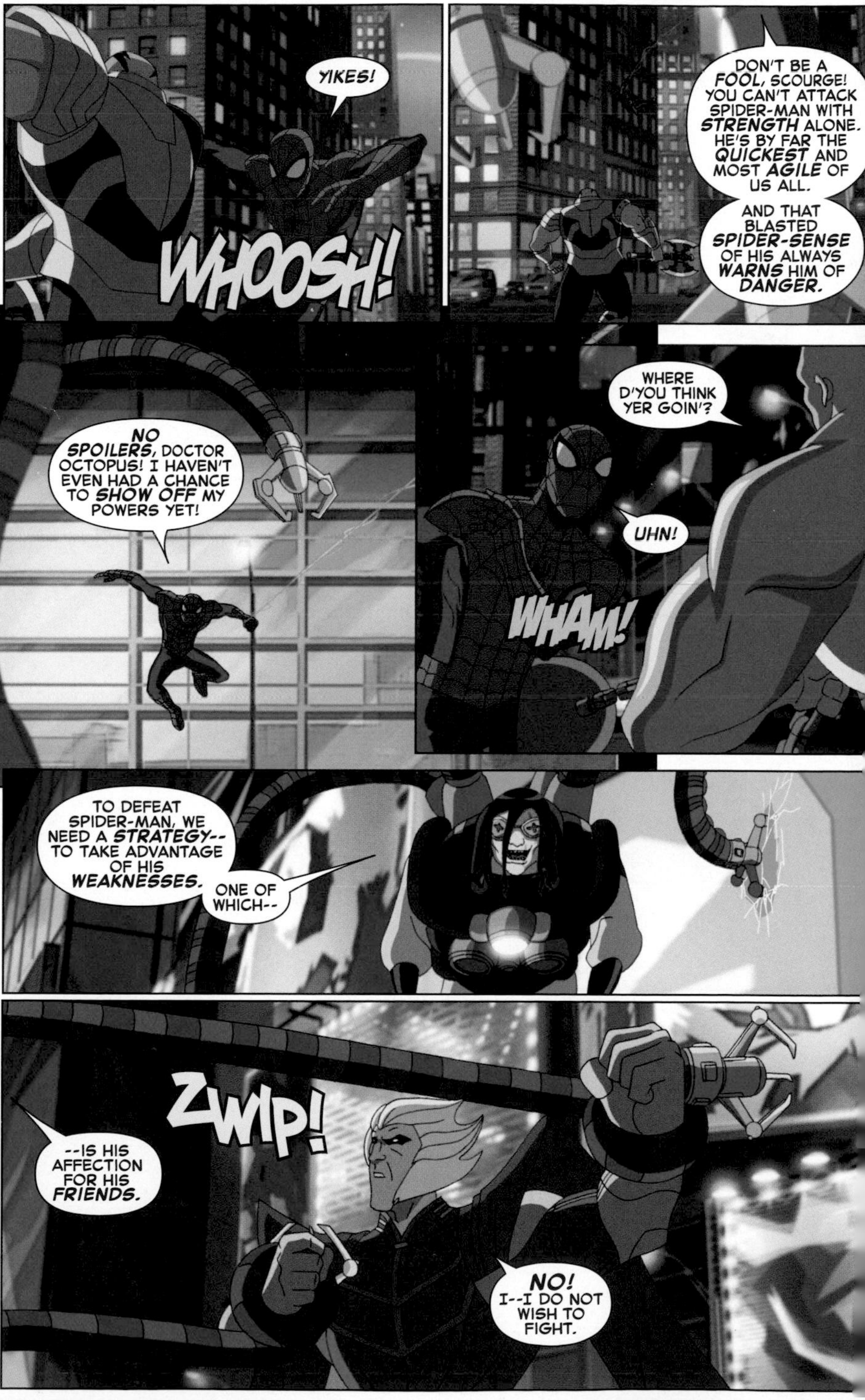
YIKES!
WHOOSH!
DON'T BE A FOOL, SCOURGE! YOU CAN'T ATTACK SPIDER-MAN WITH STRENGTH ALONE. HE'S BY FAR THE QUICKEST AND MOST AGILE OF US ALL.
AND THAT BLASTED SPIDER-SENSE OF HIS ALWAYS WARNS HIM OF DANGER.
NO SPOILERS, DOCTOR OCTOPUS! I HAVEN'T EVEN HAD A CHANCE TO SHOW OFF MY POWERS YET!
WHERE D'YOU THINK YER GOIN'?
UHN!
WHAM!
TO DEFEAT SPIDER-MAN, WE NEED A STRATEGY-- TO TAKE ADVANTAGE OF HIS WEAKNESSES.
ONE OF WHICH--
ZWIP!
--IS HIS AFFECTION FOR HIS FRIENDS.
NO! I--I DO NOT WISH TO FIGHT.

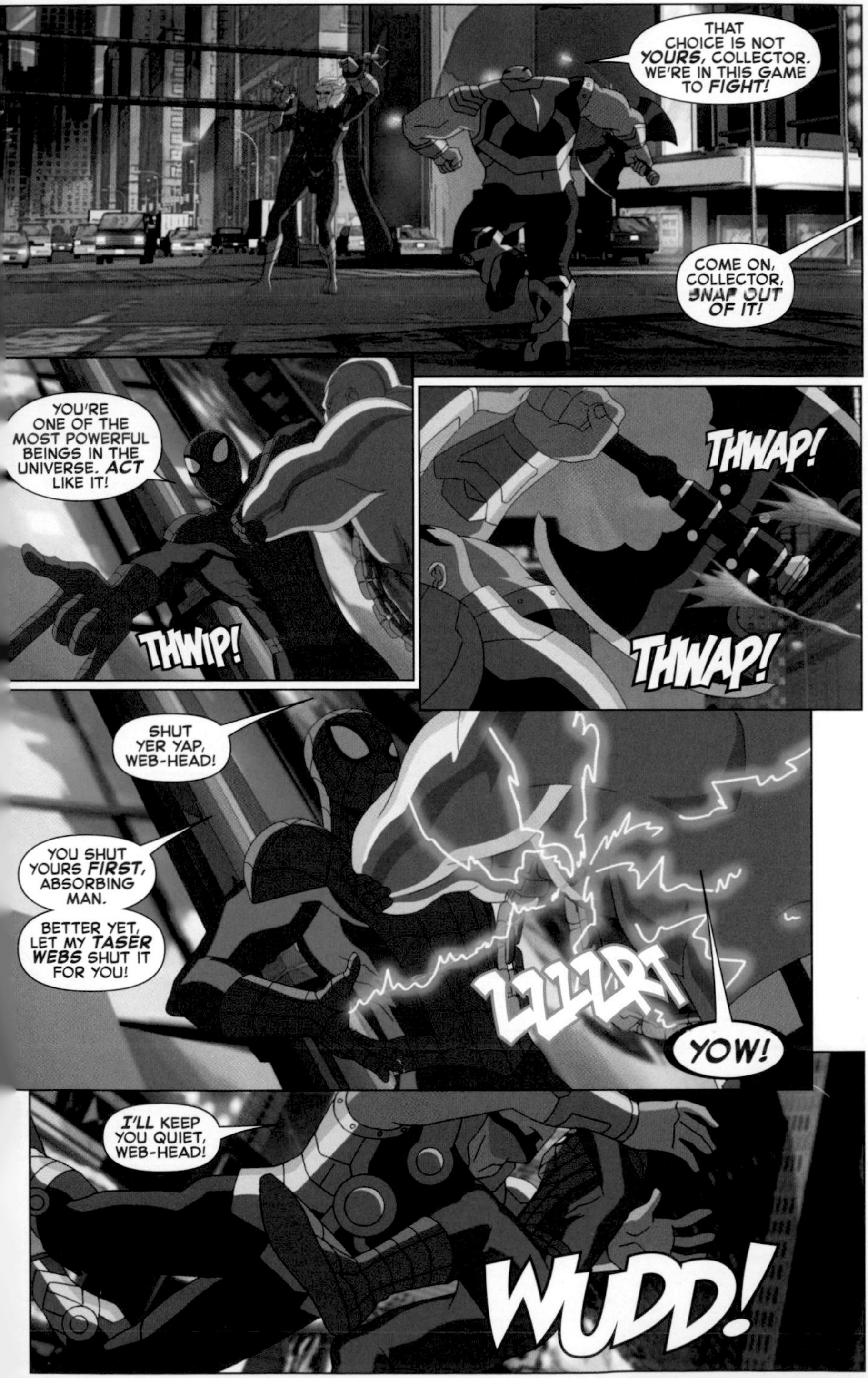
THAT CHOICE IS NOT YOURS, COLLECTOR. WE'RE IN THIS GAME TO FIGHT!
COME ON, COLLECTOR, SNAP OUT OF IT!
YOU'RE ONE OF THE MOST POWERFUL BEINGS IN THE UNIVERSE. ACT LIKE IT!
THWIP!
THWAP!
THWAP!
SHUT YER YAP, WEB-HEAD!
YOU SHUT YOURS FIRST, ABSORBING MAN.
BETTER YET, LET MY TASER WEBS SHUT IT FOR YOU!
ZZZZZRT
YOW!
I'LL KEEP YOU QUIET, WEB-HEAD!
WUDD!

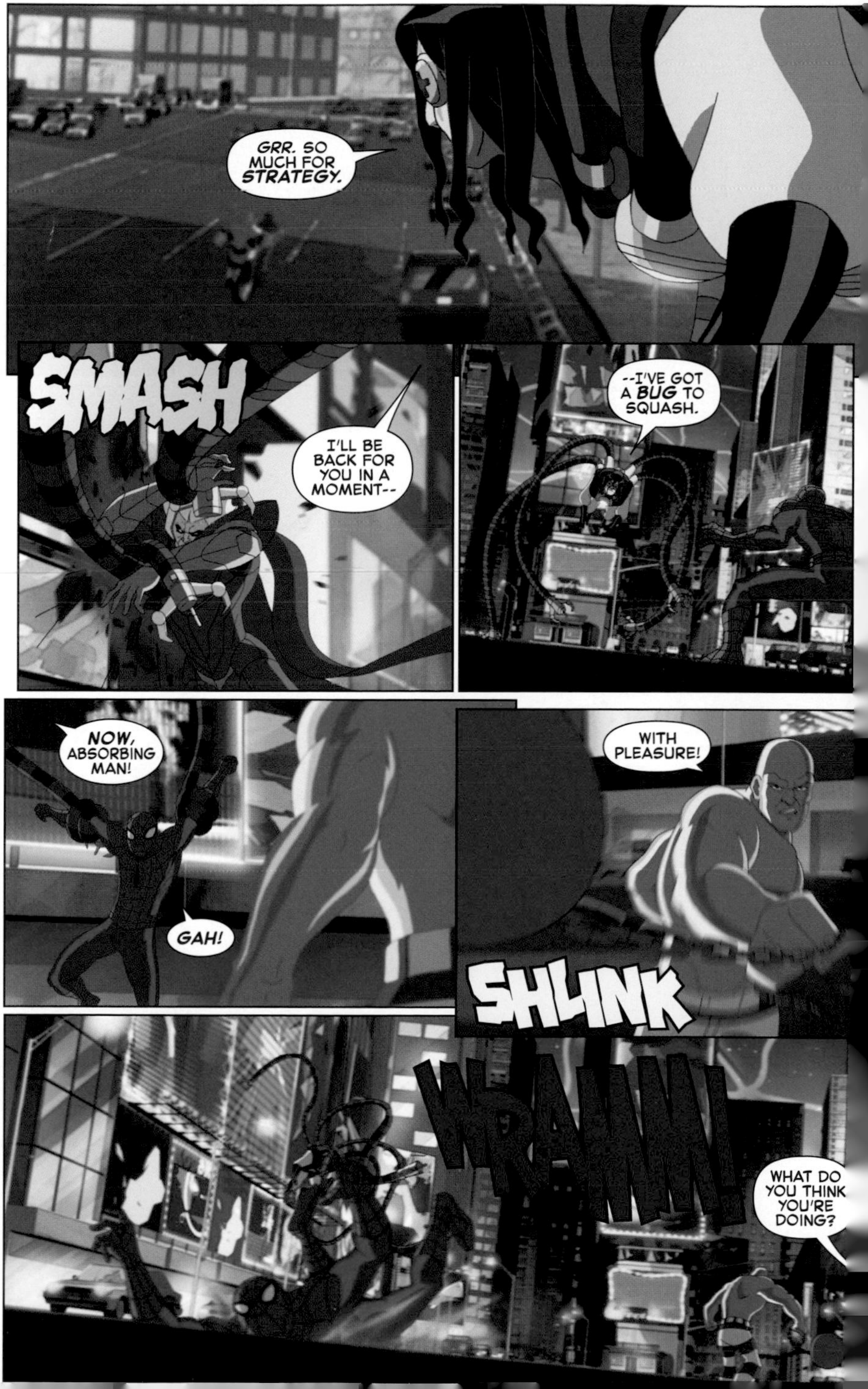
GRR. SO MUCH FOR STRATEGY.
SMASH
I'LL BE BACK FOR YOU IN A MOMENT--
--I'VE GOT A BUG TO SQUASH.
NOW, ABSORBING MAN!
GAH!
WITH PLEASURE!
SHUNK
WHAT DO YOU THINK YOU'RE DOING?

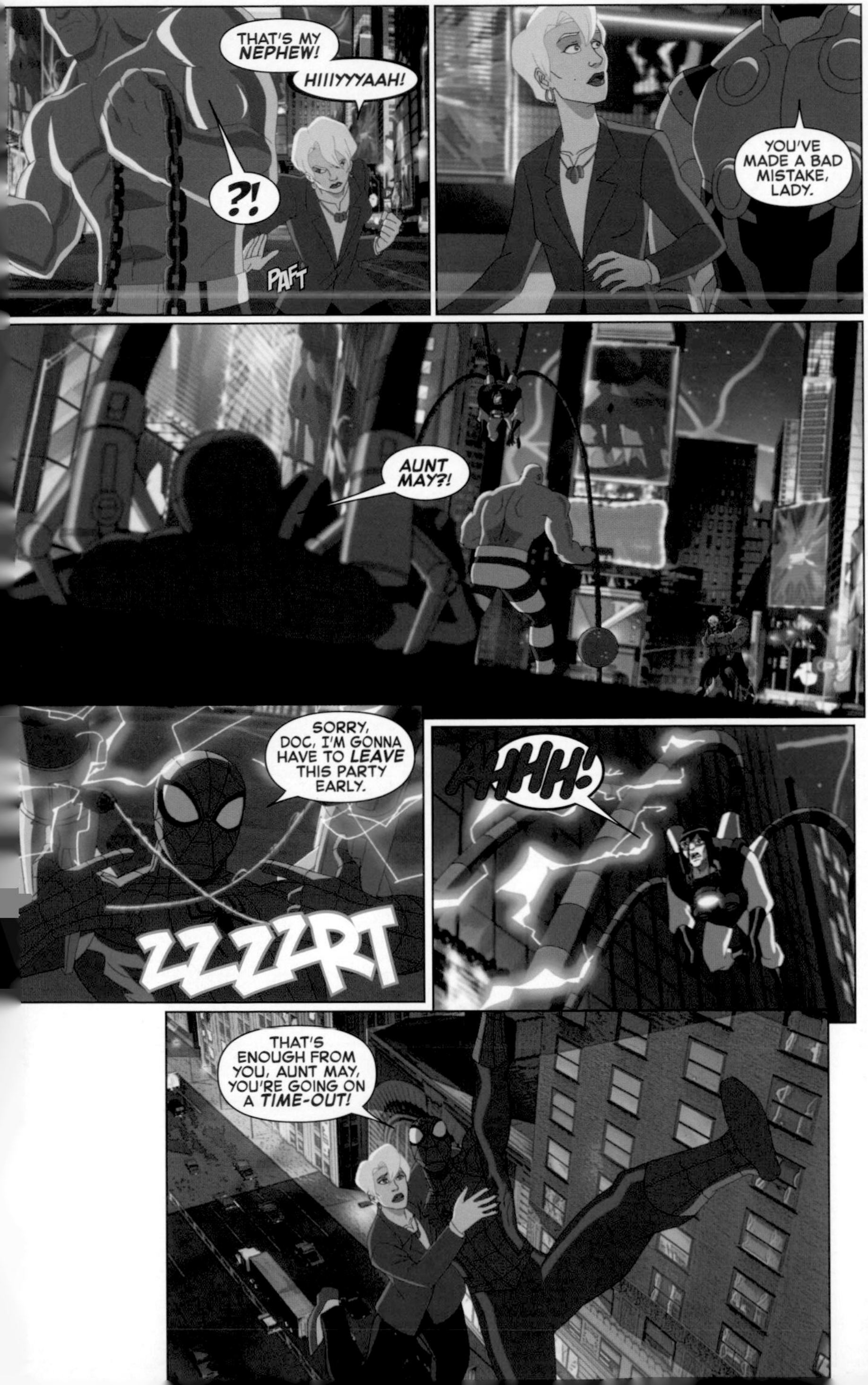
THAT'S MY NEPHEW!
HIIIYYYAAH!
?!
PAFT
YOU'VE MADE A BAD MISTAKE, LADY.
AUNT MAY?!
SORRY, DOC, I'M GONNA HAVE TO LEAVE THIS PARTY EARLY.
ZZZZRT
AHHH!
THAT'S ENOUGH FROM YOU, AUNT MAY, YOU'RE GOING ON A TIME-OUT!

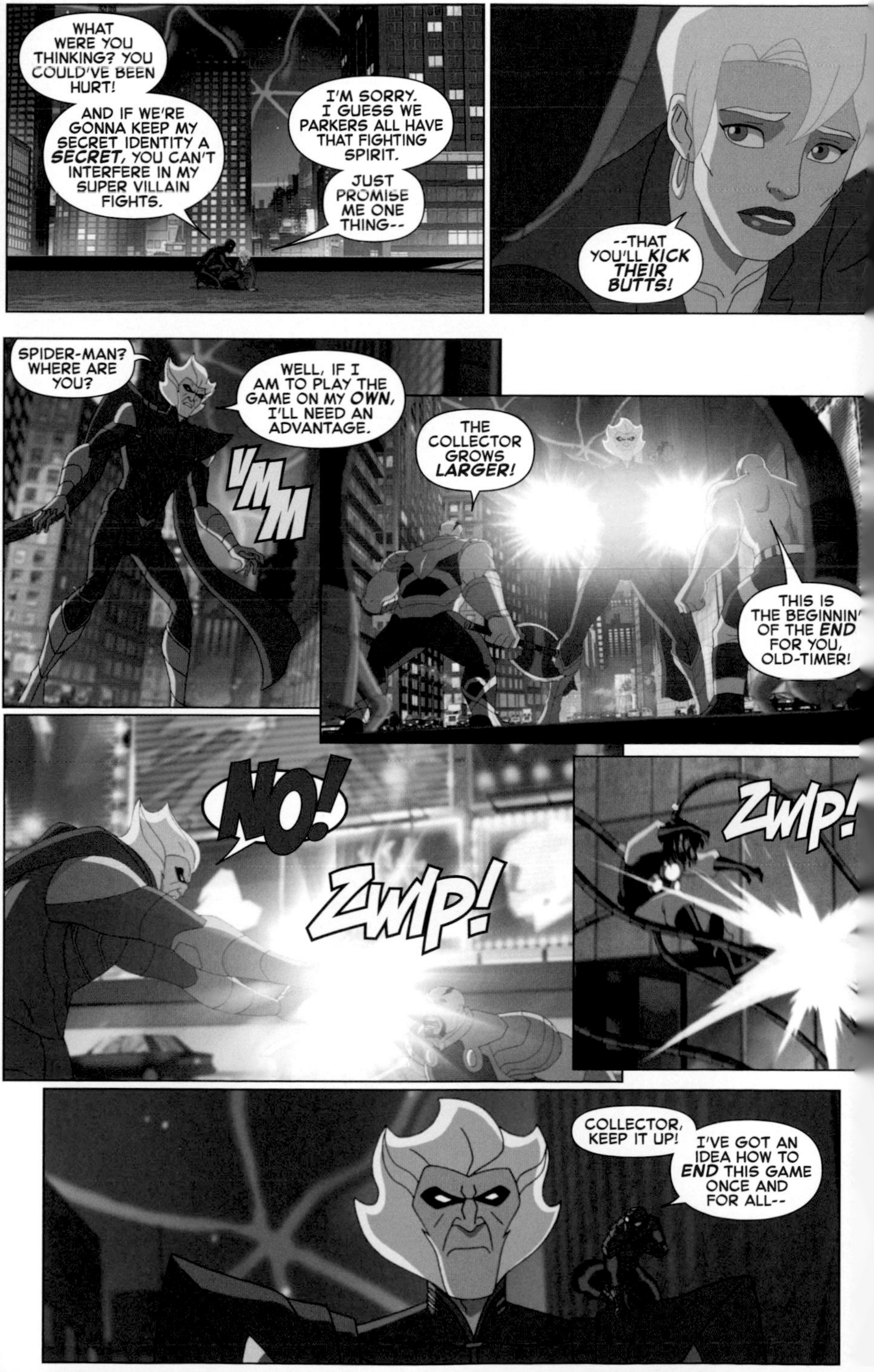
WHAT WERE YOU THINKING? YOU COULD'VE BEEN HURT!
AND IF WE'RE GONNA KEEP MY SECRET IDENTITY A SECRET, YOU CAN'T INTERFERE IN MY SUPER VILLAIN FIGHTS.
I'M SORRY. I GUESS WE PARKERS ALL HAVE THAT FIGHTING SPIRIT.
JUST PROMISE ME ONE THING--
--THAT YOU'LL KICK THEIR BUTTS!
SPIDER-MAN? WHERE ARE YOU?
WELL, IF I AM TO PLAY THE GAME ON MY OWN, I'LL NEED AN ADVANTAGE.
VMM
THE COLLECTOR GROWS LARGER!
THIS IS THE BEGINNIN' OF THE END FOR YOU, OLD-TIMER!
NO!
ZWIP!
ZWIP!
COLLECTOR, KEEP IT UP!
I'VE GOT AN IDEA HOW TO END THIS GAME ONCE AND FOR ALL--

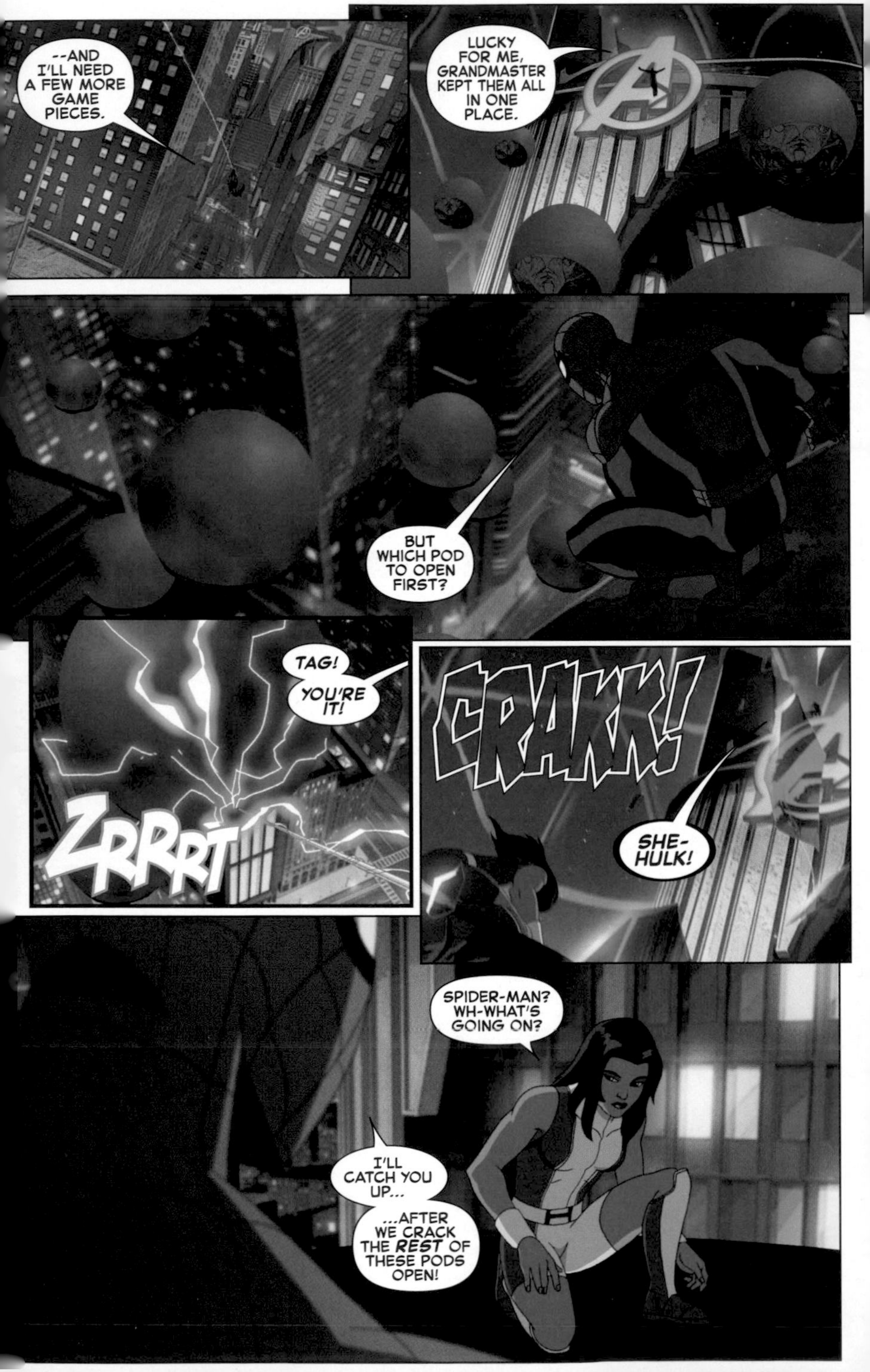
--AND I'LL NEED A FEW MORE GAME PIECES.
LUCKY FOR ME, GRANDMASTER KEPT THEM ALL IN ONE PLACE.
BUT WHICH POD TO OPEN FIRST?
TAG!
YOU'RE IT!
ZRRRT
CRAKK!
SHE-HULK!
SPIDER-MAN? WH-WHAT'S GOING ON?
I'LL CATCH YOU UP...
...AFTER WE CRACK THE REST OF THESE PODS OPEN!

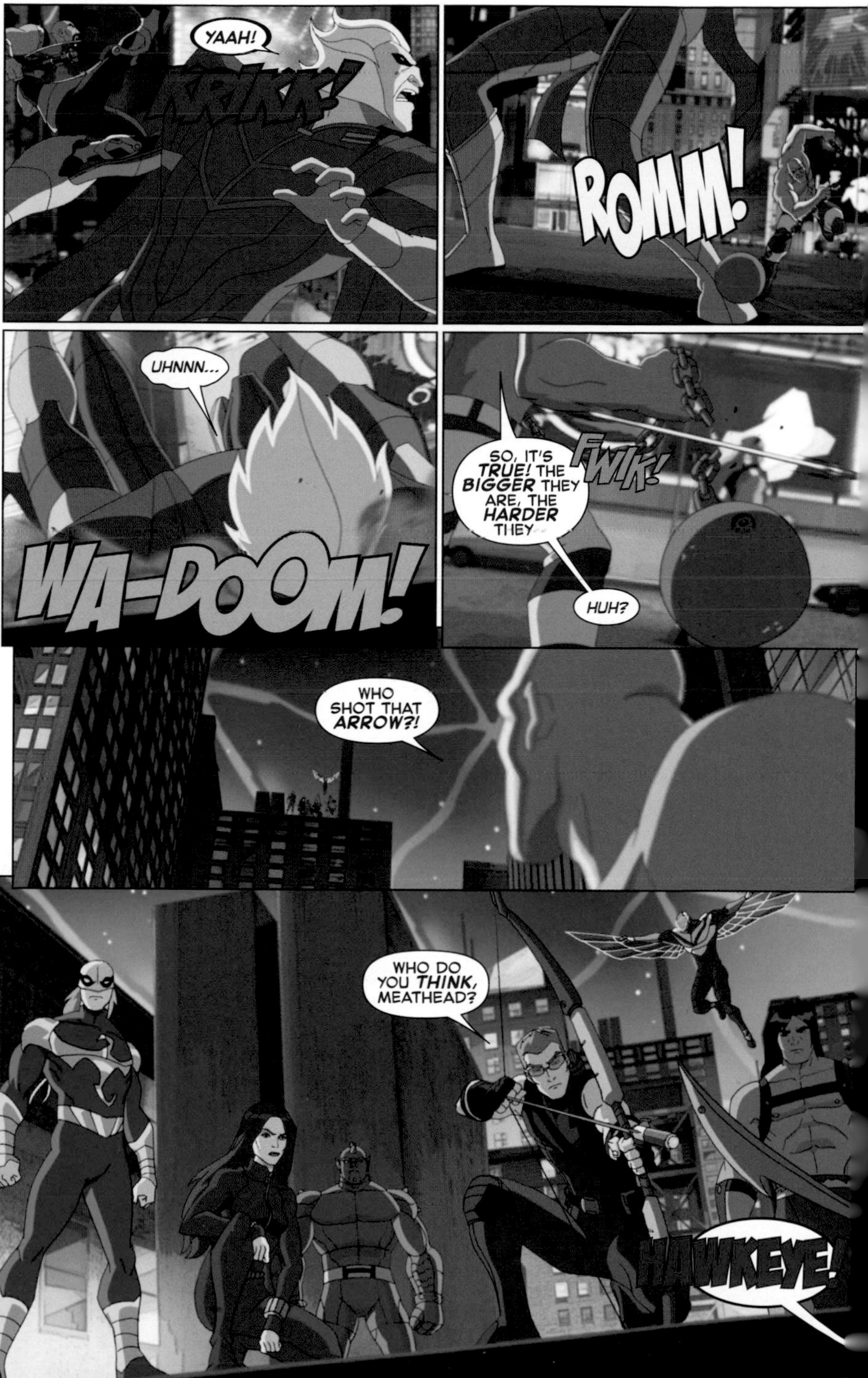
YAAH!
ROMM!
UHNNN...
WA-DOOM!
SO, IT'S TRUE! THE BIGGER THEY ARE, THE HARDER THEY--
FWIK!
HUH?
WHO SHOT THAT ARROW?!
WHO DO YOU THINK, MEATHEAD?
HAWKEYE!

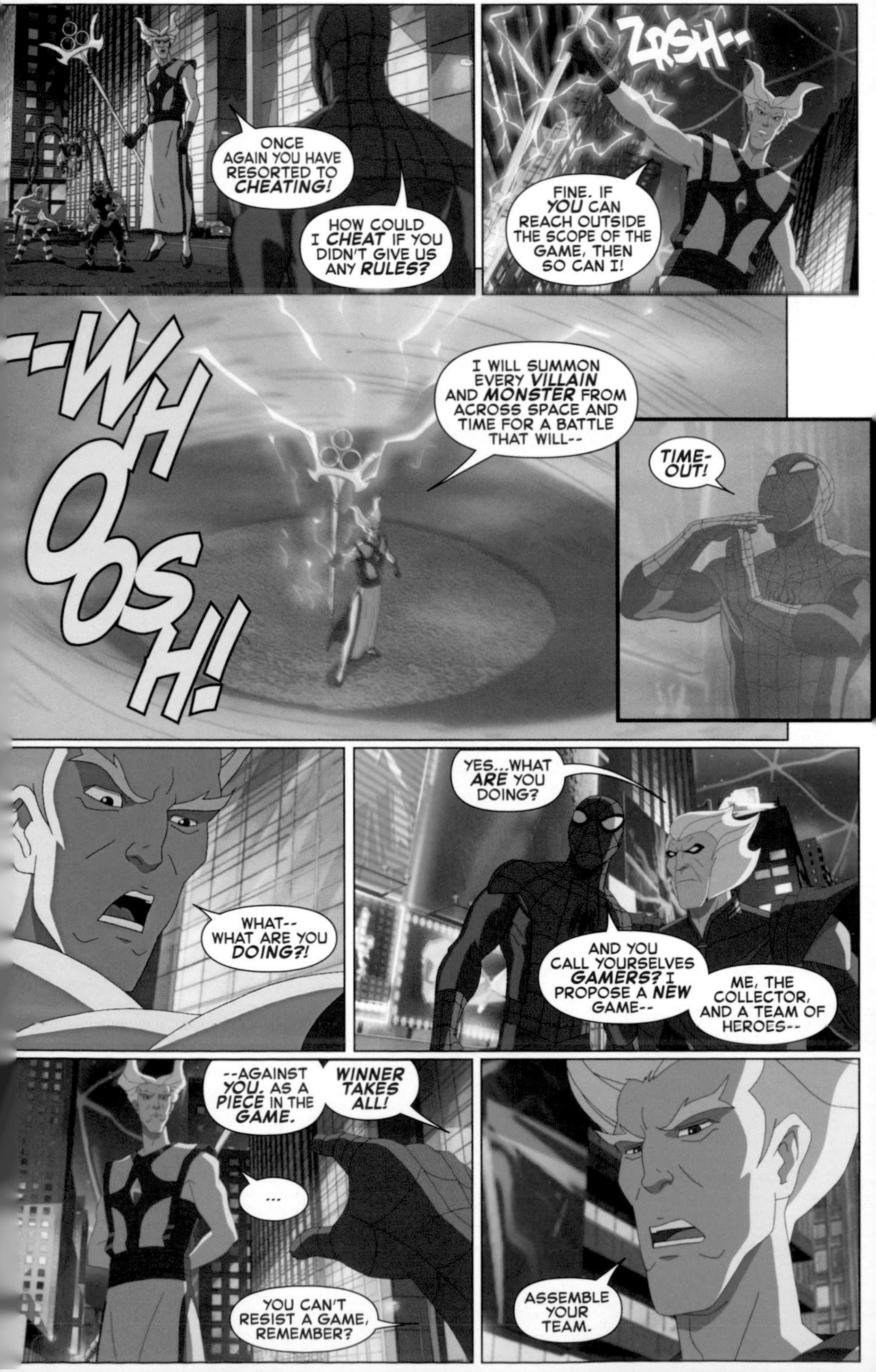
ZRSH--
ONCE AGAIN YOU HAVE RESORTED TO CHEATING!
HOW COULD I CHEAT IF YOU DIDN'T GIVE US ANY RULES?
FINE. IF YOU CAN REACH OUTSIDE THE SCOPE OF THE GAME, THEN SO CAN I!
--WHOOOSH!
I WILL SUMMON EVERY VILLAIN AND MONSTER FROM ACROSS SPACE AND TIME FOR A BATTLE THAT WILL--
TIME-OUT!
WHAT-- WHAT ARE YOU DOING?!
YES...WHAT ARE YOU DOING?
AND YOU CALL YOURSELVES GAMERS? I PROPOSE A NEW GAME--
ME, THE COLLECTOR, AND A TEAM OF HEROES--
--AGAINST YOU. AS A PIECE IN THE GAME.
WINNER TAKES ALL!
...
YOU CAN'T RESIST A GAME, REMEMBER?
ASSEMBLE YOUR TEAM.

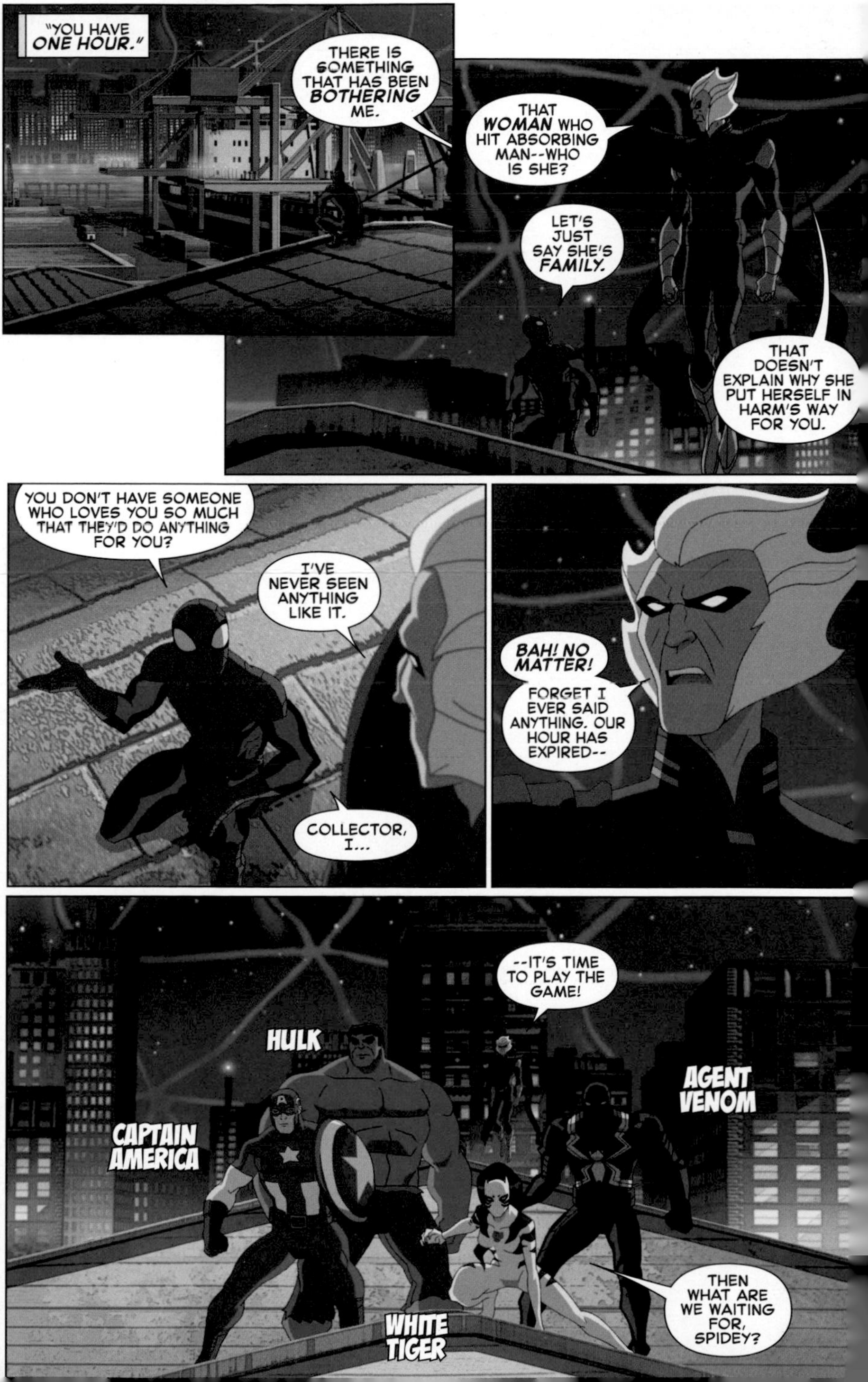
"YOU HAVE ONE HOUR."
THERE IS SOMETHING THAT HAS BEEN BOTHERING ME.
THAT WOMAN WHO HIT ABSORBING MAN--WHO IS SHE?
LET'S JUST SAY SHE'S FAMILY.
THAT DOESN'T EXPLAIN WHY SHE PUT HERSELF IN HARM'S WAY FOR YOU.
YOU DON'T HAVE SOMEONE WHO LOVES YOU SO MUCH THAT THEY'D DO ANYTHING FOR YOU?
I'VE NEVER SEEN ANYTHING LIKE IT.
COLLECTOR, I...
BAH! NO MATTER!
FORGET I EVER SAID ANYTHING. OUR HOUR HAS EXPIRED--
--IT'S TIME TO PLAY THE GAME!
HULK
AGENT VENOM
CAPTAIN AMERICA
WHITE TIGER
THEN WHAT ARE WE WAITING FOR, SPIDEY?

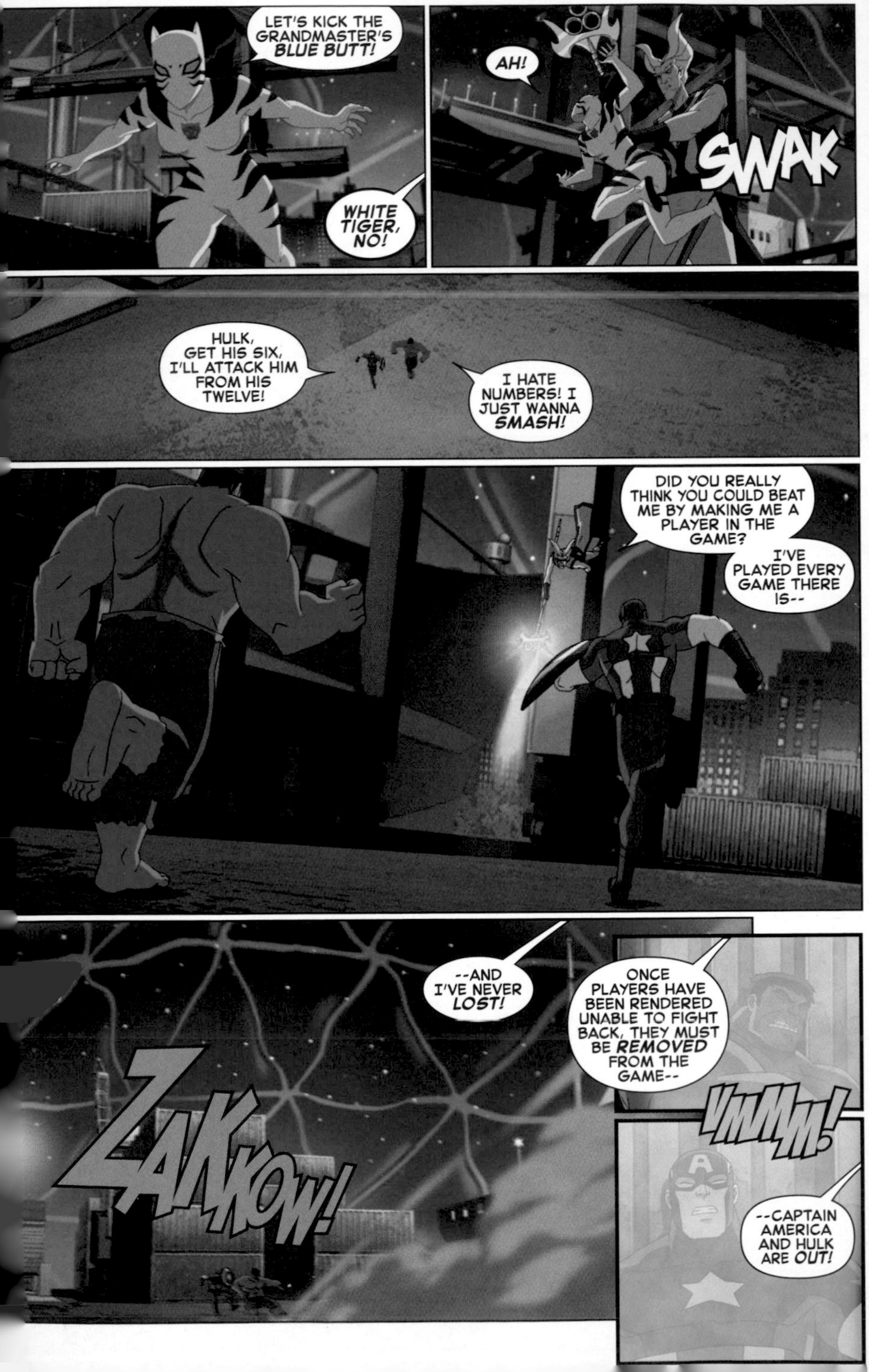
LET'S KICK THE GRANDMASTER'S BLUE BUTT!
WHITE TIGER, NO!
AH!
SWAK
HULK, GET HIS SIX, I'LL ATTACK HIM FROM HIS TWELVE!
I HATE NUMBERS! I JUST WANNA SMASH!
DID YOU REALLY THINK YOU COULD BEAT ME BY MAKING ME A PLAYER IN THE GAME?
I'VE PLAYED EVERY GAME THERE IS--
--AND I'VE NEVER LOST!
ZAKKOW!
ONCE PLAYERS HAVE BEEN RENDERED UNABLE TO FIGHT BACK, THEY MUST BE REMOVED FROM THE GAME--
VMMMM!
--CAPTAIN AMERICA AND HULK ARE OUT!

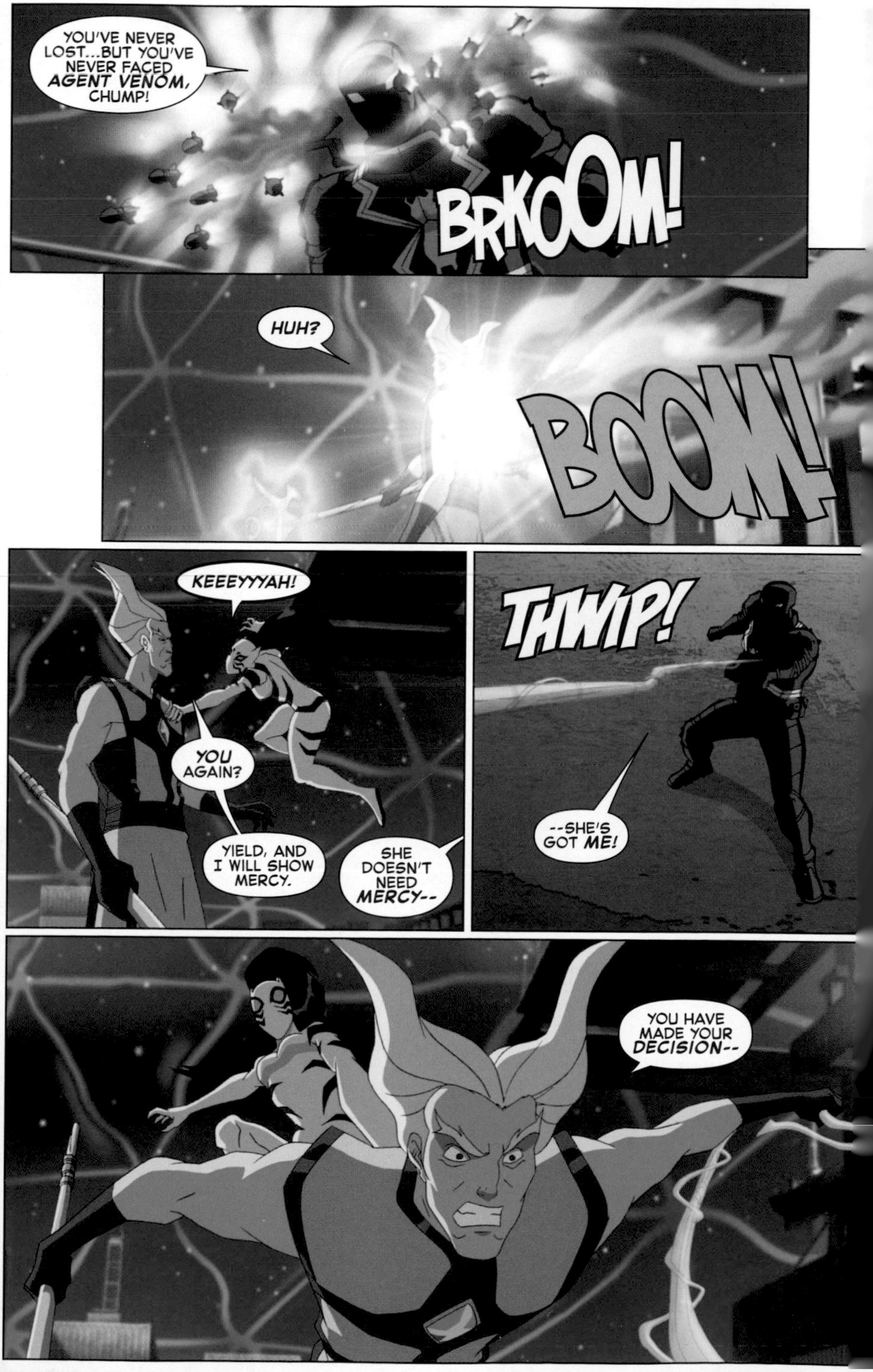
YOU'VE NEVER LOST...BUT YOU'VE NEVER FACED *AGENT VENOM,* CHUMP!
BRKOOM!
HUH?
BOOM!
KEEEYYYAH!
YOU AGAIN?
YIELD, AND I WILL SHOW MERCY.
SHE DOESN'T NEED *MERCY--*
THWIP!
--SHE'S GOT *ME!*
YOU HAVE MADE YOUR *DECISION--*

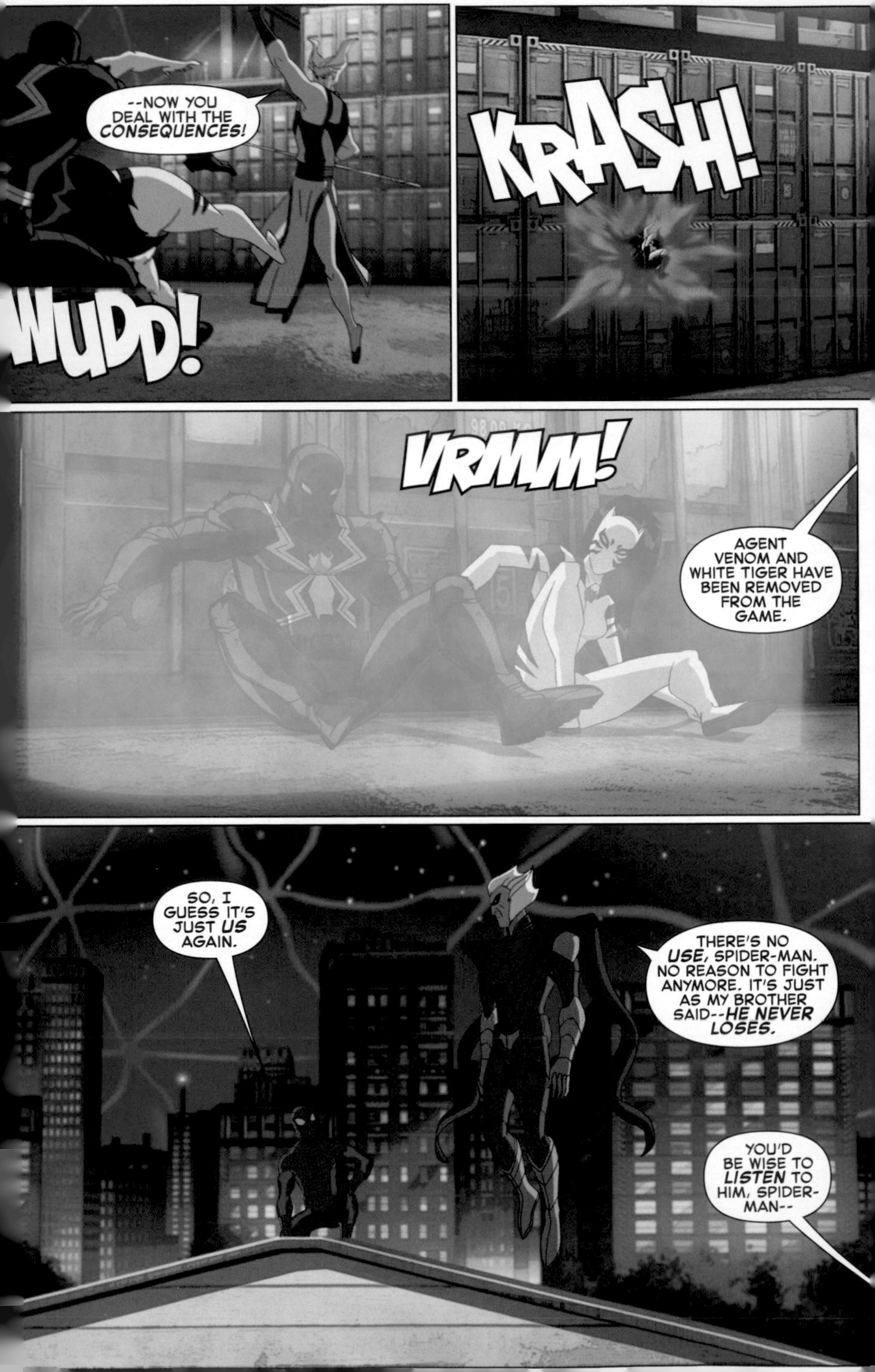
--NOW YOU DEAL WITH THE CONSEQUENCES!
WUDD!
KRASH!
VRMM!
AGENT VENOM AND WHITE TIGER HAVE BEEN REMOVED FROM THE GAME.
SO, I GUESS IT'S JUST US AGAIN.
THERE'S NO USE, SPIDER-MAN. NO REASON TO FIGHT ANYMORE. IT'S JUST AS MY BROTHER SAID--HE NEVER LOSES.
YOU'D BE WISE TO LISTEN TO HIM, SPIDER-MAN--

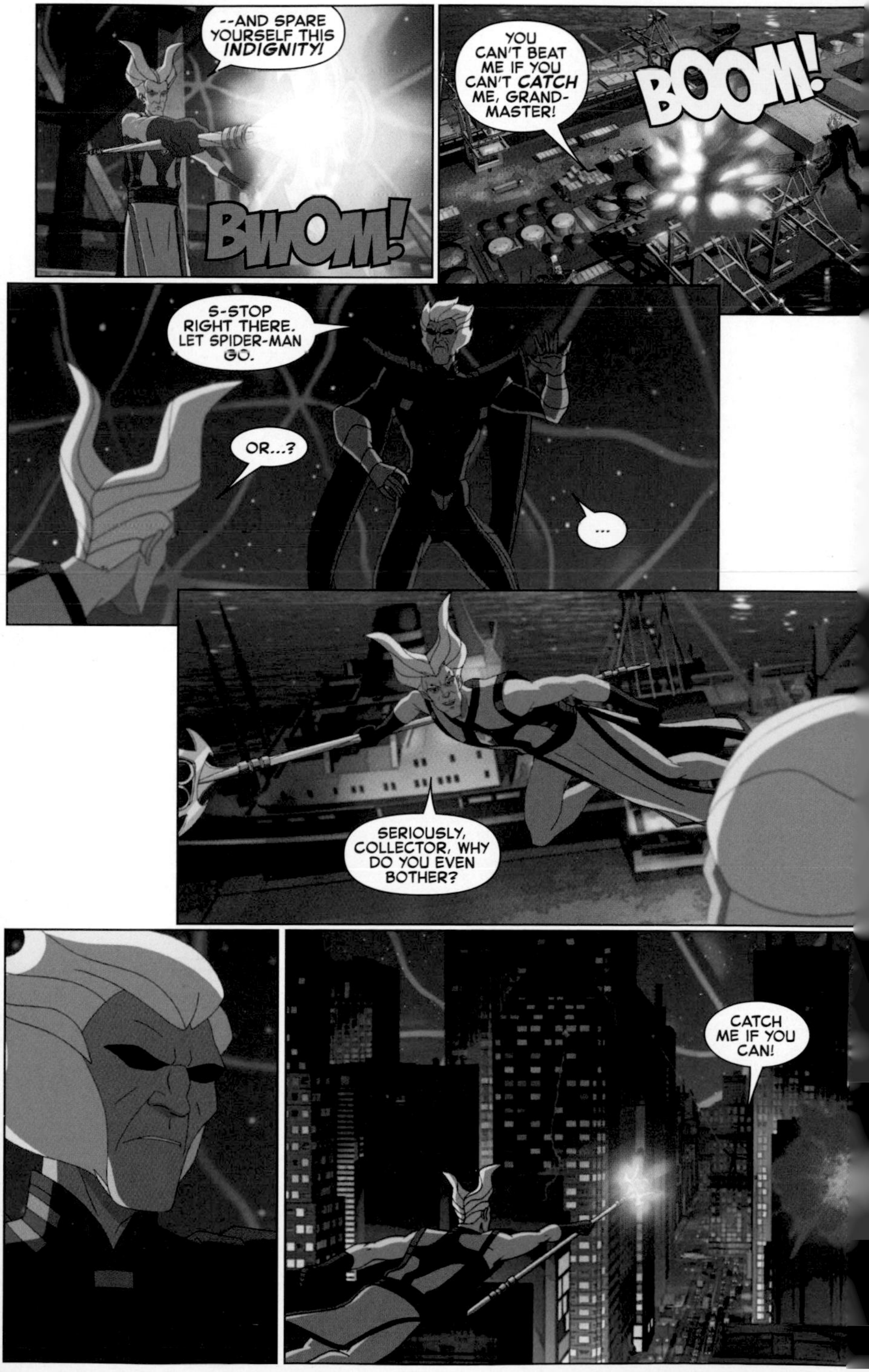
--AND SPARE YOURSELF THIS INDIGNITY!
BWOM!
YOU CAN'T BEAT ME IF YOU CAN'T CATCH ME, GRAND-MASTER!
BOOM!
S-STOP RIGHT THERE. LET SPIDER-MAN GO.
OR...?
...
SERIOUSLY, COLLECTOR, WHY DO YOU EVEN BOTHER?
CATCH ME IF YOU CAN!

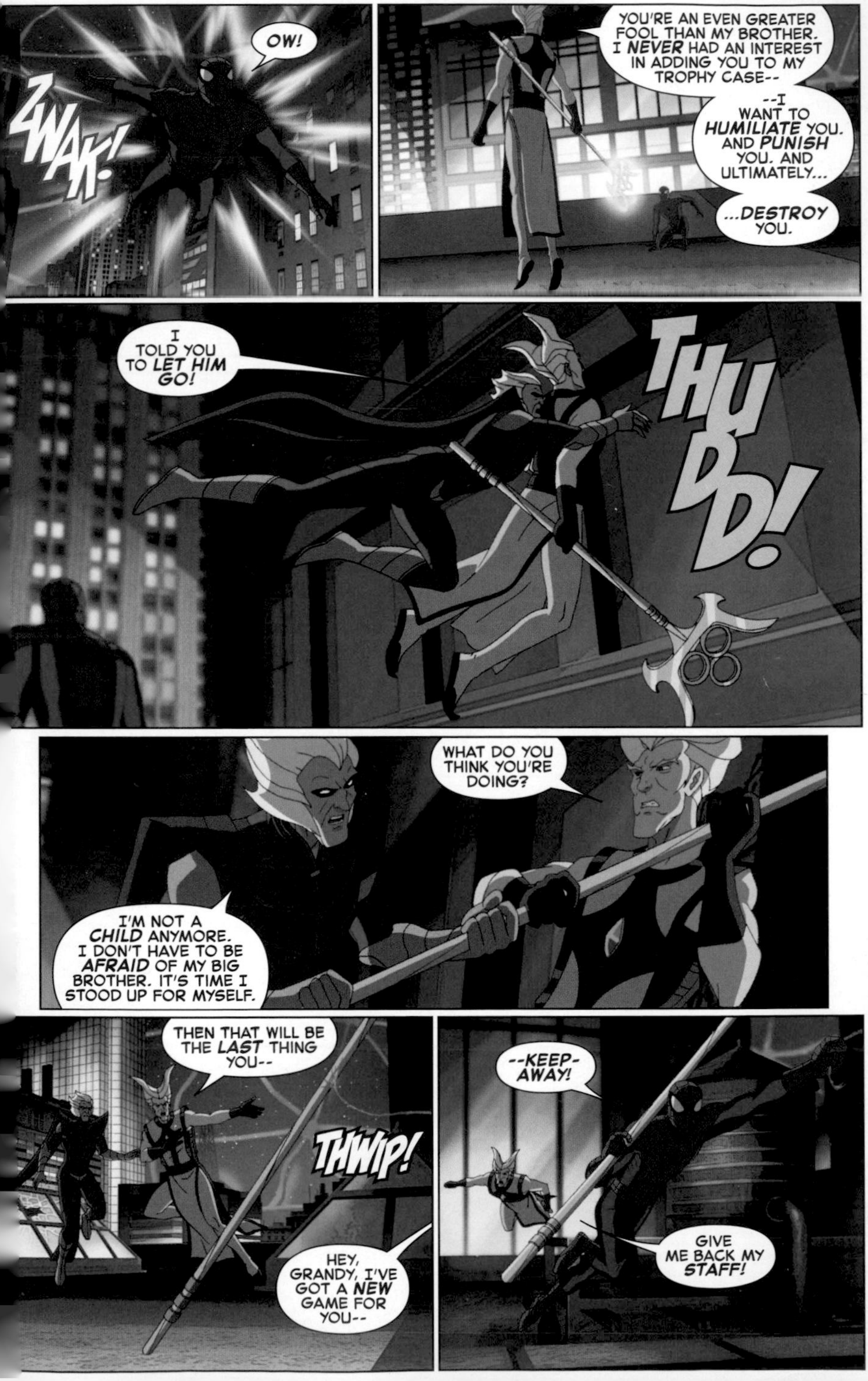
OW!
ZWAK!
YOU'RE AN EVEN GREATER FOOL THAN MY BROTHER. I NEVER HAD AN INTEREST IN ADDING YOU TO MY TROPHY CASE--
--I WANT TO HUMILIATE YOU. AND PUNISH YOU. AND ULTIMATELY...
...DESTROY YOU.
I TOLD YOU TO LET HIM GO!
THUDD!
WHAT DO YOU THINK YOU'RE DOING?
I'M NOT A CHILD ANYMORE. I DON'T HAVE TO BE AFRAID OF MY BIG BROTHER. IT'S TIME I STOOD UP FOR MYSELF.
THEN THAT WILL BE THE LAST THING YOU--
THWIP!
HEY, GRANDY, I'VE GOT A NEW GAME FOR YOU--
--KEEP-AWAY!
GIVE ME BACK MY STAFF!

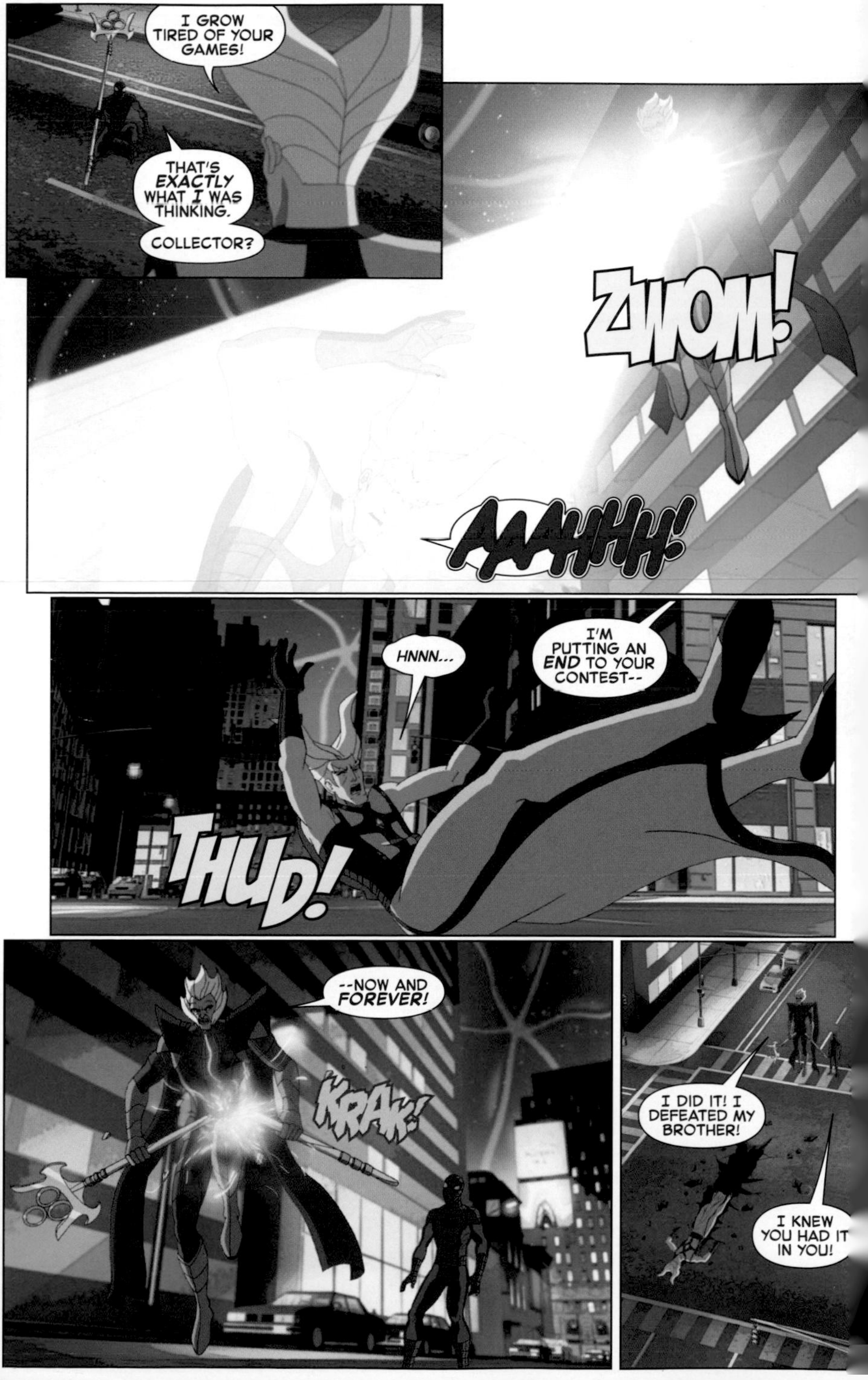
I GROW TIRED OF YOUR GAMES!
THAT'S *EXACTLY* WHAT *I* WAS THINKING.
COLLECTOR?
ZWOM!
AAAHHH!
HNNN...
I'M PUTTING AN *END* TO YOUR CONTEST--
THUD!
--NOW AND *FOREVER!*
KRAK!
I DID IT! I DEFEATED MY BROTHER!
I KNEW YOU HAD IT IN YOU!

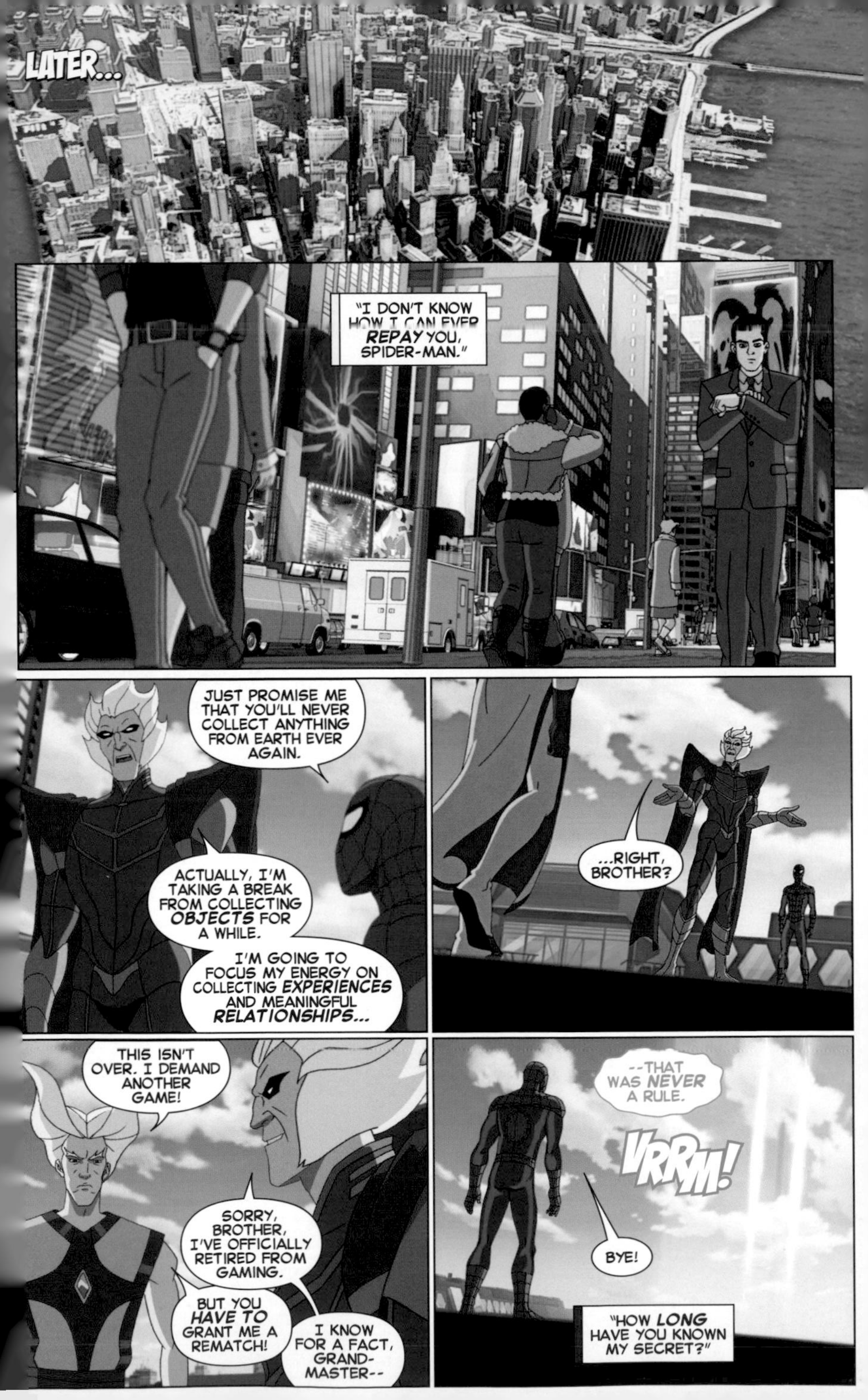
LATER...
"I DON'T KNOW HOW I CAN EVER REPAY YOU, SPIDER-MAN."
JUST PROMISE ME THAT YOU'LL NEVER COLLECT ANYTHING FROM EARTH EVER AGAIN.
ACTUALLY, I'M TAKING A BREAK FROM COLLECTING OBJECTS FOR A WHILE.
I'M GOING TO FOCUS MY ENERGY ON COLLECTING EXPERIENCES AND MEANINGFUL RELATIONSHIPS...
...RIGHT, BROTHER?
THIS ISN'T OVER. I DEMAND ANOTHER GAME!
SORRY, BROTHER, I'VE OFFICIALLY RETIRED FROM GAMING.
BUT YOU HAVE TO GRANT ME A REMATCH!
I KNOW FOR A FACT, GRAND-MASTER--
--THAT WAS NEVER A RULE.
VRRM!
BYE!
"HOW LONG HAVE YOU KNOWN MY SECRET?"

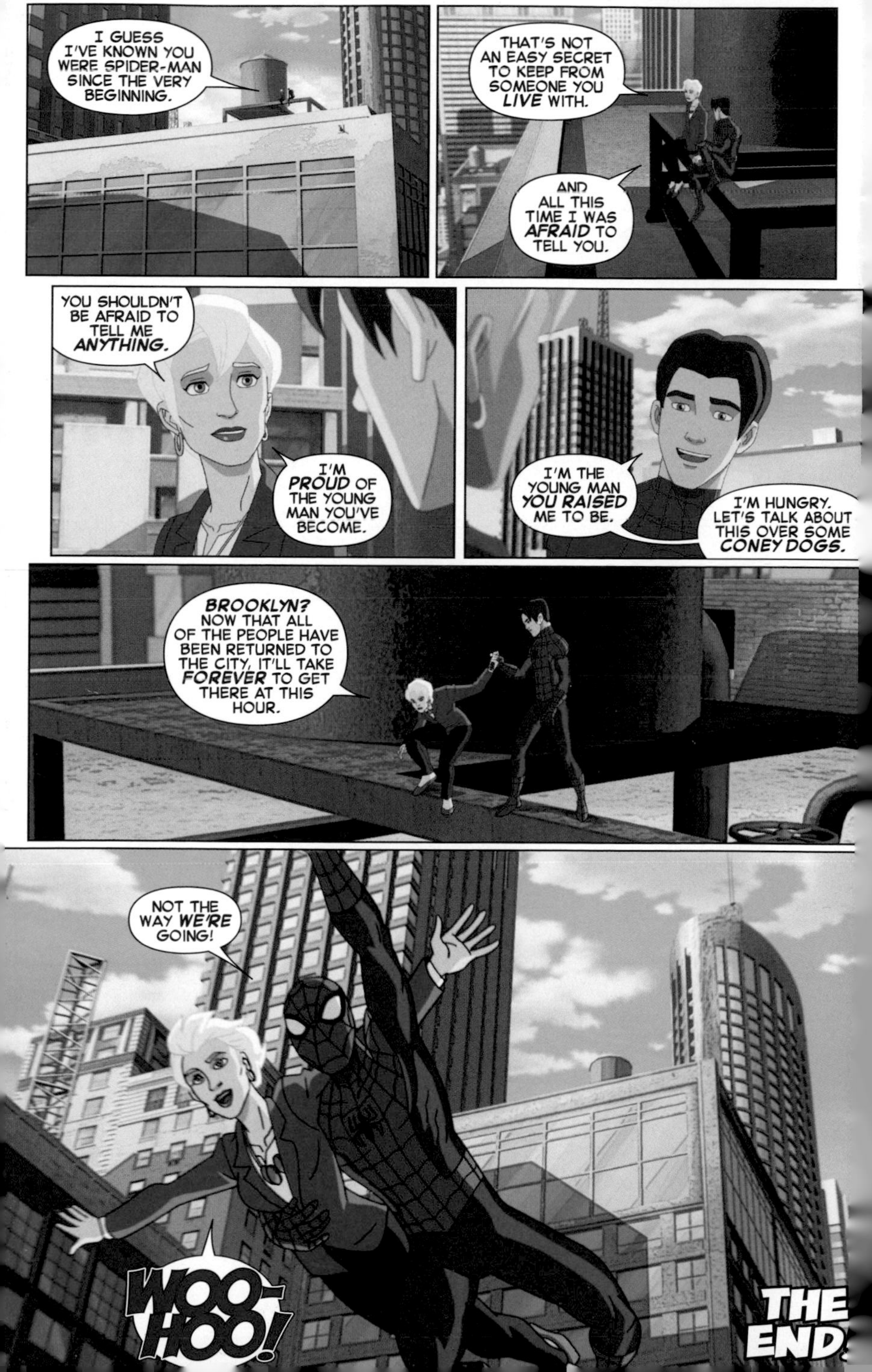

I GUESS I'VE KNOWN YOU WERE SPIDER-MAN SINCE THE VERY BEGINNING.
THAT'S NOT AN EASY SECRET TO KEEP FROM SOMEONE YOU LIVE WITH.
AND ALL THIS TIME I WAS AFRAID TO TELL YOU.
YOU SHOULDN'T BE AFRAID TO TELL ME ANYTHING.
I'M PROUD OF THE YOUNG MAN YOU'VE BECOME.
I'M THE YOUNG MAN YOU RAISED ME TO BE.
I'M HUNGRY. LET'S TALK ABOUT THIS OVER SOME CONEY DOGS.
BROOKLYN? NOW THAT ALL OF THE PEOPLE HAVE BEEN RETURNED TO THE CITY, IT'LL TAKE FOREVER TO GET THERE AT THIS HOUR.
NOT THE WAY WE'RE GOING!
WOO-HOO!
THE END

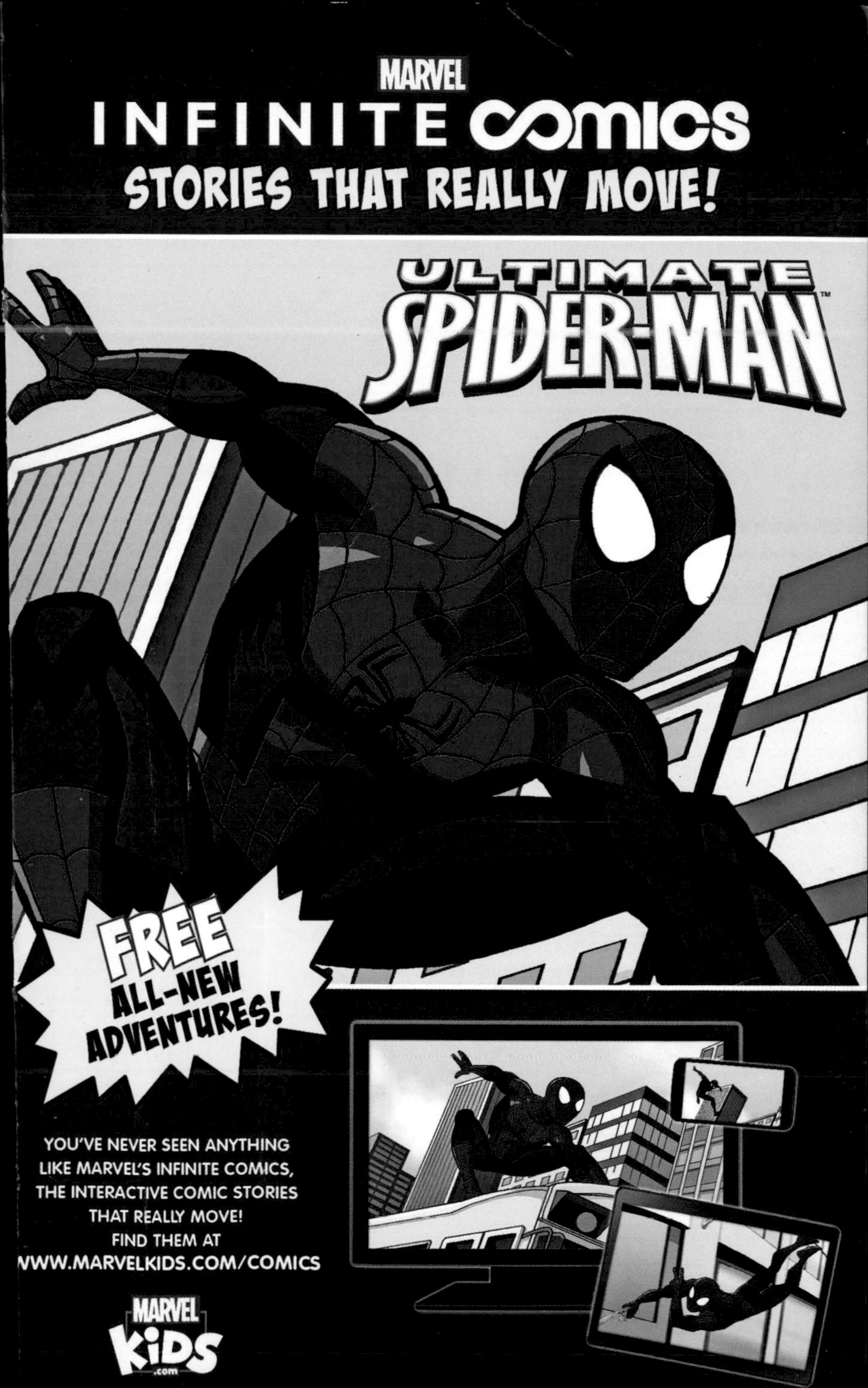

MARVEL
INFINITE COMICS
STORIES THAT REALLY MOVE!
ULTIMATE SPIDER-MAN™
FREE ALL-NEW ADVENTURES!
YOU'VE NEVER SEEN ANYTHING LIKE MARVEL'S INFINITE COMICS, THE INTERACTIVE COMIC STORIES THAT REALLY MOVE!
FIND THEM AT WWW.MARVELKIDS.COM/COMICS
MARVEL KIDS .com